THE
MELANCHOLY
OF SUMMER

Louisa Onomé

FEIWEL AND FRIENDS
NEW YORK

A Feiwel and Friends Book
An imprint of Macmillan Publishing Group, LLC
120 Broadway, New York, NY 10271 · fiercereads.com

Our books may be purchased in bulk for promotional,
educational, or business use. Please contact your local
bookseller or the Macmillan Corporate and Premium Sales
Department at (800) 221-7945 ext. 5442 or by email at
MacmillanSpecialMarkets@macmillan.com.

Library of Congress Cataloging-in-Publication Data
Names: Onomé, Louisa, author.
Title: The melancholy of Summer / Louisa Onomé.
Description: First edition. | New York : Feiwel & Friends, 2023. |
    Audience: Ages 13 and up. | Audience: Grades 10–12. | Summary:
    After seventeen-year-old Summer's parents go on the run, she is
    placed in the care of Olu, a cousin she barely knows, but with Olu
    and friends' efforts, stoic Summer eventually learns to open up.
Identifiers: LCCN 2022046325 | ISBN 9781250823564 (hardcover)
Subjects: CYAC: Abandoned children—Fiction. | Cousins—Fiction. |
    Friendship—Fiction. | Adjustment—Fiction. | Self-acceptance—
    Fiction. | African Americans—Fiction.
Classification: LCC PZ7.1.O656 Me 2023 | DDC [Fic]—dc23
LC record available at https://lccn.loc.gov/2022046325

First edition, 2023
Book design by Trisha Previte
Feiwel and Friends logo designed by Filomena Tuosto
Printed in the United States of America

ISBN 978-1-250-82356-4
10 9 8 7 6 5 4 3 2 1

THIS ONE'S FOR CHYAH, THOUGH SHE DOESN'T KNOW IT YET. I WISH YOU COULD EXPERIENCE THE JOY IN SLOWING DOWN.

CHAPTER ONE

SHE TELLS ME HER NAME is Gardenia, and then she waits as if she's expecting a question she's been asked a million times before. I don't move, immobilized by both my own fear and the sterility of this office. I hate bureaucracy. Or, corporations. The stuffiness of it all, the way people wear dress clothes as if it makes them more trustworthy when it really just reinforces the fact that I—in my worn-out tennis shoes, basic rose-colored summer dress, and box braids that desperately need to be redone—don't belong here. And that's fine because I *don't* belong here and I'd give anything to leave, to just pick up my backpack with all my possessions and go back to Tanya's for the week. But I can't because Gardenia is waving a document in front of me now and I am terrified.

Just like when she introduced herself, she's tempting me to ask a question the more she waves this paper in front of me. I keep quiet.

When I don't bite, she sighs and sets down the paper on the desk. I let my eyes shift a little so I can see the letterhead. "York University." We look at each other. "Sorry?" I croak out. My voice doesn't belong here, either.

"Do you know what this is?" she asks.

I'm tempted now to really look at the paper. It's some sort of letter from York, a school I applied to at the end of last semester for their criminology program. Ironic, now. I don't trust the legal system and I don't care about criminology, but I just needed it to look like I was thinking about life after high school, you know? I didn't want to draw anyone's attention, so I applied to a bunch of stuff. Criminology here, psychology there, all programs that a person who is really thinking about their life would apply to. The guidance counselors at school didn't bat an eyelash when I told them about my plans, and I told them about *all* of them, even though half of them weren't true. Parts of me were so open. I'm not sure if that version of myself exists anymore.

It doesn't matter.

I was almost free.

Gardenia is still watching me, so I answer, "A letter from York?" as innocently as possible. I still don't know what kind of trouble I'm in.

She tilts her head, purses her lips, and it looks like she's judging me hardcore. I am used to this look. "Apparently, the school has been trying to get in contact with you about a deferred payment program, and when they couldn't reach your household, a very lovely adviser went out of their way to contact your high school guidance counselor."

"I graduated already," I say, almost like a challenge. For what, though, I don't know. "In June. I'm seventeen now."

"Seventeen doesn't make you an adult," Gardenia says,

equally as bold. She sighs in that way adults do when they're about to say something they hope will get an emotional rise out of you. "I'm here to help you, you know. It may not seem like it, but I've been in your situation."

I bristle. *Bristle*. This nasty, creeping, prickly feeling whips up my spine. Anger floods my senses, coaxing me to shout and snap and curse at her until I run out of breath. She's staring at me with these kind eyes and it makes me even madder. So what, then? She's been in my situation, so what? She isn't me, and I'm not like those other screwed up kids she's probably seen before. I was *fine*—I was almost free.

So I say, "I'll be eighteen in, like, a month, so."

She frowns, tilts her head again as if to say, *Really?* Then she sighs a second time. "Almost eighteen is not eighteen, and there are rules . . . Listen, Summer." She clasps her hands together and leans toward me across the desk. I lean away on impulse. "Mr. Gordon, your old guidance counselor, rang your house many times and tried to get ahold of your, um, your g-guardians . . ." She stumbles on the word. Her eyes, flashing to the windows before settling back on me, betray her in a second.

She wanted to say "parents."

"B-but," she presses on, faking composure. "The number was no longer in service, so naturally, he was concerned."

I glance away. "S-sure."

"He had no choice but to go to the authorities, and by that, I mean reach out to us . . ."

"Us" being Child Protective Services. Because that's what I am to these people: a *child*.

But I am almost eighteen and it may not mean anything to Gardenia, who I'm sure can no longer remember what it's like to be young with a sense of style, but it means everything to me. I didn't crumble under the pressure; I didn't break when my life went to shit. After last year, after last summer, when . . .

Doesn't she see? I can do this on my own.

What should be arrogance turns to fear, and my hands begin to tremble with uncertainty, with the realization that I was found by Child Protective Services and I may be in trouble. I'm sitting in a social worker's office. Gardenia is a social worker. I am almost eighteen. These sorts of things don't go well for girls like me.

I mumble, "So are you making me go to a shelter or something?"

"No."

Silence.

"I—I want you to know that I'm not living on the street or whatever," I offer. "My friends have been real good. I've been bouncing back and forth for a while now. Tanya, Sid—honestly, Sid's like my best friend and I've been staying with him more than the others. He lives closer to my old school, so it was easy for me to get a ride with him and stuff."

"Well, your friend Sid is also a minor, yes? So that doesn't really help your case," she tells me.

"Not *just* him," I say with a click of my tongue. "He lives with his parents, and they're actually so legit. His mom is a stylist and his dad sells cars. They're really good people. No drugs, no drinking, nothing." I want to also say *and they're white*, just in case that matters to these people. It probably does.

"They're good people but they let a teenager couch surf?" Gardenia asks, eyebrows raised in disbelief. She doesn't have to say it; I can already hear her thinking, *Some moral citizens they are*.

I open my mouth to "yeah, but . . ." my way into an argument, but I figure there's no point. I don't know what will help, so I ask again, "Do I have to go to a shelter?"

Gardenia shakes her head. I'm so confused. "I'm going to have a talk with Sid's parents and do a home evaluation, so leave me a number for how I can reach them." She's writing now, taking notes on the laptop beside her. A privacy screen and the glare of sun from the window prevent me from reading what she's typing. When I look at her computer, all I see is a dark reflection. "If they're approved, you can stay there and *only* there temporarily, but unless they're going to resolve this payment deferral situation for you . . . I mean, ultimately, it would be best to locate a relative as soon as we can."

I scoff. I don't mean to, but the thought is laughable. Our family had a few family friends here and there, but they all dipped after last summer. We don't have any blood relatives locally anymore, either. I had an aunt, Amaka, who used to live here on and off, but we haven't heard from her in a few years. Both my parents' families, their siblings and cousins, either live in other provinces, other countries, or back in Nigeria where we're from.

Gardenia's eyebrow twitches at my scoff, like she's reached her limit on dealing with teenagers for today. She stops typing, trying to keep her cool. It's not working. She's tan, but her skin is still burning pink. Sucks. "We'll need to locate your *parents*, then," she tells me as if it's a threat.

Go ahead, I want to say, teeth gritted, eyes narrow. *Go and find them if you can.*

God knows I've tried.

CHAPTER TWO

GARDENIA'S OFFICE IS ON THE fifth floor, and the ride down to the front desk feels extremely painful for some reason. I'm not sure why.

Wait, never mind. I figured it out.

It's the stares. I don't get them all the time, honestly. Sometimes when I'm out with my friends, skateboarding up and down the block, people will tilt their heads back to watch us. Maybe they've never seen a Black girl on a skateboard before. Maybe they're unnerved by the fact that I'm actually really good. Not sure.

But sometimes when I get that double take, when that glint of knowing sparks behind someone's eyes and their faces become withdrawn, I shiver. I know who they see when they look at me. The same height, the same smallness. The same confidence, the same regret. It's all there. I am my parents' daughter, after all, and sometimes I feel like everyone can see it. They can all tell.

I keep my eyes down until I make it to the front desk. The attendant there makes me sign my name in all caps to prove I'm actually me. I scribble *Summer Uzoma* without looking and set down the pen. The entire time, she's looking at me like she's got something to say, but she doesn't speak. The threat of conversation sticks in the air between us. I know what her conversation would consist of, most likely. Her and everyone else.

Then, she reaches behind her desk to slide out my skateboard. I grab it, practically wrenching it from her grasp, as I take off.

Outside is hot and humid as hell. Sickening and sticky and unwelcoming. Summertime in Toronto means haze and heat until you're dead. Sun that burns your skin beneath a thick smog that coats your lungs. I sweat the second I step outside the building.

Quickly, I pull my backpack over my shoulders and let my skateboard's wheels hit the pavement. Looking around, squinting in the sun, I have a better idea of where I am. This busy street corner is filled with pristine office buildings, like those new types that are all glass and are supposed to make you want to work there. I hate them. Now I can't equate them with anything else but this . . . this social worker. Gardenia. If she's actually planning on making a stop at Sid's place, it'd be better if I was actually staying there this week. I gotta get out of here, head back to Tanya's, and grab my stuff.

But first, there's somewhere I really want to go.

It doesn't take long for me to look up a bus route that'll take me to my old neighborhood.

Everyone keeps asking me if I still go there often. They don't believe me when I say I don't, and to be honest, I wouldn't believe me, either. Anyone can tell I'm a liar.

I get on the bus, tucking my board under my feet as I find a seat near the back, and mentally prepare for the long journey to my old home. I consider calling Sid, giving him a heads-up that someone may be calling his house soon about me, but I don't. If I remember correctly, he's probably hanging with Kirsten, his girlfriend. It's not that she'll mind if I call or anything—Sid and I used to be *way* closer, and it's not her fault, honestly, but just—I don't know. Gardenia will call his house regardless. Me giving him a heads-up when he's not even home feels trivial. I mull it over until the bus approaches my old street.

The house belongs to someone else now. There's a red sedan in the driveway, a symbol that the owners are home, so I don't bother getting close. Sometimes, I think one day there may be a sign, something that tells me Mom or Dad is looking for me. Like, maybe they'd leave a message for me, telling me everything will be fine and once I turn eighteen, they'll . . . I don't know. It's stupid.

Forget it.

I ride my way to the community mailbox across the street, fishing for my key in my pocket. When I left the house way back then, I held on to the mail key, just in case Mom or Dad would use mail to contact me. I have to check the mail quickly so no one sees me lurking. I don't think anyone around here would call the police or whatever, but it's better to be safe.

So I turn the key, pull open the box assigned to my old house, and stick my hand in for any letters. There are three. Flipping through them quickly, I see two addressed to who I assume is the current owner, someone named George Glass. I put those back in the mailbox.

The third one makes my heart skip a beat. It's a bit bulkier and the address looks like it's been written quickly, but that's not the thing that makes me pause.

It's been returned to sender, clearly never making it to its intended location. And it's addressed to "Oluwadara Akindele."

Auntie Dara.

"Auntie *Dara*?" I repeat, flipping the letter over in my hands. Why is there a letter to Auntie Dara in my old house's mailbox?

The letter had apparently been sent months and months ago, as evidenced by the semi-faded ink, and from the looks of it, it was sent by someone in my house. Otherwise, why would it be returned to sender and end up in our mailbox?

I open it quickly. There's not much to it; just a hand-written note for Auntie, saying, "Send this to the lawyer if you don't hear from me," and some numbers below that don't make any sense to me. They must be relevant for this lawyer, though, whoever they are. It could be a claim number or a . . . a client number. Right? The handwriting kinda looks like my dad's . . . or my mom's . . . I don't know. It's hard to tell, as if the person writing was trying to disguise themselves somehow.

Auntie Dara and my parents weren't on the best terms for a while. And I haven't heard from her since—

My phone buzzes and in the distance, I hear a door

push open. Both sounds startle me and I fumble the letter into my bag, slamming the mailbox closed. My hands are jittery. When I look over my shoulder, I spot someone coming out of a house across the street. I don't see which, but still, I drop my skateboard to the ground and push my way out of there. What if it was the person who lives in my house now? What if they call the police?

I fix my sunglasses on my face and ride harder down the road until the overbearing smog starts to feel like the slightest breeze on my face. Each time my feet collide with the pavement and I propel myself forward, I think of flying. That's what this is to me. Soaring. Unabashed freedom. I think it's the thing I want most in this world: to be free. And at least, for a moment, I thought I was well on my way. I thought I had it. Now with this social worker thing and this weird letter, I feel like I'm being rooted back in a place I don't want to be.

Tanya lives near Centennial Park, which isn't too far from my old neighborhood. I have to catch—I count on my fingers—two buses? Three? Either way, I'll be a sweaty corpse upon arrival. "Don't think about it," I grunt to myself. Truly, the less I can think, the better. I skate to the first bus stop, tap my transit card, get on, sit. I get off at the next stop, wait for the second bus, tap my transit card, worry about how much money is still left on there . . . get on, sit. As I feel the ground rumble underneath the bus, I realize my jaw has been clenched this entire time. Trying to relax is hard. Tanya's mom always says, "You don't *try* to relax. You just relax." I don't get it.

11

Finally, I jump off at the last stop, the one closest to Tanya's house, and take the back roads to the convenience store at the corner of her street. Two kids on bikes hang around by the doors, eyeing me while I make my way past them.

I take my skateboard in, holding it under my arm as I weave through the cramped aisles. They moved the card rack, the one that sells gift cards, top-up cards, and pre-paid credit cards, to the opposite side of the store. Khalid, who owns the place, doesn't trust a lot of the neighbor-hood kids, but for some reason, he doesn't give me a second look when I walk in. He's watching a small TV bal-anced on the corner of his counter. CP24, the news chan-nel, shows a constant stream of people getting arrested or the government doing the bare minimum. People are protesting again, downtown and in other cities. In rural communities. Politicians are joining them, which is so stu-pid, honestly. It has very "help *me* stop *me* from ruining society" energy.

I need to ration what I have for my phone and my tran-sit card, but Khalid only does phone top-ups here. I grab a top-up card and bring it to the counter. "Hi."

He grunts in response, taking the card, scanning it, and reading out my total: "Twenty even."

I hand him a crumpled bill and he taps the counter, tell-ing me to leave it there. His eyes are homed in on the TV. I glance at it—just another news report—as I take the card and disappear.

Tanya's house is a corner house, so her front yard is

huge. The family uses it more for parking, though. She has so many relatives and they're always visiting, parking half on the lawn and half on the driveway to fit everyone's cars in. "Zim people, African people," she would say, tsking and shaking her head. I wanted to relate so bad. My family is an anomaly as far as Nigerian families go. We never really had a large community of friends and family here. My parents always kinda kept to themselves, only letting a few people in.

The sweet smell of spices in the air greets me when I step into Tanya's. Her mom doesn't work, so she tends to be at home, letting something simmer on the stove. When I first stayed over, she looked me in the eye and said, "Sorry, I can't make your traditional Nigerian food. We're from Zimbabwe," in a voice that made me feel I had done something wrong. Tanya's mom has always been really cool with me, but it took me a while to realize she meant it like she wished she could do more. She didn't need to. They let me stay. That was more than enough.

Voices chatter in the living room on the other side of the wall as I slip off my shoes and set down my bag. My socked feet pad their way down the hall. The closer I get to the living room, the quieter it gets, until Tanya appears, almost bumping into me—blocking me from the doorway. She stumbles, her long, dark hair settling messily around her shoulders, and she smiles at me, nervous and awkward. "Yo, Summer," she greets.

My eyes flash behind her head: her parents on the couch and CP24 on the TV.

Then, back to her. The panic in her eyes.

Within moments, the TV is shut off and quiet drapes over the room.

I know what they were watching, so I spare her the discomfort. Instead, I carry it on my own, feeling my stomach twist and lurch at the idea of another report on my parents. Another public plea from the police to find them.

Another shameful reminder that they're on the run.

My throat feels like it's closing up. It's so hard to swallow, but I do so anyway, just so I don't sound as hoarse. "Uh, h-hey. Hey. Can I . . ." My words get stuck in my throat, too. I don't even know what to ask her. Just trying to fill the air so this whole encounter—the both of us pretending that the people she saw on TV with a big WANTED marquee under their faces aren't my parents— will feel more palatable. Luckily for her, I'm a pro at this. Sidestepping, weaving, maneuvering. I do it so easily, both on and off my skateboard.

Suddenly, I think about Gardenia and how serious she was about finding my parents, finding me guardians who could deal with my tuition deferral. Then I think of my home, how I probably won't be able to go back to it the way I used to, and how I found a letter addressed to the last person on earth I ever thought I'd hear of again. It hits me all at once.

"I gotta go," I tell her, my voice uncharacteristically high. I turn on my heel and backtrack to the door.

Tanya follows, practically stepping on my heels as I

make my way to the front hall. "But you just got here! You don't have to leave. You said you'd stay till the weekend, right? Is it because of the news? Man, I swear, that shit was just on TV, like, we weren't actually watching it. Plus, it's kinda everywhere again, you know, now that new details have come out . . ." She goes on forever. I hate how guilty she sounds, when in reality, it doesn't even matter. It's on TV. It's on my face. Everyone can see it. *Everyone* knows about my parents. And I don't—I don't care.

"No, no, you're good," I manage to get a word in. My voice cracks with my own nervousness. I slip my shoes on and throw on my clunky backpack. When I straighten back up, Tanya's face is scrunched with regret. I say again, "It's cool. I'll explain later, but there's this thing with a social worker, so I might need to go to Sid's at some point."

She raises an eyebrow. "Oh, wait, what?"

"I'll explain later, I said."

"Yeah, but—" She reaches out for my arm to stop me from running. "Is it serious? What happened?"

I let my weight shift from one leg to another, while Tanya's grip on me loosens. "It's . . . They just need . . . They found out I was on my own," I say finally. Her brows furrow, drawing creases in her forehead. With this, she looks just like her mom: always a bit panicked at every little thing. "And now, they might be calling Sid's parents to see if I can stay there."

Tanya's concerned-auntie face doesn't let up. "That's major, my friend," she utters. "Will you be okay? Should—

hey, you know what, hold up." She taps her chin, nodding. Ideas piece together in her head. "Are you headed there now? Maybe my mom can drive you—"

"No!" I say at once. "N-no, it's fine, honestly. Don't worry about it."

Tanya frowns. "Yeah, but—"

"I said don't worry," I shoot back. My voice can come out sharper than I mean it to sometimes, but Tanya doesn't even flinch because she knows this already. She just tilts her head, stares at me. I'm the one who shies away from her gaze. I didn't mean to be so harsh, but I just, I mean, I wish people wouldn't make such a big deal about this. About any of this.

I avoid her searching gaze, saying, "I'll be back," while I slip out the door.

My backpack feels extra heavy as I'm heading down the road. I drop my skateboard and begin a steady glide back to the bus stop, ignoring the beads of sweat that have started forming along my nose. I feel lotion and sweat moisten along my arms.

A lot of the buses heading out of Tanya's neighborhood serve the business areas, so they're always packed with people who have career jobs. Consultants and lawyers and managers. Executives. People like that.

I tap my transit card and shuffle my way to the back, trying not to hit anyone with my board. The dirty stares are too many to count. People slip back to let me slide through as much as they can, but whenever the board under my arm knocks someone accidentally, they kiss their teeth and start muttering under their breath. I keep my head down.

My skateboard slips a little just as I shimmy past a mother and her stroller, and the wheels knock a passenger behind me.

"Damn, *ow*, watch where you're going, fam."

I freeze at once. My shoulders hunch with crippling anxiety and my heart starts pounding louder and faster. I'm too terrified to look at their face or to acknowledge their voice. People nearby avoid my eyes like they don't want to get dragged into a stress-fueled argument outside the West Mall. And me, I wish I could disappear forever. I hate the attention; I hate so many people staring at me.

Suddenly, someone—the guy who called me out—grabs me by my shoulders from behind, shaking me while he—he laughs. "Yo, did I scare you?"

I shrug his hands off and shuffle around to see Jet staring back at me, wide, toothy grin, lip piercings, and all. The last time I saw him, his high-top fade was looking a bit janky, but it looks as if he's fixed that up now. He skates, too, and I see him at the park sometimes. We're not really friends, though.

Jet is like me—or, he's not really like me, but sometimes I feel like he wants to be. Displaced. Who would want that?

He looks unfazed, as if he didn't almost cause me to have a heart attack on this bus full of corporate white people. I open my mouth, still in shock from the scare, but nothing comes out. The bus lurches forward and I brace my feet before I go flying into him.

He's still snickering like a fiend. I give him a playful shove in the arm and stutter, "Wh-what's your problem?"

"I seen you get on all sketchy, head down and stuff, and I wanted to scare you," he says easily. Everything Jet says is easy, like nothing matters. "Where're you headed?"

"I'onno," I tell him, adjusting the strap on my backpack. He nods to it. "That heavy?"

"No," I say. "Just not a lot of room on here." The bus slows toward its next stop and I dread the new wave of passengers trying to get on and off in such a cramped space. Not to mention, these small bus windows aren't bringing in any new air. I feel like I'm baking.

Jet cranes his neck, probably to check the number of new passengers getting on. "Should've taken a rideshare or something," he says as the first of the riders begins to shimmy down the aisle.

The corners of my mouth lift in a subtle smile, but it's gone as soon as it comes. I'm seriously running low on money. The bus and my skateboard are really my only options, and I like to save bus trips for longer distances. I need to make sure that three dollars and my two-hour transfer window stretches.

There are so many things I had to start doing the moment I left home. Plan bus routes (plan when I can get away with not paying), pack light (know what to leave at friends' places and what to take along), always wear comfortable shoes (distribute my weight evenly so the soles last longer), carry five dollars in change (mostly quarters), avoid the TVs (don't wanna see), avoid the radios (don't wanna hear)—don't look too hard at anyone in case they see a bit of *them* in me. They could recognize my high forehead, my soft chin, my sharp eyes, the brownness of my skin, my last name. And they will know right away. Then, there would be nowhere I could run where they couldn't find me.

Bodies squeeze onto the bus, turning us all into one long limb. Jet and I have to shift farther down. One of his feet is on the step to the raised level in the back, and the other is awkwardly sandwiched between my feet. I hug my board to my chest so the wheels don't smack anyone else in the arm.

When I look up, the top of my head almost knocks Jet in the chin. He's taller than I am, which isn't too surprising, I guess, but I'm so used to everyone being shorter than my five eight. It's almost a relief to look up to someone.

He glances down at me. I say, "Next stop," and he nods quietly. The person closest to our right, closest to the back door, stifles a frustrated groan, likely because that means he has to move out of the way soon.

The bus crawls to our stop. The moment it's safe, we push open the back doors and wrestle our way outside. The outdoors smells like the indoors. There's no respite in this shitty weather. Not in this city. Not in the summertime.

Jet takes a huge gulp of the smoggy air and stretches his long limbs. I readjust my backpack again, whipping it around briefly to make sure it's still all zipped up. Jet chuckles and says, "Man, and that wasn't even a rush hour bus," while he does a few exaggerated lunges.

I just shrug.

"Need help?" he asks, gesturing to my backpack.

"It's honestly not heavy," I tell him, but he approaches and helps me slide it off, anyway. I feel the difference immediately and my back straightens up. "Thanks," I utter.

"All good."

"So where are *you* headed?"

He chuckles as if I said something funny and continues to walk like he's the one leading. The backpack looks like it costs him nothing to sling over his shoulder while he carries his skateboard under his other arm. I adjust my board under my arm, too.

Jet doesn't say anything until we get to the intersection. Sid's house is farther west, but I haven't decided if I'm going yet. I know he's not home, and even if he was, he's probably busy so, once again, there's no point going. Instead, I decide on the skate park. I'll hang around for a bit until I head back to Tanya's.

Slowly, I let my feet shuffle down the street. Jet follows.

He stays quiet in that way kids do before they're about to blurt out a big secret. When we get to the park, he hands me my bag back and makes sure he's composed enough before he says, "Don't pay the news that much attention, you know? People . . . They'll say whatever, man. It doesn't matter."

At one point, I couldn't escape my parents' faces on TV. The roundness in Mom's cheeks—usually lit up with the fullness of her laugh—suddenly sunken and colorless across the news. My dad's usual sharpness, dulled behind the weight of shame. Everywhere I went, it was a reminder that maybe I should be a little bit ashamed, too.

But Jet is right.

"I know," I tell him with a small smile. "It doesn't matter. Not much actually does."

CHAPTER THREE

I DON'T MENTION TO SID that a social worker may be calling his house until I see him on Friday. I text to ask if we should go skate and he says yes, so at least I know he's home. Then, I say: *A social worker might come looking for me at your place btw*, and he sends back a long string of question marks.

Tanya and I get a ride from her mom, who spends the majority of the ride glancing at me in the rearview mirror. She is unreasonably quiet the whole way there, and when we climb out of the car, she only waves with a press-on smile. "Okay, you two be careful," she says, and drives away fast.

Over the past year, I've spent so much time at Sid's house, but I feel it always welcomes me back the same way: with cautious smiles. Overcompensation. Mr. and Mrs. Costanza are okay people and they were awesome to let me stay here so often, but I still can't help but feel as if I'm intruding. As if I'm taking up space where I shouldn't.

When I sit down to meals with them, I try to finish all of it. It's a guilt thing. I feel guilty for being here when I shouldn't be; I feel guilty that they're looking after me when they don't have to. Me and this feeling are together all the time these days, and it comes out in my voice, when

I utter a soft but guttural thank-you after every meal, or when I make sure to wash, dry, and put away the dishes before I go to bed. It's hard.

But then, when I come here, I have Sid.

And he understands me in a way I wasn't sure was still possible.

We've been close all through middle school and high school. Even though we don't hang out as often as we used to—or spend as much time skating as we did before—it's still nice to know we have each other.

He doesn't judge me, either.

When he sees Tanya and me, he can probably sense immediately that I'm tense. I'd been putting off telling him about Gardenia for many reasons, but mostly because I didn't know how to bring it up at first. I mean, the reality is this: Gardenia knows who I am, knows who my parents are, and she may not let me jump around from house to house anymore. I'm so freaked out, so hyper-aware that I'm being perceived by a system I didn't even know existed, that I can barely balance on my board. After wobbling off too many times, I sit on the curb outside Sid's house while he rides back and forth, up and down the street on his skateboard.

Tanya's farther down the curb, on her phone, while Kirsten sits beside me. She's leaned back, balancing awkwardly on her forearms—like, there's just no way she's actually comfortable. Every now and then, she shifts and pushes her thick, straightened hair over her shoulder, but her gaze is always trained on Sid. She watches him like she's studying, her eyes following him like they're being pulled by an invisible string. So she and Sid are dating. Whatever. She doesn't have to be this damn creepy.

Adding to that, she's kinda the worst. She's literally nothing like us: She doesn't skate, she doesn't play video games, she hates superhero movies, and she can't stand lo-fi hip-hop. Sid's last girlfriend was Black, too, but she wasn't *this* bougie.

Oh, and somehow, Kirsten knows about the social worker thing. I bet it's by osmosis—or, Sid showed her the text I hastily sent him about the situation.

Every time Sid skates past us, he throws out random words when he's in front of me. It just ends up sounding really garbled.

Swish! He skates by and, "Soisthisladygonnahelpyou findyourdadorlikeIdon'tknow . . ." and then, *swish*, he's too far for me to hear.

"Sorry, what?"

Kirsten sits up straighter, dusting off her forearms.

Sid skates over again, readjusting his hat, and, "Areyougettingadoptedorputintothesystemorsomething?"

Okay, I heard that one. "No one's getting adopted, relax," I tell him, though I'm not too confident that won't be the case. Gardenia did specify that I'm underage and I can't jump between my friends' places anymore. She also said they'd try to find my parents. "Try" being the operative word here. I've tried—I've *been* trying.

The police have been trying, too. Ever since my parents were wanted for credit card fraud.

I hadn't heard . . .

I mean, I guess I *had* heard the word "scam" being thrown around my family before, if I'm being honest. It didn't mean much to me because Dad would call everything a scam.

The dentist insists I get braces? Scam; he just wants more money.

The mechanic says we should fix the brakes on our car? Scam; the brakes were working just fine a minute ago.

My parents made it seem like everyone was out to get something. *Who would do something for free?* Dad would say. God, he would always say it. When I'm rocking myself to sleep, biting my tongue to keep the bad memories at bay, that's still the first thing I hear in his voice. No one does anything for free. No one ever helps for nothing.

The police never came to our house or anything—at least not until it was too late. It was all really hush-hush. On that day last summer, I remember hearing my parents' voices get louder and louder as the hours went on. Whispers turned into eruptions by the evening. My mom's voice vanished first. She probably took off earlier than I realized. The doorbell rang, loud and unforgiving—I heard some more talking, a voice I recognized, like an auntie or an uncle. And then, they were all gone. Dad, too. Of course, I didn't think it was out of the ordinary. That's what I told the police when they came way after: *Why would it be suspicious? It was just, like, a regular evening.* Did I remember hearing anything odd? *No, I was watching a movie with my friend in my room.* So there was someone else there with you? *Nooo, like, she was on the phone watching from her house and we were texting. Yeah* . . . So many questions. I didn't get what the big deal was.

But when I saw my parents' faces on the news the next day, their names, Jacob and Mabel Uzoma, in bold, with WANTED and CREDIT FRAUD streaming across the bottom of the screen . . . I got it. I understood as much as I could in that moment, at least. They were in trouble. Or maybe, they *were* the trouble. The scam.

The details are wonky, and everything I know about this, I've learned against my free will. There's an influencer named Holland Jericho, who goes by Holly, and she does . . . or, she *did* mediocre reviews of beauty products on her YouTube channel. My parents, I mean, they always told me they owned a company that sold face creams. Mom would refer to the many small white boxes around the house as "the cream," and I was never really interested in it past that. They would send off the cream in droves every week. That was their livelihood. And our house was nice, so you know. I didn't ask. I never asked any questions.

One day, Holly decides to look into the cream after being sent a sample. Before her exposé? She got ten thousand views a video, usually. After she dropped her twenty-minute rant on how this cream contained harmful chemicals and was, essentially, not fit for use on humans? Five hundred thousand, easy, and it only grew from there. The beauty community was rabid, and the business community, even more so. Because her dad owned a company and that company happened to be responsible for assisting with regulations on beauty supplies sold in Canada.

Once he got involved, it was the beginning of the end.

Each week, Holly would release a new video, digging more and more into my parents and their company. They revealed that it was a shadow company, a place that existed only in name, and that the bulk of the transactions that went through the company were carried out by credit cards that had recently been canceled. All stolen cards. That's when the police got involved. That's when the news cycle started.

Mom and Dad aren't in jail. I know that much, otherwise the media would stop reminding me every damn day that they still haven't been caught. It's worse knowing they're out there. Since the disappearance, I've heard nothing from them and nothing from the family friends they used to keep so close—aside from Auntie Dara, who they never really got along with, anyway. She dropped off a tray of jollof rice the Saturday after my parents split, and she hasn't contacted me since. She's keeping her distance, the way people in our community do when there's something bad going on, when there's something that gives us a bad rap. In our culture, nothing is worse than shame; no act worse than losing face. My parents, the scandal surrounding them, was cliché, but it was my life. That didn't make a difference to anyone, though. It didn't make me sympathetic to them; it made me a stain. Valueless, just like my parents.

The police stopped coming around, too, once they

realized I knew nothing. They didn't ask if I had relatives; they didn't ask if I would be okay. I could tell in their eyes, the way they talked to me, that they didn't really care. So they let me be. I was on my own.

At first, living alone was pretty cool. I got to do whatever I wanted, watch whatever I wanted, and stay up late playing music until I fell asleep in the middle of the living room floor. None of my teachers asked for my parents' signatures on permission slips, probably because they didn't wanna upset the girl whose mom and dad were suspected criminals. Whatever. I also never let my grades drop because average or high grades meant that my teachers would never ask questions. No one worried about me. I was set. It was fine. I almost covered that hole, that emptiness, that reminded me at every turn I'd been left behind.

But then the food started to run out. No problem, no worries, I had money. I had at least $500 saved up in my room from different birthdays and holidays. I also started to sell stuff around the house, like the sofa, my bike, some books I didn't want. Then, I'd have enough to drop $10 here or $30 there buying groceries. Who knew fruits and vegetables were so expensive? Who knew how fast $500 could turn into $100? Could turn into $50?

And I'd just wait. I didn't even know what I was waiting for. My parents to come back? The police to show up? My school to call? Someone to actually give a shit about me?

Because of the news and all the YouTube shit, I'm willing to bet all my friends knew from the jump, but none of them said anything to me. Maybe they didn't know how. I don't blame them. I couldn't talk about it, either. At first, every time I tried to tell anybody, it's like this hole in my chest grew bigger and bigger. It swallowed my emotions; made my thoughts disappear. Forced me to say things like "It's not that deep," when Sid would ask, or "Don't worry about it," when Tanya would suggest I stay an extra night at her place. Sometimes it hurt, but most of the time, this emptiness didn't feel like anything. Couldn't bottle it, couldn't pinpoint it.

No one asks me about my parents anymore. It's like an unspoken rule and I'm cool with it that way. What would I say, anyway? How my parents are wanted criminals, they're both missing, and I was too scared to tell people that no one was taking care of me anymore because I thought that would mean I'd be sent away to God-knows-where—and I just wanted to stay here, party with my friends until my senior year was done, and figure out the rest later, when I turned eighteen and would become invincible? And I *would* figure out the rest because that's how I am: strong, resilient. Nigerian.

This—being uncertain, being cold and scared in an August breeze—isn't me.

But I don't know what to do about it.

Kirsten chortles beside me, bringing me back from the awful memory of my family, of Auntie Dara, of that weird letter. Now I'm stuck in the awful present of having to converse with Kirsten. "So are they gonna go through the police to find your parents or something?" she snickers.

I shrug. My throat clams up.

"Girl, shut up," Tanya groans with a roll of her eyes.

Kirsten gasps, arched eyebrows and wide eyes feigning shock. "Whaaat? I meant it seriously. Because they're, you know, *wanted* by the police." She whispers the last bit as if it makes a difference. As if her quieter tone won't make my heart thud with fear.

Sid circles back around to the curb, slowing his pace before he flips up his board and catches it with his hands. Then, he comes to sit beside me. Not Kirsten; me. I feel the tension immediately. Kirsten leans back on her forearms, I'm guessing to make her torso look longer or something.

"You think they can find them?" he asks.

I grunt. "I dunno."

"I mean, they found you, after all."

"Yeah, but . . ." *I wasn't trying to disappear.*

I look down, focusing on my bare knees glowing brown in the summer sun. The thick air makes it a little harder to breathe, so I inhale and push out a breath from the cracks between my teeth.

Sid watches me but says nothing. He pulls his cap from his head and ruffles his wavy brown hair. We stare out in front of us, across the street to the other set of houses that look just like the ones behind us. In the distance, there are birds and cars, but none of them makes their way to the place we're in.

Then Sid asks, his voice quiet like it's only the two of us, "Do you think you're sad?"

The way he says it makes me feel like he's talking about a different kind of sadness. Emptiness. I push it away and force a scoff that sounds more painful than casual. "Tch, no? Why?"

He looks at me. We used to stare into each other's eyes because we have a hidden language that doesn't need words. He's looking for it there now, but I turn away, focusing back on my knees.

"I think I would be," Sid says finally, "if I were you."

I shift, feeling my hands and feet prickle with unease. My back sits taller and I grab my unused board, setting it on the grass behind me instead of on the road. "Yeah, well . . . ," I mumble, still rearranging myself here and there. Yeah, well.

Sid doesn't push it. He leans forward, touching his forehead to his knees, and when he comes back up for air, he pushes his hair back and fixes his hat on his head. "D'you wanna go?" he asks, gesturing down the road. "At least once around the block."

"Oh my god, again?" Kirsten pouts. "You said we'd watch a movie if I came over."

Tanya frowns. "I thought you hated Marvel movies? Did—did no one tell her that's what we're watching?" she stage-whispers to me. I bite my tongue to keep from smiling too wide.

Sid jumps to his feet. "This'll be, like, five minutes. Ten tops." Then, he reaches for my hand to pull me up. I get up on my own. The last thing I need is Kirsten breathing down my neck because of a helpful gesture.

Kick, push, and we're off. The smogginess intensifies as Sid and I weave through the summer haze. I can't feel the wind on my scalp, and it reminds me again that I need to redo my braids. The breeze flutters my skirt and tickles my bare shoulders until I can barely even remember the sadness Sid was asking about.

But still, I spend the afternoon thinking about it and what it feels like. What it smells like and sounds like. Maybe I am sad and don't know it.

Tanya calls as we're making our way back to Sid's place. Confused, I bring my phone to my ear. "Tanya?" I say when the call connects. "Are you good?"

"Friend, my Summer," she says coolly, and then clears her throat as if she's bracing herself for a difficult conversation. Maybe she is. "My mom wants me to pick up something from my uncle nearby, so I gotta dip for a second. I'll be back, though."

"S'cool."

"Mmm," she hums. I push against the road again, letting her hum fade into the sound of my wheels ripping against the pavement. She says, "Actually, now that Kirsten isn't hovering, I wanted to ask you . . ."

I ignore the heightened tension, the tightened muscles in my throat, at the feeling this is a conversation I don't want to have. "O-oh?" Then I deflect. "Hey, um, did we check the bus schedule yet? What's the last bus for today, was it eleven or twelve, I can't remember . . ."

"I don't know. I'll google it," she says, brushing my nervousness aside. "What's going on with the social worker? Do you know if they called Sid's parents—"

My heart thuds, a resounding *boom!*, in my ears.

"—or if you have to leave? Mom has been wondering. Actually, I've been wondering, too," she goes on like normal, but all I can hear is a dull throbbing in my head. I try so hard to home in on Tanya's words, but these anxious feelings won't let me.

I shake my head. Big mistake. The throbbing gets worse. Deep breaths. Count to ten.

"Not yet," I tell her in a faraway voice.

"'Not yet' they haven't called or 'not yet' you won't have to leave?" she asks. "I'm just worried, my friend. Remember when you used to go back to your old place all the time? You don't still go there, do you?"

Boom-boom-boom.

"N-no," I sputter out. "Why would I?"

Tanya is silent for a moment, taking in my lie. She knows. About slipping by my old house, peeking in windows, checking the mailbox, hoping to see a glimpse of *something*. Even though I didn't care.

Now, I have this letter addressed to Auntie Dara. Even though I *don't* care.

My foot pushes against the ground again and I try to think of a way to change the topic. The last thing I want to talk about is my parents.

"Like, this social worker getting in touch with you out of nowhere," she continues, wistfully. "It's too much of a coincidence. Isn't it almost a year to the day—?"

No.

"I—I gotta go," I sputter out.

A *year*.

"Sorry, I just—I gotta go." My fingers start to tremble as I pull the phone away from my ear. *Boom-boom-boom.* "See you later, don't be mad, I'm sorry," I blurt out and hang up.

I do another lap around the road without telling Sid. I just need to get my nerves out, need to calm down. By the time I circle back to his house, he's sitting by the curb and, luckily, Tanya is nowhere to be found. He jumps to his feet when he sees me. "The hell? Where'd you go?" he asks, confused. "I looked back and you just disappeared."

"I—I just needed to clear my head."

His brows furrow deeper, but he doesn't push it. I'm happy he doesn't. I already feel like an asshole.

Behind him, I see his mom appear on the porch of their house. She gestures me forward and I take this opportunity to jog past Sid so I can't see the disappointment in his eyes.

"Summer . . ." She smiles, slow and wide. "Can you come in here for a second, please?"

"Sure," I say, and disappear into the house without a second look behind me. As I walk, I take deep breaths. Try to count to ten. My feet and hands move on autopilot, but inside me, there's a storm.

I set down my board and make my way into the kitchen, bright and expansive with chestnut-colored cabinets and sparkling white floors. It's always clean in here. There's never a crumb out of place. Seeing its perfect geometry helps put me at ease. I count cabinets; I count tiles.

Sid's mom stops me, reaching out a hand for my wrist

before I get too far into the room. "Actually, there's something I wanted to talk to you about . . ." She guides me over to the kitchen table where she's left a handwritten note and her glasses.

Oh no. That note could be about anything, but my mind immediately goes to the worst-case scenarios: someone's dead, someone's been murdered, it's my real birth certificate and I'm actually only sixteen!

I tremble as I watch her put on her glasses and unfold the note, peering at the scribbles. The kitchen is filled only with the sound of a pot simmering on the stove before her voice cuts in. "Someone named Gardenia Cruz called for you—well, *about* you today."

"Gardenia?" My heartbeat quickens as I take a shaky step forward.

She glances down at the note, skimming over the words. "She says that if you can't call her today, that's fine, but she has our address . . . You know." She pauses, resting a hand on her hip. "I thought she would want to come by, but she didn't seem too interested in any of that. All she said was she, and I quote, 'found and vetted a match,' and that she'd be by Monday morning to 'escort' you."

"What?" I spit out. This wasn't on my list of scenarios at all. My eyes fall to the paper, then Mrs. Costanza, then the paper again. "She . . . Sorry, what? She found my parents?"

I want to look at Sid's mom's note, but before I can take a step closer to it, she lifts it to her face and starts reading again. "'Found and vetted a match, Hikari Ol . . . Oluchi?

Arai?' Does that name sound familiar to you? Gardenia says they're a relative of yours."

Well, there's a name I haven't heard in forever. "That's . . . my cousin," I say, dumbfounded. My cousin Olu is my auntie Amaka's daughter. She's like two years older than me, and apparently she's famous in Japan or whatever. Japan, where she *lives*. There's no way she'd be back here. "There must be a mistake," I say. "Olu doesn't live here. Her and my auntie Amaka and uncle Ken moved away ages ago. I barely know her. And she's, like, my age."

"Well, this Gardenia says your cousin now has a residence in the Port Credit area."

"Ew, Port Credit?" I grimace. Okay, there's nothing wrong with Port Credit; it's just not my scene. Too stuck-up for my tastes. Everyone thinks they're worth something just because they live by the water. I don't know what that says about Olu, though. "Wait, is she sure?" I step forward and look down at the note to confirm. It's all there: "found and vetted a match, Hikari Oluchi Arai in Port Credit, coming at 9:00 A.M. on Monday to escort Summer."

Sid's mom smiles, though it looks apologetic. "I don't want you to think we don't enjoy your visits," she says, reaching out to give my shoulder a squeeze. "We do, dear. But, I mean, legally, we haven't been approved by any sort of association . . . A-and we wouldn't want to get you in trouble, you understand, by keeping you here longer than we're allowed to. I don't know. The whole thing confuses me, if I'm being honest. So this is great news. It sounds like maybe this cousin of yours can offer you a permanent residence."

I doubt it. Best-case scenario? Olu knows what happened to my parents and is here to gloat. Worst case? She has no idea I'm even coming.

CHAPTER FOUR

KIRSTEN HANGS AROUND A LOT when I'm at Sid's, as if she thinks I'm scheming to steal him away from her. On a normal day, I don't care. On a day like this, when my mind is so wrapped up in this social worker and my cousin—my *cousin*—showing up, it makes me restless. I can't take her sideways glances as I move through the house, so I grab my board and head out into the muggy air.

I kick and push my way down the road, nothing but the sound of my wheels skirting along the sidewalk to comfort me. Kick, push, breathe. It's medicine. It helps me clear my thoughts, too.

Thoughts about this social worker: She's really pushing it. She must see hundreds of kids a day, all with their own different sob stories, so why latch on to mine? I'm not a sympathetic victim. My parents hurt so many people. They stole so much money. I think, anyway. Like I said, the details are wonky, and everything I know, I've learned against my will.

This funny thing happens to my body whenever I hear about my parents or see their faces on the news. My breathing gets slow and fast at the same time, as if my brain has forgotten to give my body instructions on how to breathe. As if it *needs* instructions: Open your mouth, inhale, fill your lungs, exhale. I met a guy once who told me that when people faint due to being overwhelmed, it's because their brain forgot to send the signal to breathe. I never faint, but sometimes I feel like my brain stops communicating with the rest of my body. Every now and then, it's not so bad, if I'm being honest. Feeling everything all the time is nothing special.

Thoughts about tuition: Maybe Gardenia wouldn't be pushing the foster kid angle so hard if she knew I don't really care about school. None of my friends really know that I just applied for the hell of it. It was too much to explain back then. Sid said he was interested in York, and I kinda was at the time, so we applied together. York is in the city; it's close enough that I wouldn't have to leave . . . I mean, not that it matters, because I'm not really going. I should come clean to Sid, but then my foot pushes against the ground and I hear the whirring of my board's wheels beneath me, and I'll do it some other time, I swear I will.

And then, thoughts about my cousin Olu: Honestly, the last time I saw her, I was ten. She had come back to Toronto for the first time since leaving for Japan, and she spent half the trip sleeping because she was so jet-lagged. Auntie Dara used to always bring rice every other weekend when she wasn't beefing with my parents, so she fed Olu and asked her a lot of questions about life in Japan. Even then, I remember Olu being hesitant to respond. Maybe Auntie Dara was too overbearing. I don't know. But after that awkward trip, Olu went back home, and the next thing we heard, she became a celebrity. Like, overnight. Commercials, TV shows, music, all of it. I used to stalk her online just to see what she was up to, but I never reached out. We don't have anything in common, so to me, she's just another stranger.

And she's *two* years older than me.

When my foot pushes against the ground again, it's with fury. Why would the social work people think staying with someone who's practically my age is the answer? If anything, at least at Sid's or Tanya's, there are actual adults to look after me.

If they can't solve this tuition issue for you . . . well . . . Gardenia's voice is ripe in my head.

So if this all goes back to tuition, then I should say something.

Even if I'm not sure if that's what I want.

Even if I don't know what I want.

Freedom—true freedom. It's the most important thing to me. Once I turn eighteen, I swear . . .

Sid's mom asks us if we want to stay for dinner, but Kirsten can't and Tanya won't. Tanya's mom doesn't let her have dinner at other people's houses. I don't get it.

Sid's mom also says I can stay the weekend since Gardenia expects to pick me up from here. Tanya doesn't hesitate to say she can ask her mom to bring my stuff over. I slap the voice in my head that's saying her mom is trying to get rid of me.

On the TV in the living room, I see the faces of my

parents again. Holly has joined some civilian task force, and they came to her with information. Apparently, someone out there knows more about where my parents are than I do.

Sid sees the news report and quickly nudges me, saying, "Come on, let's go upstairs." I'm finally able to exhale when we get to the top of the second floor.

We go eat in his room while rewatching every movie he watched with Kirsten earlier. We're uncharacteristically silent through the movie marathon. I eat fast because I'm starving, but I also want an excuse to sleep early.

"Excited for Monday?" Sid asks while I'm slurping the last of my fettuccine.

I shrug. "Not really."

He sets down his bowl and reaches for his phone. "Should we look up your cousin? Just in case she's some kind of creep," he snickers.

I shake my head, a nervous chuckle sputtering out of my mouth. "Nooo, we don't have to. I mean, I don't care."

"If she's a creep or not?"

About anything.

"Yeah," I say with a forced smile. "Plus, the info might not even be in English, so . . ." Sid waits for a deeper explanation, tilting his head and gesturing as if there's more to tell. I begrudgingly launch into what little I know of Olu's life. "Uh, she's—like, her mom is my mom's sister, and her father is Japanese, so when she was young, they moved to Japan. She's come back to visit a few times, but she lives there . . . well, she did until now. She's also a legit celebrity." His eyes pop when I say that. "Yeah, yeah, like I'm sure the last time I heard about her, her song had just gone to number one on some chart and she was singing an intro song for this movie or whatever. That was a few years ago."

"Are you serious?" he gasps. "You've had a rich, famous cousin this entire time and you never told me?"

"I mean, I don't think about her ever," I say bluntly. "She has her own life."

He snickers again. "It's about to be *your* life."

"Enough," I groan, rolling my eyes. Biting back a smile.

Olu's life is probably so different from mine. I bet she's always had Auntie Amaka and Uncle Ken to look out for her. I bet they drove her to auditions or made sure she was being treated properly by producers. They'd reassure her when she was wary. They wouldn't abandon her.

In the evening, I take my place in the spare room, surrounded by my backpack and other stray items that couldn't fit inside it. This room is almost bare in comparison to Sid's room. It belonged to his older sister when she lived here, and now it's practically devoid of personality. The moon filters through the shutters to shine over my face. I stare at the ceiling for so long that I fall asleep without realizing it.

Sid is busy all day Saturday. "Kirsten's cousin has this thing and she wants us to go," he says in a quiet voice, as if he's still undecided. I stand in the doorway of his room after breakfast while he roots around for his phone. "You'll be good on your own, right?"

I cough out an incredulous laugh. "Yeah, obviously. What, are you worried about me or something?"

He grimaces. "I mean, I wouldn't say 'worried' . . ."

"I'm good," I tell him with a bit too much bravado, tossing my hair over my shoulder, crossing my arms.

"Tch, yeah, sure." Something in the way he looks at me says he doesn't exactly believe me. He finds his phone, stuffing it in his pocket, before he shimmies past me out of the doorway. I follow, counting the steps till the ground floor. "We'll hang tomorrow," he says.

"You don't have to, like, look after me or anything, you know," I say, meaning it to be cute and tongue-in-cheek, but as I hear the words, I realize I sound panicky. Distant.

Thankfully, he chuckles, reaching over to squeeze my shoulder. "Relax. It's not like I don't know where you go when I'm not around."

"Uh, and where's that?"

"Home," he says.

I feel cold the moment he removes his hand. In my ears, I can hear him shouting his goodbyes to his parents in the kitchen—I can hear him saying goodbye to me—but my body is locked down. At the last second, I raise my hand to wave before he disappears out the door.

"I don't always go back home," I grumble aloud in the silence of the front hall. Tanya thinks all I do is skate to my old neighborhood and wait for my parents to come back. Sid, too. I bet even Kirsten thinks the same thing.

It makes it sound like I'm stuck, like I can't move forward. As if I stare at the letter my parents meant to send to Auntie Dara with jealousy and anger and—and I don't know! Why can't everyone see that I *am* looking forward? On my birthday, by the time I turn eighteen, everything will change. They'll see.

"I'm going out to the park," I tell Sid's parents out of courtesy. They've never really been strict on letting me go out, but I figure I owe them that much since I'm staying at their house. When I'm at Tanya's place, her mom wants to know where I'm going, for how long, and, if I'm not with Tanya, who I'm meeting. "African parents, eh?" Tanya would say with a cringe, and we'd laugh together until it got uncomfortable for me to reminisce.

My parents were never really . . . like that. They knew who my friends were, so my mom might say, "Be safe," as I left, or "Come back before nightfall," while she watched her favorite evening game shows. She was fair that way. She never really—I mean, neither her nor Dad were very controlling. Or overbearing.

I shiver. It's useless to think of this now. What good will it do? I can't reconcile those memories with my reality. Instead, I grab my board and skate down the road, bringing out my phone to call Tanya. Sid might be busy, but I bet Tanya will have a bit of free time.

Or, maybe not.

"Sorry, my Summer," she croons over the line. So dramatic. "I have to do some stuff for Mac's orientation. I've been putting it off for *days*."

I push against the sidewalk, feeling a slight breeze on my forehead. "No worries. You're good."

"Oh, and I know I still have to help you with your hair, so just tell me when."

"Mmhmm."

"You outside? Where're you going?" she asks suddenly. I'm being extra sensitive because the second she says it, I start panicking, thinking she'll accuse me of heading to my old neighborhood. To my old house.

My shoulders hunch at the thought of having to drag my way through this conversation, so before she can get another word in, I tell her, "To the skate park, the one closest to Sid's. Thought I'd waste time there for a bit."

"Hey, when you're done, call me," she says. "If I'm done with this McMaster stuff, we can hang."

The tension eases from my shoulders as my foot pushes against the ground again. I'm propelled forward with a whoosh. "Yeah," I sigh, and stifle a yawn. "Yeah, let's link up later."

"Gotcha," she says, and hangs up before I do.

The skate park closest to Sid's place isn't the nicest, with its worn-down rails and rough ramps, but it's better than nothing. The terrain is better for bikes, so younger kids with their BMXes maneuver up and down the structures with ease. A few groups of middle schoolers do tricks on the rails. One nearly trips but makes a solid recovery. His friends start cheering, rushing to clap him on the back.

I circle the perimeter, feeling uneasy. That's like my constant state of being: a mild panic. It's there I run into Jet and a group of his friends, fellow high schoolers who I've seen from a distance but never met, as they're perched on a bench beneath a tree. Jet spots me but I ride faster, pushing against the ground to speed up so I won't have to stop and talk. I'm hyper-aware of how he watches me skate back around. I don't know why I don't just run away or something. Instead, like an idiot, I'm circling back to the rail closest to Jet and his friends.

He calls out, "Yo, I know you're not gonna pretend like you didn't see me!"

I force a regretful smile, which feels more like a wince, as I jog off my board and carry it over to them. Jet is grinning, hands clutched on the straps of his backpack, as I approach. He reaches out and we bump fists even though I don't want to. His friends nod at me, alternating "W'sup?"s filling the air. I nod back, then avert my eyes.

Jet grins. He is always grinning. "We're headed to the beach. Wanna come?"

"Why?"

"Uh . . ." He chuckles nervously. "Like, why we're going to the beach or why we're asking you . . . ?"

"Both, but mainly the former," I snort.

"Well, it's packed here," he says, gesturing around at the groups of younger kids. I know it's not possible, but they seem to have multiplied since I last turned around. When I turn back to Jet, he nods at my disturbed expression. "Exactly. So we thought we'd go chill for a bit, you know, see the water and stuff."

"But you can't skate there," I say as if they're missing the most obvious point.

"Yeah, but you can see the water and stuff," he chides,

as if I'm the one who missed the point. "I bet you've never been to the water before."

I slide back onto my heel, getting defensive right away. "So?"

"So?" he teases. "Come with us. It's not that far from here."

Behind us, a kid squeals when he wipes out on the rails. One of Jet's friends grimaces, so I know it's bad without having to turn around and see for myself. Then, Jet's friend says to me, "You wanna end up like *that* kid? That's what'll happen if you stay here, girl," and I laugh.

I laugh so suddenly that it scares him; I laugh so boldly that it freaks me out, too. Quickly, I press a hand to my mouth to stop the sound, but it's too late. Jet is grinning again, nodding heavily; he must know the second they leave, I'll be right behind them.

We skate to a bus stop. I feel awkward around Jet's friends, gliding in pace with them but not a part of the pack. They are boisterous and loud, just like Jet: a gaggle of Black and Asian kids who know how to fly in a way I haven't learned yet. One of the boys spreads his arms wide as he picks up speed, laughing because he has a split second to avoid a car before he crashes into it. And the sound, the laugh, is so full of life. I find myself just listening, unsure how to talk to these people who feel so different from me.

By the time we catch a series of buses, I realize we're headed to the Port Credit area. Ironic. As I sit next to Jet on the bus, watching the scenery catch up with us, something in me wants to tell him that I'll be moving here soon, that I'll be living in Port Credit with a cousin I barely know and this beach will be close to my backyard.

I've never seen the water, but the closer we get to the beach—the first steps off the bus, crossing the street, heading down a twisty, tree-lined path—the more I hear it. The waves. Jet and his friends cackle and shove each other, their pace picking up the closer we get to the clearing. The moment we're free of the trees, the moment we can no longer hear the busyness of the road behind us, the beach comes fully into view.

It's not spectacular, but . . .

The waves of the lake wash upon damp sand in an enclave surrounded by distant trees. The sun catches the water, which seems to move closer and closer like a sheet being pulled to shore. A few other people pepper the shoreline, standing with bare feet at the edge of the water, pointing at boats and birds in the distance.

It's not spectacular, but it's the stillness that gets me, that roots my feet in place while Jet and his friends run to the water. I hear waves and I hear wind, but not much else, and it's calming in a way I can't really describe. It's electric.

It's lonely.

I look down at my feet, unsure if I should . . . I mean, I could take off my shoes so I don't get sand in them. I could see what it's like to walk barefoot along the beach, like the groups of people near the shore. Like Jet's friends, too.

My feet shuffle forward, tracking more and more sand in my shoes. By the time I get to the shoreline, one of Jet's friends has already fallen in the water. Jet crows obnoxiously, and he glances at me when I settle in beside him. "This place is so close to our hood. It's *sick*, right?" he asks, like I've never seen water before.

"Yeah," I say. "It really is."

On Monday, I'll be living closer to this place. On Monday, I'll be in a new house with a cousin I barely know, a cousin who probably doesn't want to look after me because she's twenty years old and she's busy living her own life. On Monday, I'll still be a little lost, a little lonely, a little adrift.

But for now, I have the water.

CHAPTER FIVE

GARDENIA HAS ALREADY SENT ME two texts by the time I wake up around 8:00 A.M. The first is so I remember that she's meant to pick me up this morning—*Please have all your things ready as your cousin will be waiting.* And the second is to confirm Sid's address. As I crawl out of bed, I figure she's probably rolling up right now.

I shower quickly and stuff all my belongings into my backpack and a small item of hand luggage I took from my house before I left. I've left books, old headphones, and tons of rings—from my "I need a ring on each finger" phase in grade nine—at Sid's place before, but I can't leave anything behind this time. Each ring gets stuffed into my backpack, and the ones that don't get squeezed in get worn. Same with the headphones, dangling awkwardly around my neck while I roll the rest of my clothes into my bag and luggage.

The doorbell rings. I hear Sid's footsteps dragging toward the staircase. I didn't even know he was awake. "Hey," I whisper, sticking my head into the hall. With sleep in his eyes, Sid turns, gives me a shrug as if to say *What?* and continues down the stairs. I wrestle my bags closed and zip them as fast as I can before I chase after him.

I spot Gardenia the moment my feet touch the ground floor. She's clutching a bag and a clipboard, as if she's planning on interviewing someone. Her press-on smile is vapid, even when she examines Sid from head to toe. She asks, "Is—are you . . . Are your parents home?"

"No," Sid grunts, his voice still groggy. He says, "They don't live here," at the exact time I say, "They're at work."

Gardenia's eyebrows shoot up. "They what?"

"Yo, shut up," I hiss, fixing Sid with a glare. He snickers and steps back. I rush to tell Gardenia, "They're at work, but they for sure live here."

"Well, that'll have to be fine, I guess," Gardenia sighs, but still looks around my head as if we're lying about Sid's parents not being here. Then, she reaches out like she's going to take my hand. "Okay, we have to get going. Your cousin should be up and waiting for us. And there might be some rush hour traffic . . ."

"Sure," I reply. I glide over to my shoes, slipping them on as fast I can, feeling Gardenia's stern gaze on my back.

Sid calls, "Text me when you get there," from the foot of the stairs.

"Yeah, of course." I hitch my backpack up on my shoulder, step back and reach out for a fist bump. Somehow it feels final. Maybe I should've spent more time taking in the details of the house, paying more attention to Tanya's house, too. Now, I'm headed somewhere that's supposed to be more permanent, but I still can't help but feel like I'm just being passed to another temporary place. Everything is temporary until I turn eighteen. Then, I don't have to listen to anyone.

Gardenia drives an old sedan that looks way below her pay grade. She unlocks the passenger side door for me once she gets into the driver's seat. "You can throw your things in the back," she tells me. I put my hand luggage in the trunk, but I still settle in with my skateboard and bulky backpack between my legs. She glances at me but says nothing while we back out onto the road.

All the streets tend to look the same going at this speed, but there's a shift in scenery driving south toward Port Credit, toward the water. Large, tree-lined roads give way to thinner roads with perfectly pruned trees at even distances. Outdoor malls turn to boutique shops that line a busy road where upper middle-class people walk dogs and sip expensive coffees and stuff like that. It's kinda nauseating. I can't believe this is where Olu moved to. But then again, maybe I *can* believe it. She's not like me, and as we pull into the visitor parking lot of a stunning ten-story condo that has its own concierge, well, I mean, it's hard to feel optimistic about fitting in.

Gardenia doesn't say a word to me as we're let in by the concierge and take the elevator up to the penthouse. I get it, though. She's the kind of person who only makes nice for a purpose. She's already got me here, she's conned Olu into letting me stay or whatever, so she has no need for small talk. We stand side by side in the elevator, but it feels like even that's too close for her.

The elevator opens at the penthouse floor. I follow a pace or two behind Gardenia as she practically flies down the hall. She glances back at me before stopping at apartment PH6, her mouth shifting as if she has words stuck somewhere in her throat. I wait. In the end, she sighs and knocks on the door.

My eyes fix on the frame; my heart beats faster in anticipation. I hear footsteps shuffling on the other side, a soft voice groaning out something like, "Whaaaaat?" and I don't know if I should laugh or feel discouraged. I glance at Gardenia. She said Olu knew I was coming. Was she lying?

The door unlocks. I hold my breath.

Olu might hate me. She might take one look at me—tall, skinny, skinned knees, rough braids—and decide I'm not perfect enough for her world. Well, that'll be fine, because I don't need to be here. I really don't.

Finally, the door pulls open. Time slows while Olu creeps out from the other side, looking both like my aunt and uncle, looking a bit like my mother—and a bit like a . . . wreck.

I used to stalk her online sometimes, but I never reached out because why would she care about me? She's so glamorous and put-together. Olu is pretty, but today she looks like she's going through it. Her eyes are puffy as if she's been crying and her curly hair is all over the place. In most of her pictures online, it's straightened, but now it's suspended wildly above her shoulders. A mess of 3C curls that tell a different story.

She says, "Come in," in a voice that's so familiar to my ears even though it shouldn't be. It's not like I really had a relationship with her and know her voice like the back of my hand or anything, but within her inflection, I can hear my auntie Amaka. I can hear my family.

"Thank you. Summer, if you would." Gardenia is at my back, guiding me into the apartment, while she rolls in my luggage. I slip off my shoes and take a step in. The air in here is crisp, probably due to an air conditioner working overtime in this summer heat.

The apartment is quaint but so stylish, black on white on teal furnishings, a lounge chair positioned by the balcony door, houseplants breathing life into the space and everything. Just like Olu usually looks like a model from a magazine, this apartment looks like it was styled through an HGTV program. And knowing the area, this place must be *expensive*.

I turn to Olu who is putting away wineglasses, placing them carefully in the sink, and moving around what looks like an empty bottle. That explains a lot. When she catches me watching, she chuckles nervously. "Ah . . . I didn't get to clean up. I'm sorry."

I shrug. It's whatever.

"Can we all have a chat?" Gardenia calls as she settles onto the sofa. "Hikari, I'm going to need you to sign a few documents. Summer, there are a few things we need to go over as well."

"Yeah, sure," I say at the same time Olu says, "Of course!" We glance at each other, so aware that we're occupying the same space. I tiptoe over to the living room area while Olu follows behind me. Then, I sit beside Gardenia, and she takes up the lounge chair by the window.

Gardenia pulls out a file from her purse and spreads its contents on the table. Lots of forms I don't really understand. She tells Olu, "These are the forms we discussed. Please have a look and let me know if you have any questions," while she pulls a set of papers from the pile. Olu reaches for them, staring curiously. I have to remind myself that she's older than me because she really doesn't look like it. And then it begs the question, like, *why* do I have to stay with someone who's basically my age? Someone make it make sense.

"And, Summer." My concentration is broken when Gardenia hands me a brochure of some kind, *What to Expect in My New Home*. I want to vomit. "I know this is a difficult transition for you, so feel free to ask any questions that will help you process this easier. We can also set you up with a registered psychotherapist who specializes in working with youth, if you prefer. There's no rush, and initial sessions will be free of cost." She says the last part to Olu, who just nods. "That offer is always on the table."

Gardenia is silent long enough that I feel she wants me to respond. "Yeah, okay," I say bluntly. I can practically see the weight, the burden of another neglected teenager, drop off her shoulders. She literally can't wait to get rid of me.

"Do you have any questions for me?"

So many questions, but how to phrase them all?

First of all, *why* did I have to leave my friends' places? She said she'd do a home visit with Sid's family, so when did that idea go out the window?

Why didn't I have a say in getting moved here? Does my consent mean nothing anymore?

And who says it's better to stay with family anyway? I was with family, if she remembers—I was with my mom and my dad, and they left. So, if we're going by track record here, family is at a negative right now and friends are currently several points ahead.

Also *why* . . . just why couldn't she have left it all alone? I was fine where I was. I'm less than one month from being eighteen. There are other kids, ten-year-olds or six-year-olds, who need the help. *I* don't. The second the clock strikes midnight on my eighteenth birthday, best believe I'm taking my board and I'm gone. I don't know where I'm going, but I know it'll be far away from here.

"No questions," I murmur, and Gardenia sighs again, more relief and guilt peeling off her. Olu also shakes her head as she signs away on the last of the documents and sets them back on the table. It's so quiet in here that I can hear the wind softly hitting the window outside.

"Well. You guys are a very talkative bunch," Gardenia chuckles alone. It takes everything in me to not roll my eyes.

"If I have any questions, I can call you, right?" Olu asks.

"Yes, of course," Gardenia says, then puts on her serious social worker voice: "So I want you to know this isn't by any means a final meeting. In about a week, I'll come by again for a visit to make sure Summer is adjusting well. I'll come by monthly after that. Not to mention, I'm always available via phone."

She shouldn't bother coming by after I turn eighteen. There won't be a point.

"That sounds good," Olu says and smiles like an adult, warm and plastic, like she's dealt with adults like Gardenia her whole life. She reaches out her hand to shake Gardenia's, and they do so awkwardly. They shake hands again when they're at the door.

And then Gardenia is gone.

The apartment feels bigger and emptier without her presence. Olu turns around, and when we lock eyes, she offers a stiff smile. Yeah, she definitely hates me. She probably can't stand the fact that I'm intruding.

"So . . ." She clasps her hands together as she approaches me slowly.

I stand, smoothing out my skirt. Olu gestures to my clothes and says, "I like your dress. It's really cute."

I glance away. "Uh, thanks."

When I look back, her eyes wash over me like she's never seen anyone quite like me before. The fatigue in her face has disappeared and is replaced by what feels like wonder, intrigue, and a bit of relief. It makes me hyper-aware of my breathing. I grasp my wrists, roll my shoulders. "Um . . ." Not sure what to say here. "S-so. Which one is my room?"

"Oh! Yeah, of course," she gasps, and spins on her heel right away. "Come this way."

I follow behind until we get to a door directly across from the bathroom. When she pushes it open, I have to stagger back, shocked at the sheer number of stuffed animals on the bed and the floor. The walls are beige but lined with fairy lights and tacky posters that say things like, "Follow your dreams." On the far wall, there's a TV hanging with a shelf of games and movies underneath. And a PlayStation. She got me a whole ass *PlayStation*? Damn, she really does have money. "What the . . ." I look around, trying to take everything in and failing horribly.

By the time I spin back around to Olu, she's grinning, like *beaming*. "Do you like it? I kept thinking, like . . . what would you be into? And I like cute things and games, so, yeah."

"O-oh—"

"Because we're close in age, so I thought you might like what I would like," she says, and then gives her brow an exaggerated wipe. "There. I said it. Now we don't have to pretend anymore."

I snicker and I think she takes that as a good sign because she shifts, looking visibly more relieved than a moment ago. But I blank on what else to say.

Olu walks over to the bed and sits down. I can tell she thinks I'm going to join her because of the small uptick her eyebrow does when I don't follow. "Is it weird for you to be here?" she asks eventually. "Like, is it weird that, um . . . that you have to live with me?"

I shrug and say, "I don't know. I'm . . . It all happened so fast, so I don't really know—"

"Oh, I *know*," she cuts in. "It was fast for me too! One second, I'm sitting alone in my apartment, and the next, your caseworker calls and says—just, like, 'Be ready on Monday.' I was so shocked!"

"Y-yeah."

"Can you believe it?" She lets out a heavy sigh and rubs her cheeks. Forward, then backward, then forward again. "But anyway, you should eat or drink something. Come on." In one leap, she springs to her feet and glides past me out of the doorway. She barely takes a second to look back and make sure I'm following.

The first thing she does when we get to the kitchen is pull open the top drawers, grabbing mugs and an array of loose leaf teas. "I have almost every tea. It's the healthiest thing in my house," she says with a quick glance toward me.

"Green tea is fine," I tell her, and she gets to work.

I slouch against the breakfast bar as she fills the kettle, measures out the tea, chooses the mugs. It feels like I'm someone else, watching a movie about a girl who woke up one day and is now living in a penthouse apartment in Port Credit. I'm waiting for Sid to show up, nudge me in the back, dare me to race him down the street. I'm waiting for Tanya to burst into song. I'm even waiting for Kirsten to talk smack about my parents again. Anything that would make this feel legit.

After Olu brews and pours the tea, she grabs the cups and says, "Let's go sit in the other room," before walking by me to the sofa. I sit and reach for my cup. I take a quick sip, feeling the hot liquid burn the roof of my mouth. It takes everything in me not to flinch.

"So," she pipes up. "Tell me about yourself. Or, ah . . ." Nervously, she pushes her hair down and tucks a tuft behind her ear. From this angle, with more of her cheek-bones showing, she looks so much like my aunt, and in a way, like my mom, too. It's unnerving and I have to look away because there's this emptiness, you know. "Maybe I should tell you about me first . . ." She clears her throat and sits up a bit straighter. "S-so. It's me," she says, and chortles. "I guess . . . you don't know much about my life, right? I'm a singer. Also, I once did a commercial for a popular car company, even though I can't drive." Oh, so she's *rich* rich.

I ask, "So then what are you doing here?"

Her eyebrow twitches. My question hangs in the air. I know at once that it's not welcome. "I'm, um." She clears her throat. "I'm just . . . relaxing."

"For how long?" I take a big sip of my tea. "Gardenia probably thinks you'll be here forever."

Her gaze is distant. Just when I think she'll give me a straight answer, she claps her hands together, the loud sound echoing through the quiet room. "Gardenia, she's so interesting, right? Anyway, y-your turn. Tell me all about Summer," she says with a fake ass grin.

I swallow, unease creeping into my throat. Even if she's being fake, her increased attention makes me squirm a little. It's weird but I really wasn't prepared to share like this. I thought she'd show me my room and leave me to do whatever while she got on with being a celebrity or something. Recording music, selling cars, stuff like that.

She waits and waits, not once wavering, no matter how long it takes me to open my mouth. I don't even know where to begin; I don't know how to act around her. She looks at me, talks at me like we're sisters, but I just *can't* seem to . . . I can't. I don't know.

I squirm again before I say, "Uh. Well, what do you wanna know?"

She snorts. Her eyes scream, *Are you serious?* "How about everything? Gardenia told me a few things, but I think it's better to hear from you."

I twitch. "Things like what?"

There's that sharpness again. Olu flinches, and I don't blame her. Even a fool could hear the accusation in my tone. My heart starts racing at the thought of Gardenia, the exact kind of person who couldn't pick someone like me out of a crowd, telling Olu anything about what happened. It's probably all lies, everything she said.

Olu shrugs and says, "That . . . you needed help, and that your parents aren't here anymore."

I raise an eyebrow. "I need *help*?"

"With money," she cuts in, as if that'll actually make this all better. "Like, that you need help with money for, uh, university fees, I think?"

I scoff, confused. "So wait, you said yes because you wanna pay my tuition?" Never mind the fact that I wasn't even serious about going to university, but this doesn't make any sense to me. "How, like, *why* would you do that? Is the government giving you money for this?"

"Oh, wait, wait." She holds up her hands in surrender. Her body language shifts and she mutters to herself in what I'm guessing is Japanese. "Maybe I'm not saying it the right way. Sorry. I just meant that . . ." She takes a deep breath. I know what's coming. I've seen that look, that hesitation, before. My body tenses like it's waiting for a blow to the chest. "I heard what happened."

No.

"To your parents."

No.

"A-and, honestly, it sounds so horrible. I don't know how I would feel if my parents were serious criminals. Stealing money, using other people's cards, and sending out fake products. That sounds like the worst thing ever. I would hate my parents if they did that to me." She places a hand on her chest, leaning into it, playing into the devastation she'd feel if she found out her parents were wanted by the police. I can't move. My breathing slows, rising and falling as if there's a second blow coming.

But there isn't.

The air is stale with the reality of my situation. Everything comes to a halt.

Olu says, "I just wanted to make sure you're okay."

A switch goes off in my mind and I enter a vortex. There's just me and this emotion, this rage. "Don't I look okay, though?" I hurl out before I even realize I've said it. Olu blinks back shock, but I interrupt before she can say anything. "We don't even know each other like that. I'm not even going to that fucking school, so it's whatever. You didn't need to say yes to the caseworker people. I'll be eighteen soon, anyway, next month."

I don't know what to expect. Olu to get mad at me and

kick me out? Her to start crying and tell me I'm valid and I matter or something?

Instead, she shoots up her hand like we're in class, and says, "Oh, our birthdays are so close together. I turned twenty this past week."

What the *hell*?

Honestly? I wasn't expecting that.

Still, it proves my point!

"See? You're *twen-ty*. This is *in-sane!*" I groan and slouch back into my chair. "Why would the social worker people let you look after me?"

She stops for a minute, contemplating her words, before she says, "Because you don't have anybody else. That's what they told me."

It hurts unexpectedly to hear those words come out of her mouth. My mind says *that's not true*, but ugh, my chest tightens again. That emptiness, it stretches, morphs, turns into panic. My heart is doing a mile a minute, leaps and hiccups and twirls in my chest. I don't want to talk about Mom and Dad. I just wanna forget everything that happened.

And I do have—I *do* have people. I have my friends. They might have their own lives, they might be preparing for the next step, university and things like that, but I have them. They haven't abandoned me. Why doesn't that count?

Olu's voice—*Because you don't have anybody else*—it stings the more it loops in my mind.

I say, "I'm gonna go skate."

For a split second, the two of us stare at each other: Olu,

confused; me, fed up. I look away, unsure if she can see the fear in my eyes. I'm so embarrassed to admit that's what it is, too. Fear that she will ask more about my parents; fear I'll have to tell her I don't know anything other than what the media reported. Fear that being eighteen soon won't be enough to keep me from the truth that I'll still be alone.

"Skate?" she repeats.

I get to my feet and head to my luggage still stuffed by the door. My skateboard is leaning against the wall behind my backpack. Olu comes over, marveling at the grip tape, the roughed-up wheels, and the pink bunny illustrated on the deck. Her expression freezes in astonishment. She says again, "*Skate?*"

I nod. "Yeah." I wave a hand down my outfit, my signature short summer dress, but it doesn't really mean anything. I just like to wear dresses and I happen to skate.

Olu glances at the board before looking at me. "But you're . . . coming back, right?"

I open my mouth to say something stupid, but the way she looks at me makes me reconsider. Sadness creeps into her eyes. Maybe she doesn't realize it, but I recognize it so well these days that it's hard to ignore. In an instant, it's there. In an instant, it's gone.

And me, I don't know why I can't just say yes.

My silence seems to be enough for her. Olu musters a small smile before taking a step back. She dips around the side of the fridge and comes back with a few bills and a small plastic card that she holds out to me. "For the bus," she says simply. "And the keycard. For the main doors."

I take them without another word and disappear out the door. Soon, I'm skipping down the hall, toward the elevators, and outside to freedom.

I lament the tea I didn't finish as I hit the pavement outside, kicking and pushing down the sidewalk. Olu's apartment faces Lakeshore, a busy, major street, so I stay off the road and ride past pedestrians, ignoring the stares they give me as I pass. I know I'm probably not what they expected to see rushing past them on a Monday morning, but I live here now, so I guess they gotta get used to it.

Or, I guess, I *kinda* live here now. I didn't agree to anything. This isn't fair at all.

I want to go home.

When I glide to the nearest bus stop and reach for my transit card, my hand brushes against the letter in my bag. My fingers poke at it, as if it will disappear otherwise. I get on the bus, preparing to map out a new route to my old neighborhood, but when I sit down, Auntie Dara is the only thing on my mind. *Why couldn't she offer to let me stay with her?* My chest rises and falls with bitterness as the bus lurches forward.

Quickly, I punch the address to Auntie Dara's restaurant into my phone. Not that I care—not that it means anything, really—but if she knows something about where my parents are, I need to hear it. For all the years I had to stomach her bland ass rice, she owes me that much, at least.

"What are you doing, Summer?" I murmur to myself.

I haven't heard from Auntie Dara since the day she

came by with a tray of rice after my parents went missing. She set it on the counter and dusted her hands off, taking one look around the empty living room. The house felt so hollow at that time. I could sense the walls closing in, and maybe she did, too. Maybe that's why she never came back.

"Take heart, Summer," she told me in that comforting but condescending way my Nigerian relatives would say it. Whenever someone died, it was always "take heart," as if I should swallow my feelings instead of letting them run rampant, unattended. And Auntie Dara was never very touchy-feely or kind to us. I swear it was like every other week, she and my parents were fighting about something. I never knew what. We wouldn't see her around for months and then, suddenly, she'd resurface like nothing happened.

Standing in the middle of the house, I remember foolishly asking her, "Wh-what now?" My voice was so small and timid, and I couldn't even look at her because I was so anxious.

She didn't give me a real answer. "Ah, I don't know, o," she sighed, dusting her hands off again. That motion, that *I'm done with this, I've done enough*, is the last image I saw of her. She left and never turned back.

Auntie Dara hasn't reached out to me, probably hasn't thought about me once, since everything that happened last summer. Me showing up at her restaurant out of the blue wouldn't be well received, and I'm afraid to look her in the eyes again and see that same indifference from a year ago.

She knows about your parents, I tell myself. *She knows something. She knows something.*

Auntie Dara owns a Nigerian "small chops" restaurant in the northern part of Etobicoke. It's not the easiest to get to from Port Credit, but I make record time catching buses and gliding down the street on my board. Man, it's *hot*. The air sticks to me, slowing me down. By the time I get to the restaurant, I'm sticky and I'm sure the smog has burrowed deep into my hair—and I remember again that I have to talk to Tanya about these braids.

My feet come to a full stop when I see the restaurant.

And then I see her. Auntie.

She's wearing a T-shirt and jeans with her apron on top as she waves to a man who's rolling a cooler at his heels. I stand perfectly still, hoping that I can blend into the scenery. Become the wind, or something. But then she sees me, and I feel something in me shatter. She seems on edge. She doesn't come closer, just squints, probably trying to confirm that I'm who she thinks I am.

I step closer. I . . .

I can't do it.

Confrontation . . . I'm not good at it.

My feet stagger back, my knees refusing to bend. In rugged steps, I move away from the restaurant, away from her line of vision, and I take off running back down the road. She doesn't call out once.

CHAPTER SIX

OLU DRINKS A LOT.

I've been at her castle in the sky for two days, sparingly popping in and out because I still feel awkward being here, and sometimes I feel like that's all I've come to know about her. She likes red wine over white wine; she always has two bottles stashed in a cabinet. No matter how many times she opens a bottle, there will still be two unopened bottles in the cabinet closest to the fridge. It's the Law of Wine—the Law of Olu-Wine.

She probably thinks I don't notice, because she has wine with food in the afternoons or she'll be sipping on a glass while she's frantically typing on her computer, but the frequency that I see empty bottles at the kitchen table is actually ridiculous. This is a liquid diet, for real.

In the nighttime, she starts her nightly singing and dancing ritual—seriously, every night, she puts on music and starts dancing and singing alone in the living room. Spoiler alert: She's drunk.

To be honest, I pretend not to notice for Olu's sake, and also because I don't want to have that conversation. But most important, because it's none of my business. She's older than me. She can do whatever she wants. Once I turn eighteen, I'll be doing whatever I want, too, and I don't want someone like Olu to say anything to me, just like I'm sure she doesn't want me to say anything to her.

Besides, I have other things to worry about.

The letter. Auntie Dara. I *know* she saw me that day, but she didn't even try to . . . Like, she didn't even wave.

And I chickened out. Naturally.

I try again to go see her. I've almost become a pro at tracing the route from Olu's to the restaurant. It makes me think of my parents and I hate that it does. Something about this devastatingly boring trip through the suburbs reminds me of how my dad used to drive: never looking at the road, making sharp turns, but always enamored with life beyond the car windows. Marveling at the buildings or the skyline, saying things like, "Wow, when did that store move here?" I scrunch my nose at the memory, let my eyes glaze over as the bus bumbles on. I can't see any buildings, any stores. Just a city that is burning under an unforgiving sun.

My phone buzzes with a call from Sid. I scramble to answer in time. "Hello—?"

"You're alive?" he asks.

I give a tired chuckle. "Yeah, obviously."

"How's the new place?" After a moment, he asks, "How's the new parent?"

"Ugh." My eyes fall to the window, watching the unfamiliar cityscape pass in a blur. I'm lulled into a trance by the sweeping scenery, the moving cars, and the thick haze of smog in the sky. "She's, like, my age. And she basically called me a loner."

"What were her exact words?"

I roll my eyes. "You're supposed to just take my side."

"You sound like Kirsten," he says with a snicker, but I can hear the frustration.

"That's offensive."

"And you're not," he adds. "A loner, I mean."

I hum in response. I should say thanks, but the words are all stuck in my throat. I should say that Olu doesn't have to do anything for me, that I don't need a sister or a new mom, and she can go back to ignoring I ever existed so neither of us gets too tangled up in this fake life we have to lead. But they're all stuck, the words.

Sid's voice cuts through the confusion in my head. "What's her name again? Can I look her up now or is that weird?"

"Hikari Oluchi Arai. And yes, but go off."

The bus lurches to a stop a street away from Auntie's restaurant, and I get to my feet, balancing my board in one hand while I cradle my phone in the other. I walk down the steps to the bus's back door, waiting for it to sweep aside once the sensor realizes I'm there. The heat outside pummels me the second my feet touch the ground.

By the time I refocus on my phone, I catch the tail end of what Sid is saying. "... *really* popular for a hot second, actually." He's probably reading Olu's Wikipedia page. "Her career kinda stalled because of some relationship, it says. It's not super clear. But damn, you really never knew your cousin was this famous?"

I shrug, feeling a pang of irritation. "Dunno. Didn't really care."

"And this entire time you could've gone to Japan to visit her or something."

"Didn't really want to." That's not true. Even if I cared, my family wasn't super big on travel. I've never been out of the country. My auntie Amaka loved being in airports, darting back and forth to different countries, but my mom liked her feet on the ground. To me, she was always practical, sensible—until she wasn't.

Why am I thinking about my parents so much today?

"I gotta go," I tell Sid the moment Auntie's restaurant comes into view. As I stash my phone, I can't help but feel like I'm being watched. Is she in the window? Will she come outside to greet me this time?

Will *I* go inside?

The answer hits me immediately. "No, n-no way." I swallow, feeling my throat dry up.

For a second, it looks like the door is opening—"Nope!" I turn and take off running. Again! I race to the closest bus stop around the corner, my heart beating frantically in my chest, while I check my phone for the bus schedule. Honestly, what the *hell* is my problem? What's the point of coming all this way if I won't even talk to her?

I get back to Olu's, swiping my keycard on the ground floor and taking the elevator up while I stew in my misery. My frustration boils over into anger when I push open the door to Olu's apartment.

There's this almost aggressive pop song blaring out from her Bluetooth speaker on the coffee table. Olu's hair is tied up in a high ponytail while she sings into the remote, dancing around the living room like she's on stage. I—I freeze. I blank. I practically shut down. Should I go? My eyes dart around the room for an escape, and that's when they land on yet another open wine bottle on the kitchen counter. My chest pulses with the anxiety of not wanting her to see me in the doorway, and the sheer stress that, yet again, she's drunk in the middle of the afternoon.

Finally, she sees me. She nearly tumbles into the coffee table from shock. I turn to put down my skateboard and take off my shoes, my lips pursed together out of nervousness.

I take two steps forward and am met with a grinning Olu. Her eyes look both distant and present, and a little spacey, like she's watching two screens at once. I squirm under her awe-filled gaze. She's acting like I came back from war or something, like I didn't just spend two and a half hours sweating up and down the city.

"O-ka-e-ri!" she exclaims, exaggerating the largest grin.

"O . . ." I teeter back on my heel. "S-sorry?"

"Welcome back," Olu says with a giggle. "You're home already? You look so shiny, wow . . ."

Shiny? "It's sweat," I tell her, wiping my forehead.

"Shiny," she repeats. "Like a baby."

I suck in my lips, suppressing the urge to chuckle.

I can't rearrange my expression in time and she gasps, pointing an unstable finger at me, taking a wavy step forward. "Ah! You're laughing, aren't you?"

"N-no," I sputter back, but I have to hide my face. She's gaining energy from this, I can tell. She's practically giddy with excitement that I'm not completely stone-faced in front of her. Quickly, I touch my hair, wipe the back of my neck—desperately try to regain composure. "H-have you just been drinking this whole time?" I ask, forcing that edge back into my voice, the wedge that creates distance.

She seems unfazed as she shakes her head. "Nnn. I went to record a song first. I told you already." She did not. She forgets that we don't really talk.

I give her a quick once-over from head to toe. "Not gonna lie, I can't tell if it went well or not."

Olu throws her hands up with ease, which is a huge mistake because she's still holding her wineglass. I step forward, ready to catch it before the swishing red liquid hits the ground, but she steadies her hand before it does. I exhale, frustrated. Olu giggles.

"It went *so* well," she says, carefully guiding the glass back to her mouth. After a hearty sip, she continues, "My manager has been really, um ... well. Hmm. Nan-ka ..." She mutters back and forth between her two languages before eventually settling on: "My manager has been looking for a new song for me, and he finally found one. It's not really my style, but I'll record anything at this point, ha!" Her laugh is high-pitched and manic, and is only interrupted by another sip of wine. A desperate sip. I watch her carefully, recognizing the nervousness in her actions. The way her hands tremble, the way her gaze spaces out. The way her eyes can't focus or land on anything for too long. The way she paces, braces herself, even when she's standing still.

It's so clear. I don't get why I didn't see it before. She's not just drunk. She's running from something.

"I'm sending over the demo to him soon," she goes on. "But if you want, I'll let you hear it first."

I'm so fixated on the grasp she has on the glass that I almost miss what she says. When I snap back to attention, she's staring at me expectantly. "Uh . . ." I shrug. "Yeah, sure, whatever."

"Mmm! Okay, okay."

This is it: This is the record for the longest conversation Olu and I have had since I got here, and she probably won't remember half of it when she wakes up tomorrow.

I check my phone out of habit, then stuff it away in my bag.

"Your phone must be *really* interesting," Olu pipes up, and mimes texting, even though it looks more like she's pretending to use a game controller. "Maybe that's why you never want to talk to me. You're always on it, in your room."

I raise an eyebrow in confusion. "What? I mean, I'm just texting . . . friends and stuff." I'm not. When I'm in my room, I'm looking at that letter addressed to Auntie Dara. When I'm on my phone, I'm watching weird documentaries about the invention of paper or whatever. But she doesn't need to know that! "What, is that not allowed now?" I growl. A challenge.

"I didn't say that," she says, and then, "Can I meet them?"

I cringe. Can't help it. "But why?"

"It would be nice to know who you spend time with."

I scoff. "It's not that important." She'll meet them, and then what? Once I stop living here, it won't matter if she knows who they are or not.

Olu tilts her head to the side, confused. "How? They're your friends, right?"

I narrow my eyes. "Yeah, but *you're* not my—"

Summer, stop it.

My jaw clamps shut, but Olu isn't stupid. In her eyes, I can see something sobering begin to surface. She knows what I was going to say. *You're not my mom, you're not my parent. You're just a kid, too.*

She opens her mouth, hesitating through thoughts and words. Maybe she wants to tell me that she's not trying to be. Maybe she's finding the best way to tell me I don't know what I'm talking about. In the end, she says nothing. We're stuck, the two of us, here. The realization that we don't understand each other washes over me. For a moment, when we look at each other, it feels like a sad version of that hidden language, the kind that Sid and I have. Something in both of us is trying to seek out the other, through layers of hurt and anger and defeat, but this realization doesn't last long.

Olu blinks and it's gone. The secret language, the knowing. She takes a sip of her drink and averts her eyes.

She doesn't want to let me in.

Well, good, because I never asked to be there, in this secret place of understanding with her.

She says, her voice clipped, "Just ask them to come over soon. I want to meet the people you hang out with. Don't forget you're in my house, you know."

I'm silent. My breathing slows, deepens. I feel my lips quiver and words begin to form at the base of my throat, but nothing comes out. Confrontation . . . I can't do it.

I can't talk to Auntie Dara. I'm too scared.

I don't want to know anything anymore.

My feet itch, beckoning me toward my room where I can just disappear, but then Olu groans, the sound of tension seeping out of her body. She begins to move like a different person, her steps more purposeful, as she crosses the room to the kitchen.

"S-sorry," she says in a voice that is gruffer and lower than usual. She immediately dumps the rest of the wine in the sink—and cringes like she regrets it. There's hesitance in her actions. Frustration, too.

I take slow steps until I hover by the breakfast bar. "Are . . . you good?" I ask.

"I'm okay." She turns to me, flashing a weak, shaky smile. "Just . . . It would be nice to meet your friends. I know you might not . . . A-actually, I don't know. I'm not sure what you're thinking. But I want to be responsible, so I think it's important for me to meet them."

I glance away. "S-sure."

"Your social worker will come for a visit soon, and I want her to know I did at least one thing right."

The heaviness of those words hangs between us. That same sobering washes over Olu as she sets the glass inside the sink.

I just nod. I don't know what else to do. We're not close, we're not friends, but so many of her actions are familiar to me. They're mirroring loudly the things I wish I could say about myself—the emptiness, again. So I mumble, "It's all good," as an attempt to comfort her. A feeble attempt. "I can ask them if they wanna come by sometime."

She sniffles, nodding. "Yeah. Any time is fine."

"Cool." I clear my throat and, after an awkward pause, I turn and slide my feet down the hall to my room. "Cool . . ." I nudge my door closed but stop at the last moment so it never fully shuts. A part of me feels like I'm doing it for Olu, but I doubt she notices.

The next day, Sid texts me about meeting up at his place to hang out and I navigate the bus route with Auntie Dara's letter burning hot in my bag. I don't know why I take it everywhere considering I don't even have the guts to ask Auntie about it.

And I want to tell both my friends about the letter and ask what they think it means and explain who Auntie Dara has always been to our family—fringe, inconsistent, outsider—but it's hard for me to get the words right. Even in my mind, through my elaborate mental rehearsal, everything is garbled and stupid. How can I tell them I found this letter that might be able to tell me what happened with my parents without saying I found it at my old house's mailbox? They'll roast me alive. I can already hear Tanya's voice get deep, saying, "Summer, *friend*," the way a villain would in a Nigerian movie.

The crew is gathered on Sid's curb like always: Kirsten scrolling on her phone, looking actively bored; Sid attempting tricks up and down the road; and Tanya film-ing while saying, "That's fuck-ing MAD, you know!" every five seconds. I roll up, reach out for fist bumps from every-one but Kirsten (she wouldn't return it even if I tried), and settle in beside Tanya.

Tanya takes one look at me, her eyes dancing from my head to the ends of my scuffed shoes. "You're looking fresh," she says, a snide chortle in her words.

If it was anyone else, I'd probably get really defensive or irritated, but Tanya and I have that kind of joking bond because our upbringing was so similar. For the most part, anyway.

I snort. "Honestly? You're wrong for that."

She laughs, tossing her head back.

"And I said I'd come to you about my hair soon, so I don't know what your problem is."

"Oooh!" Kirsten leans over, excitedly. I brace for the attack. "I got a cousin who could do faux locs for you and she does them real good. You'd look cute and fresh, just like an island girl."

Tanya and I exchange a look. She's the first to jump over Kirsten's words. "Since when is Nigeria an island?" she stage-whispers. I have to bite my lip to keep from laughing out loud.

"I'm just saying," Kirsten goes on with a roll of her eyes. Then, she leans in further and says, "She does them for three hundred. *So* much more affordable than this other girl—four hundred. Is she serious? Like . . ."

Kirsten's words float around us while I zone out. I'm

trying my hardest to temper my mood. Can't let her know that her words, her assumption that $300 is affordable for me, are getting to me. I can feel Tanya's glances burning a hole through my skull and I can almost hear her voice, too. *Can you believe this ho? Why would she say that to you when she knows your situation?* And, also, *I could do faux locs for cheaper than that!*

Then, Kirsten says, "Plus, you wanna look dope for school, right? York in the fall and everything," with a voice that pulses through me. It feels loud, like she's yelling, and I am shifting inside even though nothing around me is changing.

I swallow, nervously. "Yeah. York."

"Mmm." She hums and settles back in her spot, keeping her eyes trained on Sid.

"McMaster is up my ass about these fees," Tanya blurts out, and then laughs. "Student union, registration, all this stuff. It's a lot—"

"*So* much," Kirsten cuts in. "Waterloo is the same. But we're close to getting our dorm assignments, so that's good."

We?

"How about you?" she continues, looking at me again. "Are you staying on campus at York? Or will you just, um . . ."

"Live at home?" I finish for her, my voice strong and blunt. She buttons up, letting her eyes fall to the ground. Tanya kisses her teeth from beside me, clearly more fed up with Kirsten than I am. I just don't get why she's like this.

It *has* to be jealousy, but once again, how is it my problem that she's not cool like us?

I get to my feet, grabbing my board before it rolls away. Tanya gets up, too. "You don't gotta leave because of her," she says quietly, glancing down at an oblivious Kirsten who's since gone back to her phone. "You know she's just talking shit because—actually, no, I don't know why."

I let my face soften to show a hint of a smile, just to make Tanya feel a bit better. I don't want her to worry about me. She doesn't really have to.

Sid skates over just as I say, "I'm good. It's fine. I'll be back."

"Where're you going?" he asks, slightly out of breath. "Should we come with?"

"No, no." I shake my head, then turn to gesture loosely in the distance. Anything to get him to not see the uneasiness in my face. "I just, um, I gotta see something. Yeah. But I'll be back, I promise."

Sid isn't convinced. When I finally look at him, when my eyes stop dancing around every other surface in the vicinity, he tilts his head like he's trying to read something on my face. Trying to see it better. I'm tempted to pull my long braids around my eyes and disappear.

"Do you wanna stay for dinner? I'm pretty sure my parents will be okay with it. Kirsten's staying," he adds, as if Kirsten's presence should inspire me to want to do anything.

I shake my head again, firmer. "No thanks, I'm good. Seriously, I'll be back, I just need some . . . space."

Sid's eyebrow twitches ever so slightly. It's so minuscule that I convince myself at first that I don't see it, but after that, he glances away, shifts back onto his heels, and doesn't look at me. He's irritated. He won't say it—no one says they're angry at me these days because they must feel like they can't be. It's infuriating. They promised they wouldn't treat me any different but it's times like these, times where I'm not afforded the full spectrum of someone's emotions, that I really feel like the poor, fucked-up orphan kid.

Quickly I blurt out, "I didn't mean it like that."

"No, I get it," he lies. In his voice, I can hear that tempering of what he really wants to say. "Text later, okay?"

"Okay."

Shame carries me farther on foot than my board can. I walk down Sid's street, turn the corner, contemplate getting on my board and soaring through this heat haze with a kick, push. But it's like the only action my body can perform is walking. One foot in front of the other. Anything else is too hard right now.

I get to the bus stop and wait. In my mind, I try to remember how much is currently on my transit card, hoping that I have at least one more ride before I . . . I don't know. I'll need money at some point. I might have some change in my luggage at Olu's place. I gotta make sure I check everywhere.

My throat constricts; my mouth waters. A wave of nausea washes over me while my thoughts linger on money, transit cards, phone top-ups, spare change, all of it. How much longer do I really think I can live like this? My friends are all going away to university soon, so relying on their kindness can really only go so far.

I mean, I guess I'll always have Sid. If we go to York together, then I'm sure I could just crash at his place. His mom would probably bring food every weekend, too.

Or, well, if *I* even end up going to York. There's just so much . . .

Forget it.

The bus comes and I wait for the doors to slide open before getting on. There is nowhere to sit, so I stand pressed against someone's sweaty back as the bus chugs along down the street. I grip my skateboard close. The bus lurches; I stumble. It's like this for ten, fifteen, thirty minutes.

I'm going to the beach.

The place that Jet showed me is close to Olu's. I'm guided by the feeling of seeing the water. It makes my last bus ride go by faster, makes my feet speed toward the tree-lined path. I get to the beach and the moment my feet hit the sand, I mentally curse myself for not bringing flip-flops. For not having flip-flops. Maybe if Olu has a pair . . . I doubt she'd let me borrow them. Or, I could take them. She'd never notice.

Jet is there because of course he is. It's so free and open here, and even though Jet isn't always my kind of person, I'm not gonna pretend that someone like him wouldn't be drawn to a place like this. As I approach, stepping carefully across the sandy path to the shore, I watch him with cautious eyes. He's sitting with his skateboard in front of him cross-legged on the sand, hunched over, speaking into his phone.

I sit beside him without a word. He glances at me, a small smile tugging at the corner of his lips, and says, "Love you too. Bye," into his phone before stuffing it away. Then, the Jet I recognize most comes back. He throws his arms open, high above his head, as he exclaims, "Summer!"

I say, "Uh, yep," like someone who's never had any friends before.

He laughs, "What'chu doing here?"

"I dunno."

"Same," he chuckles, and peers out toward the water.

The words *It's . . . calm here, you know?* roll off my tongue into the waves. "I just wanted to be somewhere quiet."

Jet nods right away. "I hear you. I come down here sometimes to call my mom. She likes to hear the water."

I frown, tilting my head as I contemplate his words. "Does she live in some land-locked place?"

"Nah, nothing like that." He sighs, glancing at me. "She's, um . . . I guess I never told you, but my mom's locked up."

My heart thuds. I force myself to nod slowly, like *yes, I understand*, even though I don't. Jet is quiet for a moment after that, and in that silence, I'm imagining what it's like to have to call a parent who's in jail. Because that could be me real soon, I think. I fear.

Jet lets out a nervous chuckle. "Aaahhh. Man, I used to be embarrassed telling people that, but whatever. Whatever, man! I still have my life. I'm still out here. And she's fine, too. She's getting out soon."

I turn to him, intrigued. "Actually?"

"Yeah," he says proudly, slapping his chest with his open palm. "Grandma's planning some kinda party. She warned me, though, I gotta take all my piercings out. Or maybe just this one." He points to his septum. "Not sure yet. When Moms went in the pen, I didn't have it, so I don't wanna freak her out."

My eyes gravitate toward his eyebrow piercings instantly. He laughs because I'm not even being subtle. "These are good," he says, gesturing to them. "Mom's a G. She's the one who told me to get them, you know."

"My . . ." I swallow down the urge to talk about my parents. There's no point. Jet's mom, she sounds real cool, even with the jail thing. Could I ever say my mom was cool? No. But maybe my dad . . . a long time ago. When I was a kid, he used to carry me on his shoulders, running around the house, and I would laugh and laugh. Then, I got too big, too tall. And he became more interested in the business, selling that cream, packaging boxes of it for shipment each week.

When Jet talks about his mom, his eyes light up, but he glances away, forcing them to dim so I don't see how excited he is. I want to tell him he can be excited around me—it's fine, it's not a problem. I don't want people to tiptoe around me. I want them to see I'm okay; I'm normal.

I let my hands dig into the sand, twisting and grasping.

Jet nods to my buried fingers. "Do you think there's crabs down there? Like those small sand ones."

"No," I say right away, but I sit still, waiting to feel a bite.

CHAPTER SEVEN

THE SMELL OF THE WAVES and the sand follows me back to the condo where I find Olu, tired and inebriated. It's a strange thing seeing the lake in my mind's eye but being confronted with my spacey cousin, slouched over her phone and a bottle of wine at the kitchen table. Her eyes seem to glaze over the phone screen she's staring at while her fingers glide messily over the keys.

When I shut the door, she startles, turning to me with a languid grin. "Welcome home," she says with warmth in her words. Must be the alcohol.

"Thanks," I utter, and readjust my bag on my shoulder. "I'm gonna shower and maybe pass out."

"Me too," Olu says with a giggle. "I'm going to pass out, too."

She must mean that literally.

The next morning, I have every intention of disappearing before Olu can catch me. For a second, I think I'm imagining it, but I realize, nope, there's a phone going off in the living room. Quietly, I tiptoe out of my room and follow the sound of the music. Olu is sprawled facedown on the sofa, an arm and a leg hanging off the side, and her phone is humming softly on the ground. My feet rush over to pick it up, flip it over, and nudge it under her fingertips. "Hey . . . ," I whisper, poking her arm. She doesn't move. I crouch down, gravitating ever so slowly to her face, to check if she's alive. She shifts slightly and, at this distance, I can hear soft, restricted breathing.

The phone rings out and starts up again. Man, this really isn't my problem. She's still breathing. It's fine. I have things to do, anyway.

As carefully as I tiptoed in, I slip out and back down the hall. If I shower and get ready fast enough, I may be able to avoid any awkward greetings when I rush out the door.

While I get dressed, the thought crosses my mind that I could just stay here and maybe check if Olu is okay. I'm not stupid. There's something wrong with her. I recognize it from that day we were arguing, the way her hands were trembling, the way her gaze would focus only to dilute moments later. I don't know how to describe it, but I can *see* it; I can recognize it as if someone was calling my own name. It's not hurt and it's not fear.

Maybe she's sad.

But she's an adult . . .

Right. She should be able to take care of herself. It's not my responsibility.

"Exactly," I tell myself over and over again while I lotion my legs a second time. "She can take care of herself. She's older than me. She'll be fine, she'll be fine . . ." Besides, I'm not even eighteen yet, and I'm doing okay. She's lived in Japan, she speaks two languages, she has a manager and stuff. Olu doesn't need me to look out for her. I mean, not like I want to.

I leave my room. At some point between my showering and extreme lotioning, Olu has disappeared from the sofa. I don't know what compels me to wait for her, but for some reason, I head straight to the kitchen instead of ducking out the front door. Like, I really don't know why. I don't want to talk to her, and I'm sure she has nothing to say to me.

She wanders into the kitchen looking completely out of it, robe practically falling off her shoulders. Once again, her eye bags are out of control. I nod to her and say, "Hey," real casual-like.

She stops in her tracks, obviously startled. "Oh," she breathes out, bringing a hand to her chest.

I say, "I'm, um, going out for a bit."

She doesn't miss a beat. "Skateboarding?"

"Yup."

She glides past me toward the drawers for tea and a mug, as if she's ignoring me. I'm hit with a pang of guilt or, I don't know. Does she expect me to try more? I mean, I told her where I was going. What else does she want?

Whatever.

"I'll be back," I mumble, and march to the doorway with my head down. I wrestle my feet into my shoes and snatch my board from the ground before I disappear.

Here goes my daily attempt to make it to Auntie Dara's restaurant. I scoff bitterly, imagining myself stepping one foot closer to the front door. Feels fake.

This time, as I turn the corner toward the restaurant, I spot Auntie Dara immediately.

The problem is she spots me too. And she waves.

I freeze.

"Summer? Is that you?" she calls, her voice sharp across the strip mall parking lot. She squints again, as if to get a better look.

"Y-yeah." I clear my throat and take a few steps forward. For the first time, my feet reach the paved lot. "H-hi, Auntie. H-how, um, how have you been?"

She straightens up and smacks her hands together. Again with that dusting motion. "He-ey, oh my god! So it's really you? Where have you been?"

I let out a nervous chuckle. Is . . . she serious? "Uhhh . . . I've been staying with friends?" I tell her, my voice turned up as if I'm unsure of it myself. She doesn't need to know I'm living with Olu now. I won't be for much longer, anyway.

She watches me as if in absolute disbelief that I'm alive and seemingly healthy. And she looks the same, too. No extra wrinkles or dark circles. I guess she's slept relatively well knowing I've been out on my own. Cool, cool, good to know.

Auntie Dara crosses her arms, still studying me curiously. "So what are you doing here?"

This feels weird—*I* feel weird. Here we are having a conversation as if no time has passed, as if there isn't an obvious reason as to why we haven't seen each other in a year. All I can think about is that letter. I carry it everywhere with me, and I'm dying to pull it out and ask why Mom sent it to her and what it means and why there are so many weird number combinations and which lawyer they're talking about and, and, and . . .

I swallow nervously and let my eyes drop to my feet before I murmur, "Um, I was hungry."

"Oh my god," she sighs, shaking her head like I'm someone to pity. "Come inside, jare. I can give you some meat pie and akara."

"I—" My phone begins to ring. I pat myself down until I find it in my dress pocket. An unknown number flashes on my screen. "What? Whose number . . ."

"And come to think of it, my girl," Auntie Dara cuts in. She's still looking at me with that pitiful look, and it's distracting amid my phone's ringing. I try to take a step back and hold out my phone so she knows I'm about to answer, but she just barrels on, "How are you getting money to be paying for your phone and such things? Do you need money?"

"W-well—"

"My driver just quit, and so I will be needing somebody to come do small-small deliveries for me until I can find a new one . . ." She shrugs, fanning her hands out. I wait for the inevitable dusting-of-hands motion and it actually doesn't come.

I blank, just as my phone rings out. "Wait, are you offering that to . . . *me*?"

She shrugs, frowning. Typical Auntie. Can't even say it with her chest.

I shrug, too, matching her energy. "Okay, how much?"

Smugness washes over her. "How much, *ke*? Okay, just twenty dollars here and there."

"F-fine," I agree. Not only will it give me a reason to come back, but I actually need the money. This saves me the absolute embarrassment of having to ask friends for bus fare. Ask Olu for more.

The same unknown number calls back. I walk away while I answer, keeping my voice quiet, "Hello? Who's this?"

"Summer, it's me," comes Olu's reply. She sounds much more awake than she did this morning. "Are you busy? I was hoping we could talk. Or, actually, I was hoping we could meet up. Spend time together, maybe? I think we didn't . . . uh." She clears her throat. "We live together now, so maybe we should hang out. I'm thinking we can go to Sherway Gardens. You know that mall, right?"

"Wait, you wanna hang out with *me*?" The words are out before I have a chance to temper my tone. I sound harsh and unforgiving, and immediately I feel guilty about that because at least she's kinda trying. She doesn't have to. I mean, she really, really, *really* doesn't need to. But she is.

If my tone bothers her, it doesn't show in her voice. "Yeah," she replies right away. "We're cousins. We're family."

If only she knew how little that actually meant to me.

My lips twist into a scowl, letting past betrayals resurface in my mind—but Olu wasn't there for any of those. It isn't fair of me to paint her with the same brush, but I can't help it. I don't know how else to be.

Auntie Dara reenters my periphery, sticking her neck out as if she's trying to eavesdrop. I scooch farther away.

"Or," Olu interrupts my train of thought. "I-if you're busy, then that's okay. I just thought maybe—"

"Yes," I blurt out. My heartbeat quickens, anxiously awaiting her response in the silence. When it doesn't come fast enough, I add, "Should I come home? And then we can head out together?"

She gives a sigh of relief that I pretend not to hear. "Text me where you are and I can come pick you up instead. It might be faster that way."

"S-sure, okay."

We hang up and I send her the address of Auntie Dara's restaurant. Auntie Dara, who was so quick to offer me this random delivery job. Auntie Dara, who might know more about my parents than she wants to tell me.

It doesn't take Olu long to get to the restaurant. She doesn't drive, but she's rich so she takes rideshares everywhere. She doesn't even do the carpool option, only the XL version where they send luxury vehicles. A sleek silver car pulls up in front of the restaurant, and Olu pops her head out of the back window, beckoning me forward.

I wave bye to Auntie Dara, who returns it, although she's distracted by the car. Olu pushes the door open for me and I get in just as she slides over to the next seat. The air-conditioning turns the space into a freezer, and the stickiness I felt from the outside air a second ago completely vanishes when my legs touch the leather.

"Welcome," Olu says with a smile when I enter, waving

her hands around the interior. "Isn't this nice? Why would anyone ever need their own car?"

She's joking, right? "Well, not everyone can afford daily rideshares," I say as I gaze around. It *is* nice in here, though. By the time my eyes settle on Olu, she's fidgeting with her fingers, pensive and nervous. Damn, maybe I shouldn't have said that. "It's cool you're rich, though." How exactly does saying *that* help?

She gives me a plastic smile and shrugs. "Eh? I wouldn't say I'm rich or anything . . ."

Great, now it's awkward.

We sit in agonizing, itchy silence as the car cruises down the street. Olu watches the road rush by from her window and I fiddle with my hands because I don't know what else to do.

Olu clears her throat.

I scratch my nose.

I see her reach for her phone, and I pipe up, "Oh, your phone was ringing earlier. Like, while you were asleep."

That plastic smile is back as she lifts the device. "Yeah, I saw."

"Cool."

She turns the phone over in her hands.

I flex my fingers.

"It was my manager calling," she says. I turn fully, looking interested enough so she knows I want her to keep talking. I want her to know I'm trying, too. Kinda.

She continues, "I tried to call him back, but he didn't answer. I guess he tried to stay up late just to talk to me. And I wanted to ask him something, too."

"What's the time difference?"

She pauses to think. "Thirteen hours, most of the time," she says.

I cringe on impulse. "That sucks."

"It does. They're ahead, so today is already tomorrow for them. Or . . . yeah, I think that's right," she tells me, and then chuckles. It's such a jarring but welcome sound. It's the kind of sound you'd expect to hear when two cousins who are close in age hang out together. Olu clasps her hands together, her phone bungled in between, and says, "Maybe you'll think this is stupid, but . . . I was kinda homesick when I came here."

"That's not stupid," I tell her.

She smiles, looking visibly more relaxed than a second ago. "Yeah, well . . ."

"Y-yeah."

"You know, I've always been traveling and doing different things for work, so I thought there's no way I can be homesick." She snorts. "But then I would speak to my manager, or my parents, and they would always tell me, like . . . 'The sun is coming up now, so I have to go to work' or 'It's getting dark, so I have to sleep,' and it used to make me feel good. Because somewhere else in the world, it was already tomorrow. So it's like . . . whatever homesickness I'm feeling today doesn't exist in their tomorrow. And it might not exist in my tomorrow, either. If I look at it that way, then being homesick isn't too bad." Then she grins, wide and vibrant. Corny, too. I can see through it in a second. She is as desperate to forget her homesickness as I am to latch on to that pain or hurt or whatever it was that I saw when we spoke in the kitchen.

"It's so hopeful," I say aloud, suppressing a cringe. Olu doesn't notice my cringing or sense my shift in mood. She just smiles at me warmly before shifting to rest her head against the seat behind us. The smile is *I know how you feel* and *You're all right, kid* wrapped up in one. It's comforting, but it's harsh, because I didn't ask for it. All my tomorrows have been just like my todays. Nothing changes, and nothing has changed since the day my parents disappeared.

We get to Sherway Gardens, and I realize it's the closest mall to where Olu lives. It's gotten some serious upgrades in the past few years. When I was very small, my parents used to take me here and it felt local and cool, but now it sprawls across an intersection, showcasing new stores for people who have more money than I do to throw around. Olu is one of those people.

"Shop first or ice cream first?" she asks the second our feet hit the pavement outside the mall.

I frown, crossing my arms. "Shopping, I guess."

She flashes a wicked grin. "Good answer."

We circle the stores with Olu dipping in and out, squealing at things that cost hundreds of dollars. I'm in awe. My parents' actions made sure we lived a comfortable life, but still, they would never entertain jewelry or clothes that were in the hundreds. Meanwhile, price doesn't seem to be a deterrent for Olu. She reaches for bracelets unflinchingly, slipping them on and asking the salesclerks what they think of them on her. I shift to the side, staying out of the way while they try to woo her, convince her to buy these things she doesn't need. Honestly, this isn't what I thought would happen when she said she wanted to hang out. What part of my casual getup told her I live for Gucci?

"Try this on," Olu says, slipping a thin silver and ruby ring onto my finger before I have a chance to protest. Her face lights up as it glimmers on my hand. "This looks so good on you! Do you want it?"

"Are you joking?" I gasp, and move to wrestle it off. "It's, like, a million dollars."

"It's three fifty. Right?" She turns to the shop clerk at the counter, a stocky woman who just nods. I manage to get the ring off and hand it back to Olu, whose disappointment is palpable. "Okay, no ring. So what else do you like?"

"I'm good," I tell her. "I don't need anything."

"Everyone needs something."

"Well, I don't *need* a three hundred and fifty dollar ring. No offense," I say to the shop clerk.

Olu does another lap around the store and buys a necklace for herself. "I need to get you something, too," she says as we exit and she balances shopping bags between her hands. "Do you want a new video game?"

I wave off her suggestion. "I don't need anything, I said," I remind her. There's a slight twitch to her eyebrow before she turns away, focusing on the path ahead of us. It's the same one I recognize in Sid whenever he's angry but doesn't wanna argue with me. It doesn't hurt any more or less coming from Olu.

As we walk through the mall to the food court, I can feel the weight of my words hanging in the air between us. I can hear her responses, too. She's probably thinking I'm ungrateful, or that I'm stuck-up and have horrible manners. She must think I'm just like my parents.

Olu orders us ice cream and we settle at an empty and questionably clean food court table. Right away, she brings out her phone, clutching it tightly in her grasp. "Wanna hear a song?"

I shrug—and then nod, once I clue in to what she's asking. "It's your demo song, right?"

A small smile comes to her lips. "Yeah. We can talk while we listen . . ." She pulls up a track on her phone under a name I can't recognize and presses PLAY. A soft melody starts up, and even in the bustle of the food court, I can still hear the beginnings of a strong voice. Olu's. She sings in Japanese with a personality I've never seen her show before. I lean in closer so I can hear her better. Something about the way she sings, the longing and desperation, hits me like a wave. The song drowns out the noise in the food court. It brings me to that beach Jet showed me, where I am the only one who can hear the waves crashing against the shore. Where my bare feet are burrowed in the sand. Where I can stare into the endless distance and it will never be enough.

Olu watches me carefully as I scoot in closer to the table, letting myself lean my head on my hand. My expression must be unreadable because she is staring at my face so intently, as if trying to gauge my reaction. I want to say, "Relax, it's good," or something like that, but I'm so taken with the sound of this song that I don't budge. It's speaking to me, somewhere. I don't understand what she's singing, but I am on that beach, *my* beach, I'm alone, and I'm okay for once. It's bizarre that it's Olu's voice that brings me there. Someone who I thought couldn't understand me at all has managed to hit on something I've been trying to avoid.

The emptiness, and all.

Olu asks me a question, but I don't hear her. "What?"

"I asked if you thought it was good," she mumbles.

I nod, hiding a soft smile that threatens to push through. If Olu notices, she doesn't say anything. Just sighs dramatically, like my approval means something to her. I scramble to sit up straight, explaining as best I can with my hands. "It's like . . . I don't know h-how to describe it. It's—it's good. I, uh . . . there's this place my friend showed me, and I go there sometimes . . ." My voice is so shaky; I sound so uncertain, so scared somehow. "This place is comforting to me. And your song is—it reminds me of . . . going there."

Olu's smile deepens the more she listens to me. I was afraid she'd think I was a loser for being so fidgety and weird and incoherent about secret places, but she doesn't hide her gratitude at all. She's so much more open than I am. I'm envious of how easy she makes it look. "It's the demo for what I think is my comeback feature song with this new rapper. It's called 'Umi-be.' Like, a beach, or sea-side. That kind of thing."

A beach.

"What's it about?" I mutter.

She swoons, touching her forehead delicately. "Oh my god, it's so beautiful," she coos, and I lean in closer. "It's about, like . . . this boy and this relationship that ends at the height of a beautiful season. Think of summertime and how happy it is, and then having to say goodbye to someone you love."

Having to say goodbye.

Not getting the chance to say goodbye.

At the height of summer.

I stiffen against the growing hollowness in my chest. Outwardly, I stare at Olu, feeling my head nod slowly at what she's saying. But in my mind, I'm in my room alone, then I'm talking to faceless police officers who treat me like I'm a liar. Like *I'm* the criminal. Like I'm not about to spend days, then weeks, then months by myself in a house that gets colder and emptier by the day. Like I deserved to be left behind.

No, no, forget it. I want to go back to my beach.

I stretch and shut my eyes. I don't know how to tell Olu that people in the summer sometimes leave without saying goodbye, and then fall comes, then winter, then spring, and you never know what happened to them. You'll never know.

And you might not even *want* to know. At some point, who cares anymore? You'll be almost eighteen and then it won't matter because you can do all the things you want without annoying adults getting in the way. You can get a car, you can rent a place, you can move up and on in the world . . . Yeah, that's it. Once I turn eighteen, none of this will matter anyway. My parents, the letter, none of it.

But that's for then and this is now, and now, I think I'm sad. A bit empty.

I know I am.

The honest truth? I'm scared. There's such a fear that eighteen is a magical number with no real powers, and none of this will mean anything. And this is the kind of fear that paralyzes.

Olu purses her lips, an emotionless smile, and pockets her phone. "Well, um . . . ," she mutters. We sit in silence for one, two more minutes before she clasps her hands together. "Hey, what else should we do? I don't have much else to do today since I sent Mr. Fukuda—that's my manager—I sent him the demo I recorded. I hope he calls me soon with good news. This kind of song . . . well, it's not really my style, but if the label likes it and they want to go ahead with the feature, then I'll do anything. This opens doors for me to record more R&B-style tracks like I want, and just like that, my career will be back on track."

I'm shaken out of my trance. "What?"

"Yeah. I'm trying not to get my hopes up because . . . well, a-anyway." She clears her throat, wringing her hands together, and continues as if that minor break didn't happen. "I always wanted an apartment in Yokohama, and I think it may be possible to move there after a comeback."

"Move there?" I ask. My voice echoes in my head.

She nods. She's doing a bad job hiding her excitement at going back to Japan. At moving away. It's not that I expected her to stay—and it's not like I *need* her to be here or anything like that, but it's just . . .

I don't know. There's no point.

Everyone leaves eventually.

CHAPTER EIGHT

I'M QUIET AFTER WE LEAVE the food court. My thoughts are in constant flux, trying to stay afloat, trying not to push too hard in any one direction. Of *course* she'd be thinking of her career first. She's twenty years old. She has a life that doesn't include me. Her taking me shopping and trying to bond with me feels kinda cheap now. Maybe she only asked so she could rub it in my face that she's gonna be on this great song that's so great and will lead her back to her great life far away from me. It's ruining the memory of my beach, the one that lives in my head. Her voice is distorting my thoughts.

We don't talk on the ride home, though I can sense her wanting to say something. I'm not angry—it is what it is. I'd rather just get back to the apartment and lie down.

The moment I'm through the door, I kick off my shoes, set down my board near the entrance, and disappear to my room. I can hear Olu walking slowly down the hall, hovering by my room door, but she doesn't come in. She will probably head to the kitchen and get a glass of wine. She'll probably celebrate singing such a cool demo song, a perfect achievement on the road to a Summer-less life. I drift off to sleep.

WHEN I WAKE UP, I go to Auntie Dara's. Her restaurant has a high counter by the window, decorated with old newspapers and local Realtor cards. Three stools are pushed haphazardly by the wall, unused as usual because no one actually sits and eats in here. They just grab their food and go.

"You're too early," she chides. She's in the back, rolling dough with her hands across a worn-out countertop. She's preparing to fry chin-chin. My mouth waters just thinking about it, but I promise myself I won't ask for some if she doesn't offer.

And she doesn't.

Auntie Dara has four orders, but only gives me two. "These are for pickup," she says of the others, even though I can see the addresses are close to the delivery orders. When she hands me a $20 bill for the two, quickly shielding and stuffing away her remaining wad of bills, I suddenly get it. She just doesn't want to pay me more money. My parents always said she was stingy, to be honest, and this proves it. It's not that I expected her to take pity on me and throw me literal crumbs, but like . . . bro, I'm homeless. What the fuck?

The two orders aren't close to each other—one is in Centennial Park near Tanya's place, and the other is close to Mimico—so I map out my route carefully in order to avoid paying bus fare twice or having to skate longer than my legs can hold up. This truly sucks. I don't actually want to do these deliveries, but with no actual income and a sketchy letter burning a hole in my brain, I don't think I'm in a position to say no. At the first house, I'm so out of breath and sweaty that I'm too embarrassed to genuinely greet the person who comes to the door. I just thrust the order in his hands and skip back down the stairs to the sidewalk.

After my final order, I go to the beach.

At this point, it feels like I'm there every day, taking in the waves. I've graduated from sitting as stiff as my skateboard on the shoreline to leaning back on my forearms, stretching out my legs and—gasp—taking off my shoes. My bare feet turn ashy, gray. I laugh, like *really* laugh from the pit of my stomach, because it looks like I'm wearing dusty ankle socks. My laugh startles me. It's embarrassing that it does. I should know my own voice. I guess it's just been a while.

I want to show Tanya and Sid the beach, but there's never a good time to bring it up. By the weekend, as we hang back at the skate park eating Popsicles that melt faster than we can lick them, the only thing they care about is seeing the place I'm currently calling home.

Sid is biting down on his Popsicle stick because he bit his way through the Popsicle. The rest of us lick ours down like normal people. "Why won't you let us see it?" he asks abruptly. When I finally look at him, he nods like I know what he's talking about. "Your cousin's place," he adds.

I choke. "O-oh."

"Yeah, eh," Tanya chimes in. "You've been there,

what, a week?" Then she snickers, leaning closer to me, "Something there you don't want us to see?"

"No, shut up," I chortle, shaking my head. "It's nothing like that. I just, I don't know, I don't hang out there."

"Why not?"

I shrug. Because it's Olu's place and not mine? Because being there makes me feel like it's just another house I'm visiting? Because it's another reminder that I don't have a place, my own place, to go to? "Because I just don't," I say.

"Man, if *I* was staying with a rich cousin," Sid begins, readjusting his hat. "I'd literally tell everyone. Like, shame-lessly. Everyone."

"Ooh, true, and I'd invite my friends over all the time, too," Tanya muses, a hum in her voice. They both sigh on either side of me. Clearly, they planned this. I can't really blame them, though. It's true, I haven't exactly been the most open about my . . . new place of residence. The place I live. It still feels awkward to even call it that. It's Olu's apartment, not mine.

Still, my friends have been so good to me this past year, so if they want to come over, then I'll make it happen. Olu asked me to invite my friends one day. I guess that day is finally here.

On Sunday morning, I get ready, tying my long braids back in a single braid, and prepare myself to ask Olu for this one, small, insignificant favor. I have to keep telling myself that she's the one who wants to meet them, so really, *I'm* the one doing *her* a favor. Still, my hands get clammy and I start fidgeting the moment I step out of my room. I haven't asked her for anything, and I maintain that I don't actually need anything from her, so this feels uncomfortable. *I* feel uncomfortable.

Olu is sitting on the sofa by the time I make it to the living room. She has her legs crossed, one knee over the other, while she frowns at her phone in the center of the coffee table. My feet tiptoe forward until she catches me in her peripheral vision. The look she gives me is harsh. There's no other way to describe it. Her jaw is set with disappointment, most likely from whatever she saw or heard on her phone, and she doesn't shake it as I slide into the lounge chair across from her.

It's hard for me to focus. I've never really . . . I don't know how to talk to Olu. One second, she's trying to be my best friend; the next, she's drunk off wine and dancing in the living room. It's like I don't know the real her, and because of that, I hesitate so much.

I inhale, then exhale a shaky breath.

"What happened?" she asks. Her tone is short, her voice, tired.

"I . . ." Asking about my friends takes a back seat the more I watch her. The more I wait, the more she softens. Squared shoulders slouch, a stiff lip bends. Her hands clasp together. "Are you good?" I ask.

"M-me?" She points a finger at herself while I nod. "Ah, yeah, I'm fine. It's just . . . stuff with my manager."

I raise an eyebrow. "He doesn't like your song?"

She puts up her hands and shakes her head as if to ward off whatever my words will summon. "No, no, I don't know yet. It's hard to get ahold of him. And I wanted to talk to him, too . . ."

I tilt my head, eyebrow still raised, waiting for her to continue.

"I want to have a show, here," she tells me, a small tug at the corner of her lips. A barely there smile, like she's not wanting to put too much hope into it. "It might be a lot of work, b-but there are these fans who keep asking me. B-because they know I'm staying in the area."

"Doesn't everyone know you're here?"

"Not really."

I grimace. "How's that possible? You're so famous, right?"

"Ah . . ." She shakes her head, a nervous chuckle slipping past her lips, while she shifts backward into the sofa. Uncertainty paints her every action. The way she ruffles her hair, unsuccessfully tucks a tuft behind her ear, and wipes her eyes are all clouded with some kind of hesitance. It's scary how fast it came over her. It's even scarier how quickly I could recognize it.

She's still wiping her eyes when she asks, "What's going on with you? I thought you'd be out all day like always."

I don't know if that's a dig or not and I'm too scatter-brained right now to care. "Yeah, I . . ." I take another deep breath before I ask. "Can my friends come over today? I know you said that you wanted to meet them, so I thought maybe we could just chill here . . ." Her hands drop to her lap. The more I speak, the wider her eyes get. Damn, maybe this was a bad idea. "You know what, forget—"

"*What?*" she exclaims, and immediately jumps to her feet. Of course she'd be pissed. Once again, this is her house, not mine.

Quickly, she holds out a hand as if she can already read the disappointment on my face. "No, no, I'm *excited*! Of course they can come! Oh, should I—should I cook something?"

I flinch. "Eww, why?"

She's not listening to me anymore. She glides into the kitchen, going straight for the cupboards. I follow. Please for the love of God, she better not start cooking. As if she can read my thoughts, she turns and says, "Don't worry, I can cook," with a wink.

"Did you just wink at me in real life?"

"I know how to make curry as long as I have the cubes. Or! I can prepare, like, a very good burger. Organic and everything. Do your friends drink sparkling water? I can get the flavored ones, too. Oh!" She smacks her hands together, the sound echoing throughout the apartment. "And do they have any allergies? That is *very* important. I don't want to, like—" Her voice drops to a whisper. "—*kill* them."

I laugh. The sound bubbles up from my gut before I can stop it—and I try so hard, pressing my hands to my mouth when I feel the urge. But it bursts through, seeping out from the cracks between my fingers, filling the space between us. Olu laughs, too, a wide grin stretching across her face.

I say, chuckling, "Olu, honestly, I've been good with scrambled eggs and toast since I got here. We can just order a pizza or something. It's not that serious."

She stops, her giddiness fading into the faintest hint of a smile. It's enough to wipe the smile off my face, too. I must have offended her.

But then she tilts her head to the side and hums. Her brows furrow while she tries to find the words. "You . . . call me Olu?" she asks.

I gulp. "Yeah?"

Her faint smile deepens with a warmth I haven't seen from her before. She glances away shyly, as she says, "Not a lot of people still call me that. J-just my mom, but only sometimes. I always hear, 'Hikari this' or 'Kari that,' but not Oluchi."

I shift my weight to my left leg. "Do you have a preference? I can call you Hikari if you want."

She's already shaking her head before I can get all the words out. "Oluchi is fine. It's my name," she says with a snort. "And it makes me feel like over here I can be a different person." Then she grins, cheesy but vibrant. Which, honestly, is kinda how I'd describe her.

I disappear to text my friends the address just as Olu's phone begins to ring. They're hovering not too far away from here, at a park nearby, so my anxiety begins to heighten knowing they could be here at any minute. I don't know if I should invite Jet, too. He's not—I mean, *we're* not real friends, the way I am with Tanya and Sid. I've known them through high school, and I know Jet is a little bit older than I am, so, I don't know, maybe they won't get along. He's also kinda weird. Maybe they'll hate him.

Maybe he'll tell them about the beach and then they'll hate *me* for not mentioning it sooner.

My finger hovers over his number, but in the end, I don't invite him. "Next time, I swear," I tell myself, though I don't know what a "next time" would be.

By the time I come out of my room, Olu has conjured up a hundred dollars to give me for food. *A hundred dollars.* Does she know how much a pizza costs?

A half hour later, the buzzer goes off, signaling my friends' arrival. It takes another two minutes for Tanya, Sid, and, unfortunately, Kirsten to come upstairs. They admire Olu's apartment out loud in a way I couldn't when I first got here. "Is this for real?" Tanya coos as she rushes to the balcony that overlooks the busiest parts of Port Credit. Sid runs his hand along the velvet of the lounge chair. Kirsten circles the kitchen, seemingly taken with the granite countertops and modern design.

And then there's me in the middle of it all. I feel kinda stupid just watching them take it all in because I don't have a right to show it off. *This isn't really my place!* I want to tell them, cutting up their enthusiasm into a million pieces.

Kirsten clears her throat as she settles on the sofa. "Wow, girl, so you're living all the way out here like this?"

Literally everything she says sounds like she's trying to fight me. "Yeah," I tell her, and turn my attention to Tanya, who's reclined and comfortable on the lounge chair. "Did you guys find the place okay?"

"Yes," she answers, pointedly. "It's not hard to follow a map."

I roll my eyes. "I meant, like, was it too far? Because I know none of you really drive, so, you know."

"Too far?"

"To come all the way out here."

Sid raises an eyebrow. "You think we wouldn't come all the way out here to see you?"

Maybe, yes. I don't say it, though with one look at Sid, I know he knows that I want to.

Olu emerges from the hallway, taking proud steps into the living room to greet everyone. She's changed her outfit to denim shorts and an oversize T-shirt and has tied her hair up in a bun. The first thing she says is, "Oh my god, it's Summer's friends, finally," and it makes me want to dig myself into a hole.

Everyone sits up straighter. If they knew Olu, they wouldn't have bothered trying to put on a front for her. Not that I know her that well, but I don't think she cares.

I clear my throat and get to my feet. "U-uh, Olu, this is Sid and Kirsten, and Tanya," I say, gesturing to each of them. "You guys, this is my cousin, Olu . . . chi. Oluchi."

Olu giggles and gives them all a wave and the slightest bow. "So nice to finally meet you all!"

Kirsten crosses her legs, leaning forward as she says, "Summer says you were a singer in Japan." How did she even know that? Sid, probably. Our eyes meet and he looks away almost immediately. Just because they're dating doesn't mean every conversation *we* have is a conversation that concerns Kirsten. He *has* to know she's nosy as hell and doesn't actually care about anyone but herself, right? That's why when she asks, "Were you, like, *famous* famous?" in that thick, disbelieving tone, I cringe. I'm so tired of this girl. She's honestly so rude for no reason.

Olu doesn't seem to mind or notice that Kirsten is

being an asshole. She laughs nervously, inching away as if being called "famous" is so embarrassing. "Ah, I guess so, but I don't really think of myself that way," she answers diplomatically.

"So then what are you doing here? Are you on vacation? And without bodyguards? Doesn't your label care you're gonna get mobbed or something?" Kirsten barrels on relentlessly. She's asking more questions about Olu than I have the entire time I've been here.

Olu clasps her hands together. Something has shifted. It's really slight, and I wouldn't expect someone like Kirsten to recognize when her intrusive questions are bothering someone—truly, that much self-awareness for someone like Kirsten would be too much—but I notice, because I live with Olu and I'm coming to know a bit about who she is. I think. So when she holds her hands like that, clasping them as if they're holding a secret, I know it's because they are. Something's wrong.

It takes a bit longer for her smile to come back in full form.

She says, "That's . . . a long story. But it's also s-so . . . *boring*," and knits her fingers together tightly. Quickly, she feels around in her pockets, then crosses the room to her bag on the counter. "A-anyway, I don't wanna get in your way. I have somewhere to go, a producer to see, preparation in case this show works out, you know . . ." She rustles through her bag for a couple of bills, at least forty dollars, and comes to press it into my hands. "Order something to eat," she instructs.

"But . . ." She already gave me money. Doesn't she remember? I don't wanna bring it up in front of my friends because someone like Kirsten would probably say something stupid—and it might push Olu further into this weird mood she's in. What's up with her, honestly?

I blink and then she's gone.

Tanya turns to me and says, "Your cousin's cool. Baby smooth skin, too, my god. What face products does she use?"

"Probably something expensive from Japan," Kirsten pipes up.

I zone in on her, my eyes narrowing in a fierce glare. "You . . ." Kirsten looks at me, eyebrow raised, ready for the attack. I don't even know what to say. All my thoughts are garbled and warped and stopping and starting at the wrong points. I'm just mad. It's one thing to say stupid shit to me about my parents or whatever, but she doesn't even *know* Olu. What makes her think—just—what makes her think she can . . .

In the end, I say nothing. As always. "Whatever," I spit out and place the forty dollars Olu gave me in the center of the table. "Y'all order something." Tanya is quick to open her take-out app and start rhyming off pizza places in the area. I keep the hundred for myself.

CHAPTER NINE

THE DOORBELL RINGS JUST AS I'm getting the rest of my hair accessories ready. Tanya promised she'd do my hair, and there's no better time than the present. I swear, she should've just stayed over last night instead of going home when she did. She, Sid, Kirsten, and I overdosed on pizza and large bottles of iced tea. We snuck into Olu's wine closet, as I like to call it, and popped a bottle of something that looked expensive. Wine tastes like ass, though, so I don't think any of us enjoyed it, but it didn't matter. I understand why people drink. I do. To enjoy, to soothe, to forget. I figured if I drank enough, I could forget how much I dislike Kirsten and the fact she was mean to my cousin unprompted. But then halfway through the night, she said, "How's your cousin's English so good?" and I cursed myself for not boxing her when I had the chance.

One by one, my friends called rideshares just before midnight. That's about the time Olu came home, too.

We said hi to each other, but even I could tell there was still something wrong. I had started to take out my braids, and she didn't even say anything about the cloud of hair on my head. Not that she would . . . I mean, it feels like the kind of thing she'd comment on. *Oh, your hair is so pretty and big!* or something, in that curious voice of hers. Instead, she floated through the room, lighting a candle on the kitchen table and then blowing it out once she realized the time. Maybe Kirsten's questions about what she's doing in Toronto really got to her and ruined her entire night. Or, maybe it was something else—something to do with her demo or her manager. I was so far gone, I didn't have the words to ask.

After she grabbed a glass and a bottle of wine, she disappeared to her room. I haven't seen her once this morning.

The doorbell rings again, and then comes a stern knock.

"Coming!" I groan as I grab my stuff and bring it into the living room. My coily hair is as dry as it's going to get after I washed it this morning, but it still drips along my shoulders as I rush to the door. I have a separate bag with combs, hair ties, leave-in conditioner, and some hair butter, just in case Tanya doesn't have any.

I pull open the door and feel my eyes bug out tenfold when they land on Gardenia.

Shit.

The visit.

My first instinct is to shut the door, but I can't do that, it'll look too suspect. So I smile as naturally as I can and wave her inside. "Hi. W-welcome," I say, uncertain if that's even the kind of thing people say when they let their social worker inside.

Gardenia enters, taking off her shoes by the door. "How are you, Summer? My, your hair is . . ." She moves as if she's going to touch it, but thankfully, contains herself. "It's *lovely*," she tells me, pressing into her words a bit too hard.

"Yep," I say, and shut the door behind her.

As she walks in, Gardenia looks around like she's inspecting the room, grading it as she goes. Her eyes glaze over the sofa. She homes in on the table where she must see the remnants of sticky drinks dried onto its surface.

"Where's Hikari?" she asks abruptly.

"Uh, she's . . ." I swallow. "She's not feeling too good."

Gardenia raises an eyebrow. "Excuse me?"

"I'll go check on her, but when she woke up earlier, she was, like, very . . . sick." I grimace, as the mental image of what Olu would've looked like this morning, had I seen her, comes to mind. I hope I'm selling it well enough. "One second." I dash down the hall, my footsteps becoming lighter as I approach Olu's room door. I don't even bother knocking because I know she's not awake.

Thick heat envelopes me as I step through her doorway. She left the window open, probably to filter out the strong smell of alcohol in here. Even with the window, I can still smell the sweetness of wine in the air. On the floor, there's a bottle overturned, its contents spilled out across the rug. I follow the trail backward, from the spill to the bottle, from the bottle to the hand dangling beside the bed, from the hand to Olu.

She's still fast asleep, breathing heavy but slow, her blanket still draped across her body. I can see sweat forming along her neck from where I'm standing. Who knows how long she was up last night, but no one drinks this much unless there's something wrong. Right?

Guilt spurs me forward as I tiptoe gently toward her. "Hey . . . Olu?"

Nothing.

"Gardenia is here for the visit," I whisper. "You gotta wake up . . ."

She doesn't move.

"You gotta stop drinking."

Her breathing hitches.

I pick up the bottle and set it on her dresser before I slowly exit the room. Gardenia is still waiting in the living room, and I can tell from the way she scrunches her brow when she sees me that she thought Olu would be making an appearance after all. "She's still . . . uh, she's not doing so good," I say, and drop into the lounge chair across from Gardenia. "I'm really sorry. S-sometimes she has these . . . flare-ups."

"Is it chronic?" Gardenia frowns toward the papers she has in her hand. "She didn't mention anything about a preexisting condition."

The way she says it, the way she examines her files, makes me feel that if Olu had a preexisting condition, I probably wouldn't be here. That gets me heated. I frown, narrowing my eyes at the papers as Gardenia shuffles them, scanning each back and forth.

"It's not that," I say finally.

"So then, what is it?"

"It's not really my business," I tell her. "I'm sorry she's

not feeling too good, but maybe you can still do the visit with just me? I've been okay here. Olu and I have been getting along really good. Um, what else?" I rack my brain for more generic things, things Gardenia would need to hear before she's satisfied that I'm not being mistreated. "We went shopping and stuff. She gave me money for a pizza."

"What about tuition?"

I exaggerate a blink. "Sorry?"

"Your tuition at York," she repeats, and taps her files. "Remember? The thing that kickstarted this relocation was that York was waiting on some information for a payment deferral plan. Has something been sorted out? Will you need the deferral plan?"

Oh yeah, university. I can't tell her I wasn't serious about going in the first place or who knows what she'll do. And besides, it's not that I'm *not* serious, it's just that, well . . . I mean, who's trying to think about school right now? I have so many other things taking up space in my mind.

I purse my lips. "Well, I'm not working right now, so probably I'll need a, uh . . . deferral thing. Oh! Actually . . . I kinda got a job," I tell her, remembering the deliveries I did for Auntie Dara. "It's not that much—I'm doing food deliveries for a restaurant now. Kinda."

Her smile is sickeningly sweet, layered and lathered with unspoken words. I've seen the kind before. She flips to another page in her file as she says, "So Hikari is going to assist with tuition, I'm guessing? Based on her salary, well, it might be, er, not optimal for your student loans application."

I shrug. "I applied for school way before I moved here, so they should honor that, right?"

"Yes, but with Hikari, you're no longer in *need* of student loans," she explains. "So I suspect York won't agree to the deferral anyway, but that's something I would've liked to discuss with Hikari had she been available." She gives a sharp, near condescending sigh as her eyes dart to the hallway.

"I can't rely on her for tuition," I say. I may not be dying to go to York or anything, but I don't want her to think I care about Olu's money, because I don't.

I add, "She might not even be staying here long-term."

Gardenia tilts her head as she listens. "Is this confirmed?"

"W-wait, no," I say. Damn, I don't want to get Olu in trouble. I hope I'm not saying the wrong thing here. "I just meant, like, she has her own life. She can't just . . . drop everything to look after me."

Gardenia starts writing. Shit! I can't see what she's scribbling from here, but I bet it isn't good. I'm panicking, feeling that itch in my fingers and feet again, that restlessness that makes me want to jump up, run away, or skate and skate until the thick, humid air starts to feel like a cool breeze against my skin.

Without thinking, I blurt out, "Forget it. I'll ask Olu about the tuition thing. I can just pay her back in the future—"

"Summer." Gardenia sets her papers facedown and folds her hands together as she speaks. Her voice is calmer. Her social worker voice. This is how she sounded when I first met her, when she was trying to get me to like her. "Hikari has agreed to look after you. Do you know what that means?"

I shrug, eyes downcast.

"It means she agreed to look after you *legally*," she tells me. "That means for financial reasons, for emotional reasons, whatever the case, she is responsible for you."

But she's just a kid, too. Don't they get that? She's twenty. She shouldn't have this kind of responsibility. It isn't fair.

"Paying her back, trying to tiptoe around important issues, you're not obligated to do these things. You're not the adult here."

"Well, neither is she," I bite back as I remember the way Olu's hands trembled, how they pressed tight into each other as if they were holding something sacred. "She's only twenty, she's practically a teenager herself, a-and maybe she's going through stuff, too."

Gardenia sighs through her nose. She re-clasps her hands, this time tighter, and says, "The offer is still on the table to speak with a registered psychotherapist. We can even let you choose one you're most comfortable with."

"I don't need a therapist. I'm fine," I grunt. She stares back like she doesn't believe me. I wish she would stop that. It doesn't matter if Olu agreed to look after me. That doesn't mean I should just take advantage of her. Getting her to pay my tuition, expecting her to drop everything and be there for me. To care about me. It's too much to ask—it was too much to ask of my parents, so why would Olu be any different?

Gardenia lets out a sigh and gets to her feet. "I'll need to reschedule with Hikari, but for now, can I take a quick look around?"

I follow behind her as she dips into my room, inspecting it for tidiness and who knows what else. She pokes her head into the bathroom, glances at a closet, and pops open the fridge, probably to make sure it's well stocked. And she keeps scribbling as she goes. We don't talk while she circles the apartment, but when she's done, she tells me, "Your job is just to be a kid. I know it's hard, but . . . Try and remember that, okay?" She gives me one more strict smile before leaving. I would've slammed the door in her face if I could.

My job is to be a kid, and I can't even do that right. I can't look the other way and let someone else take care of me, because when I did, I came downstairs to an empty house and distant sirens closing in on my front door. I spent a year with a void I didn't know how to fill with anything other than the wind on my face when I skate through the park. But at some point, even that stops being enough. Even that starts to sting.

Anger bubbles up in the pit of my stomach. It tugs and pulls the strings loose, airing my frustrations like they're nothing. Frustration that I'm in this situation to begin with, anger at my parents, anger at myself. Anger at York, like, damn, leave me alone! Anger at that old guidance counselor who didn't know how to mind his fucking business. Like, I graduated high school already, I'm not his responsibility! I'm not anyone's responsibility.

I march back to my room and grab the rest of my stuff. As I reach for my bag, the letter to Auntie Dara falls out, gliding gently to the floor. Something about the creases, those numbers, the fragile way it sucks up all the air in the room but refuses to take up space forces tears from my eyes. I inhale, I cry. I'm bawling now.

This crying feels so foreign to me. I haven't cried like this in a while—not when my parents disappeared, not when I had to leave home—and it hurts so much. The shame of it crushes me, rooting me in place, and forces me to hang my head. I think of Olu finding me like this, trying to console me, and then me pushing her away because no one can fix this for me. The thought makes me so mad. I don't need any consoling. I don't need anything from anyone.

Just forget it, Summer.

It's all useless.

I wipe my face frantically, eager to do away with any remnants of sorrow, this shame in crying. Tanya's expecting me—I should've been on a bus half an hour ago.

I bring my board to Tanya's place so I can get off the bus a few stops early and skate the rest of the way. I need to do this to relax and recenter my thoughts before I'm seated in Tanya's stuffy basement watching old-school African movies for the next seven hours while she braids my hair. I ride faster and farther down the sidewalk, swallowing down my unease, pushing away any insecurity. This isn't the time for that.

As usual, Tanya's driveway is crammed with cars from relatives who are visiting or staying over from their travels. She always has to do so much *Tetris*-ing of the cars.

I stop before I slam into one of the vans that are parked on a slant and kick up my board, grabbing it before it touches the ground again. Tanya's house has a separate basement entrance so I don't bother going up the main steps; instead, I slip around the side of the house and follow a set of concrete steps leading to a door. I knock three times. "It's me," I say.

Tanya opens, greeting me with a smile and a bowl of grapes. She snacks on one as she nudges the door with her hip. "Friend! Ooh, I love this." She reaches out and touches my hair, sinking her hand into it. "You could rock a blowout, you know."

I snort. "Not in this humidity."

She cackles. "I hear that. Get in."

I still feel raw and screwed up, but hanging with Tanya makes me forget. I fake normalcy while she loads up the first of what I'm sure will be at least three movies, an old village-style Nigerian movie called *Mark of Royalty*. "One guess as to what this is about," she snickers as she pats the seat in front of her. I sit on the sofa and she sits on the sofa's back, hovering above my shoulders so she can get a good view of my head for braiding.

I sigh as she parts my hair, detangles it, and separates strands of Kanekalon hair to braid onto my own. Tanya's braids are always tight, so I wince as she tugs and twists at my scalp. Every so often I laugh at something in the movie, but then Tanya flicks my ear with the rattail comb and says, "Don't move."

"Oh my god, but I'm dying," I fake-whine.

She mimics my whine and then starts to chuckle. "How's your cousin?"

"Eh. She's good." As good as possible, I guess.

"Cool, cool," Tanya says. "I'm trying to get on her good side. She seems like a lot of fun. And she's got money, still."

I glance at my hands. "Y-yeah."

"She'll set you up real nice since you're not working and all."

I tilt my head to glance at her, but she flicks my ear again. "Ow—I *am* working, actually. One of my aunties asked me to run some deliveries for her until she hires a driver."

She chortles. "You don't have a car."

"They're extremely local," I lie. "I skate to places, mostly."

"You and this skateboard life, man," Tanya sighs. "I'd just mooch off my cousin but go off. What's her net worth, anyway?"

"What makes you think I'd know that?"

Tanya nudges my arm with her knee. "You haven't googled her? We're about to do that right now."

I groan. "Hell no—"

"Either you do it, or I do it, but between the two of us, I'm the one who needs to focus," she says, her voice carrying every hint of a person who knows she won.

She lets me reach for my phone before she gets started on another braid. I pull up a browser and type Olu's full name into the search bar. "Happy?" I grunt, to which Tanya giggles behind me. I can feel her shift and lean close over my shoulder so she can see more of my screen. But I don't think either of us were really ready for the first search results.

"JAPANESE SINGER EMBROILED IN AFFAIR WITH POLITICIAN"

"Excuse me?" Tanya gasps. Her eyes dart around the screen. "What . . . Are you sure you searched the right name?"

"Yeah, obviously, like I don't know my own cousin's name." I kiss my teeth, feeling my fingers tremble around my phone. How is this possible? Sid looked her up the other week, but there was only a vague mention of some relationship. I check the date of this article: It was posted two days ago, but states that the original Japanese blog from which this article was translated has been up for . . . months. Two months. What the *hell*? Olu hasn't said anything about a politician. And she hasn't even said anything about an affair. She's just—she's not that type of person.

I click into the first search result and, there it is, a promotional picture of Olu. I can't believe it. Beside it is a picture of a decent-looking guy wearing a suit and ducking into a building. Below that is a blurry picture of what I assume is the two of them together. Shiiiiit.

"Read out loud," Tanya says.

I scroll a little to where the article begins. "'Nineteen-year-old Nigerian-Japanese singer Hikari Arai, known to her fans as Kari, has issued a formal apology through her agency regarding her . . . her relationship with thirty-year-old Yuuto Tanaka, whose father Seto Tanaka is a Tokyo councillor, and whose budding political career is . . .' Sorry, I can't read this." I kiss my teeth, staring on in disbelief. "This is bullshit. She's—He's . . ."

"Thirty? He's so *old*." Tanya shudders.

"And an affair, though? With *this* guy?"

"Scroll some more," she tells me, and I do so reluctantly. "Is there a picture of the wife? Ooh, yep, there she is, there she is!" Tanya practically slaps my arm to stop me from scrolling past the grainy picture of a woman whose face is shielded while she walks into a building.

She must be the woman whose life Olu ruined.

And it's undeniable now, skimming the article and looking at these pictures. Every time I asked what she was doing here, Olu wouldn't answer. And if she was forced to give an apology, then it has to be true. Why else would she apologize, especially if she did nothing wrong? Why else would she come here, if not to lay low, avoid, run?

I lean back into Tanya's knees while she braids fast. Fuck. It's all making sense now. Olu isn't stressed at having me around; it's guilt that's weighing her down. She got herself involved with a guy who was married, and then she ran away, back to Canada, because facing the truth was too shameful for her.

I don't know how I feel about that.

Actually, I don't know how to feel about any of this—Olu, Auntie Dara's letter, York, the future.

Tanya's fingers on my scalp distract me from my thoughts, and I'm able to fully sink into the movie. The more I get into this "poor village girl meets rich prince" narrative, the faster Tanya is able to work. We don't talk much aside from her commenting, "How?" every time there's some twist we both didn't see coming. I can barely roll my eyes when they realize the village girl is actually royalty. Tanya doesn't stop saying, "You . . . you have a mark of royalty," in the king's deep voice for the rest of the afternoon. It's lowkey annoying, but I don't care enough to tell her to quit it.

By the time she's done my hair, the sun is still bright in the sky. I check myself out in the mirror, tossing my fresh, long braids over my shoulder—and wincing as they reveal just how tender my scalp is.

"Ibuprofen," she says with a nod.

"Definitely."

"Let me grab you some. Hold on." She turns to jog up the stairs to the ground floor.

I gravitate to my phone again, pulling up the Google search results. My head is empty, as if every thought that was in there has just tapped out. It's so fitting. Besides, there isn't much else to think. It must be in our DNA, right? Running away from our problems.

CHAPTER TEN

I DON'T WANT TO GO back to Olu's.

To think she could be capable of something so selfish and disrespectful is hard for me to stomach. This wickedness, it must be in our genes. It got her the same way it got my parents. And maybe one day, if I don't run fast enough, if I don't skate hard enough, it'll come for me too.

As I leave Tanya's place, feeling the touch of a breeze along my newly styled head, I contemplate what to do—if I even *can* do anything. Immediately, I imagine running to the beach, throwing myself at the shoreline, and letting the waves tickle my feet. Letting them bring me back home. I imagine hanging with Jet, who is always there, always lurking in places I least expect him to be. I think he might tell me about his mom, if she's out of jail or not, and what that's like for him. I picture him asking if I want to meet her.

Somehow, my feet don't get the memo. They trace the familiar but unwelcome route back to Olu's whether I like it or not.

Quickly, I try Auntie Dara's number. Running deliveries is the exact distraction I need, but she isn't picking up. "Please, for once . . . ," I grumble to myself while on the bus back to Port Credit. What kind of business owner doesn't answer her phone on the first ring? I call again and again and am met with her voice mail each time. My frustration grows with each dropped call.

Auntie Dara doesn't pick up until I'm literally on the penthouse floor, my hand pushing gently on Olu's front door.

"Summer?" she answers, short and brusque.

I tiptoe into the apartment, glancing around to make sure Olu isn't sitting in the living room. The coast is clear for now. "Auntie?" I whisper. "I was wondering if you needed anything delivered. I'm—like, I'm not close by, but still."

"Why are you talking so quiet?"

"Me?"

"I can't hear you."

I groan inwardly and speak a bit louder. "Can I come in and run some deliveries for you? If you have anything, anyway."

"Eh heh!" she exclaims, her voice bursting through my phone. I have to move it away to protect my eardrums. How annoying. *She's* the one who hasn't been answering her phone for the past hour, and she's acting like *I* have the communication problem. "Yes, I was just thinking you should be coming in. I have the delivery people from that app, but sometimes customers will be calling the restaurant and they don't want to pay high delivery."

"S-sure," I answer. "I can come in now. It might take a while to get there, but yeah."

I plan to leave as quietly as I tiptoed in, but that plan is ruined the second I notice Olu appear in the hallway. She looks tired, like she is either still drunk or has been crying. I wonder if it's both.

I hang up on Auntie Dara. Olu and I look at each other, neither of us really knowing what to do or what to say. I can sense her uneasiness because it's my uneasiness, too. The feeling that if she steps forward, I will step back, or if I start to run, she might catch me. Her bottom lip begins to quiver, and I want to roll my eyes, annoyed that she thinks she can gain sympathy from me after what I learned about her—after I found out the real reason she's here.

She gives a strained smile and says, "Summer, hi. Welcome back."

I tilt my head, turning up my nose. My jaw begins to tremble so I bite down hard, trying not to show it.

She takes a careful step forward. Somehow the distance between us stays the same. "I'm trying to get ahold of Gardenia to reschedule. Maybe this Friday, she can come back. I will be . . . *totally* awake for it," she says through a tired exhale.

I stay quiet.

"I'm so sorry, Summer," she breathes out.

All I can do is stare back, unflinching, afraid to let my uncertainty and frustration come through. Afraid for her to see me.

My heart says, *Accept the apology, you idiot! She's* trying.

My brain says, *Fuck that.*

Trying is not . . .

It's just *not*.

I pocket my phone and avoid her while I duck to the door.

"I heard you on the phone," she pipes up, taking a hurried step toward me. "You said you need to go somewhere, right?" I don't turn around, but I slow my movements while I put my shoes back on. My brain wants to hear her out. My heart doesn't understand why. She continues, "Let's go together. Or, I should go to Gardenia's office anyway, s-so it makes sense for us to get a car together. It'll be faster."

She's right and I hate that she is. Auntie Dara is expecting me soon because I didn't have the heart to tell her it'll take, like, an hour plus to get to her place with the bus and my skateboard. Going with Olu will be way faster, but on the downside, that means being trapped in a car with her. My frustration gets the better of me—heat rises in my chest, threatening to break out. I can't even look at her, so this will be hard. Still . . . It will be free.

"Sure," I grunt, and grab my things.

She takes ten minutes to shower and get ready, and when she emerges, she looks less like a troll and more like the Olu in her pictures. The pictures of her and that guy.

After I give Olu the address, she calls a car and we head downstairs, into the sticky summer air, in complete silence. We get into the car in silence. The driver isn't talkative, either. He taps his phone a few times so the route will update, and then pulls back onto the road, his eyes narrowed in the sun's glare.

Olu and I sit as far apart as humanly possible in the back seat of the car.

Twenty minutes feels like twenty hours. I sit, sweating in my anxiety, stewing in my frustration.

By the time the car pulls into the parking lot of Auntie Dara's place, my jaw is so tense that it makes my head throb. I hadn't realized how bad I've been clenching until now. Every muscle in my face is sore, and I feel like I have to train my face on how to relax. Things like, "take a deep breath, let your jaw hang, soften your nose" run through my head, but none of them seems to work.

The second the car stops, I leap out. Auntie Dara is standing at the door, squinting at the car, and she watches us both get out. My brain snaps—*My god, I hope she's not following me into the store*—but then I see Olu calling another rideshare to wherever it is she's going.

Auntie Dara beckons me forward. "Good that you came just now. I have two orders: one is ten minutes from here, the other is five. Come, let me give you the addresses." She ushers me into the restaurant, casting a furtive glance or two over her shoulder at Olu like she's some enemy. It's weird. Wouldn't they know each other? Olu would've seen Auntie Dara before when she came to visit all those years ago. I'm pretty sure that happened . . .

Auntie goes back out to talk to Olu. I stand on the inside of the restaurant, watching their exchange. It's hard to hear. Olu is cautious and curious, tilting her head and taking half steps forward as if Auntie is saying something she can't make out. And Auntie Dara is always the same, standoffish, unmoving. Solid. Making everyone come to her.

At one point, Olu peers around Auntie to look in my direction. I panic and disappear farther into the kitchen.

Auntie Dara joins me five minutes later, dusting her hands on the apron around her waist. "Who is that?"

I turn when I hear her voice behind me, but I don't really care to answer. I'm busy looking over the containers and receipts she's assembled for me to deliver. None of them are packaged, so I don't touch anything. One is an order of meat pie for an apartment; the other is an order of spring rolls, meat pie, akara, and plantain for a house on "Random Street." Like, that's actually the name of the street.

And there are numbers written.

Of course, it's just the order number, but . . .

"Summer?"

"Hnn?"

I tilt my head toward her, but my eyes are so focused on the fast scribbles. All these numbers are written the same way as that code from the letter in my bag. The one addressed to Auntie Dara.

I turn to face her.

She puts her hand on her hip, waiting for my answer.

My lips pursed, I mumble, "What did you ask me? Sorry . . ."

"I said who is that?"

"Olu."

"Eh heh, and since when has she been here?"

Honestly, Auntie Dara has some nerve getting all righteous, as if Olu was supposed to tell her she arrived in Canada the second she did. It's not like Auntie has been super close with our family consistently. Olu doesn't owe her anything.

Wait, why am I sticking up for her, anyway? Olu doesn't owe *me* anything, either. Not even the truth of what she's really doing here.

Auntie Dara gestures like she wants me to answer her question. I say, "A few months? I don't know."

"Wow." Her shock is so fake.

"S-so which ones are going where again?" Slowly, I turn back to the counter with the orders, the orders that look curiously more and more like the numbers written on that letter. I'm emboldened by their resemblance, being so close to something so clearly off, that I point at the first set. My voice cuts off the beginning of Auntie Dara's explanation. "Who wrote these?" I ask.

"Ah ah." She frowns. After a beat, she says, "Who else? It was me, of course."

My heart bangs in my chest. *Boom-boom-boom-boom—*

Without thinking, I dig into my bag for the letter and set it on the counter between us. She immediately recoils when she sees it, and after getting a better look, her facade breaks. "What is this?" she nearly snaps, her face contorted with disgust, confusion, and anger.

My jaw tenses up again while I point to the paper. "Did you write this, too?"

"I said, what *is* this?"

"I found it."

Her frown deepens. "Where?"

"I can't remember," I lie. "But it's addressed to you and these numbers are supposed to be for a lawyer, but . . ." As I talk, my eyes home in on the letter and the orders scrawled just to my right. The resemblance is ridiculous. If she wrote those order numbers, then she definitely wrote this stupid letter. But then, *why* would it be addressed to her from my parents? That's the one thing I'm not getting. I take a deep breath. "Aun—"

Without warning, Auntie Dara snatches the paper, bringing it right up to her nose. She spends too much time looking at it, considering there's nothing much to read. And, especially since we already deduced the fact that she wrote it herself.

Eventually, she pulls the paper away, setting it down carefully. Her expression softens, though she still seems confused. It makes me feel prickly. When she utters, "I don't understand," I feel my heart sink.

I take a step forward, pressed against the counter. "That doesn't make any sense. It's addressed to *you*. And the handwriting is, like, the same."

"Ah ah." Auntie's mouth twists into a frown. "I don't *know*. What do you want me to do, na?"

I swallow down my anger. My brain is fighting with me: *She's lying, she's fucking lying, she has to be . . .* But she says she has no idea what this is. She's looking at me like I conjured this shit out of nowhere, like I'm the one who's being sketchy here.

"Forget it," I grunt, and reach for the orders.

Auntie Dara kisses her teeth as she steps up to do it for me. She begins to wrap the appropriate containers in each bag, stapling the receipts to the tops of them. She talks as she works, "Be fast. I don't want the food to get cold."

"Sure." I reach out for the letter, but her hand stops me. "What—"

"Look, my dear," she coos, a somber look on her face. All the while, she's inching the letter from my hand. The worst thing is I let her do it. I watch as she folds it in her grasp, tucking it away out of my reach. "I know you're very concerned about this . . . this letter of a thing. Eh? So, I'm going to try and help you. Don't worry."

I frown. "H-how?"

"Leave this with me," she says, jutting her lips toward the letter. "I will look into it. I don't know this number, but if this letter was for me, then I have to figure out why."

"I . . ." My feelings are all over the place. I try to reach for the letter again, but she moves it farther away. "What's . . . a-and why . . . I just . . . u-um, but . . ." I don't even know what to say. I should feel more relieved, but confusion grips me. I shut my eyes momentarily, trying to recall the letter's contents. Those numbers looked just like these. *Those* numbers looked just like *these*. Right? They did, didn't they?

"It's all right," she says softly. "I know you're very worried. I will solve it. I'll fix it."

Something in her words makes me listen. The certainty. It silences the voices in my head, my rising anxiety, all of it.

"O-oh . . ." I clear my throat. "Are you sure?"

"Yes, na." She gestures toward the doorway. "Now, go. I don't want you to be late."

I leave and run the deliveries, including two extra that come in. By the time I head home in the late evening with eighty dollars in my pocket, the day's events begin to feel like a distant memory. When I close my eyes, I can still see the letter in my mind, but now I'm not so sure if I saw those order numbers properly. I'm not so sure of anything.

"Come back tomorrow," Auntie Dara told me, so I do, bright and early. I don't want to stay home and have to deal with Olu, anyway. It's for the best that I stay outside as long as possible.

"TODAY IS SLOW," AUNTIE SAYS when I arrive on Tuesday. She gestures to three packed bags that each have receipts stapled to them. "It's just those three, and then you can go home."

"Oh?" She nods at my inquisitiveness. "Are you sure? Because I'm not doing anything today."

She snickers, giving me a wry look. "You? Nothing else?"

It feels weird that she's trying to joke with me. I want to say, "Yeah, nothing else," and disappear. Shut my eyes and try to remember the numbers again. It's the strangest thing, but now, when I reach for a delivery, I notice all the new order numbers are written differently. Almost like they're in cursive, or something.

Why would that be necessary?

Auntie Dara turns to head to the kitchen, dusting her

hands on her apron, when I rush back to the counter and slam my hand on it. It gets her attention—and makes my hand hurt. She opens her mouth, probably to ask what's wrong with me, but I throw out, "I wanted to ask you something," before she can speak.

Her eyebrows furrow. "Okay, ask."

Way easier said than done. I try to look casual when I say, "It's because of the letter I gave you. Remember? It made me think of my parents a-and I was wondering, you know, have you . . . maybe spoken to them at all? It's random, I know . . ." My voice trembles, betraying the confidence I thought I was faking well.

When I'm finally able to look at Auntie Dara, she's staring me straight in the eyes. Fear holds me in place. "No," she says simply. God, it makes a shiver run down my spine. There's something so icy, so direct, about the way she's speaking. I really don't like it. "Why would I? Have you?"

"N-no," I stammer.

She doesn't move, but the way her eyes wash over me, cascading from my head to my toes . . . She's suspicious. Oh my god, does she think *I* have anything to do with what happened? That's impossible. Out of everyone, I lost the most.

I back away from the counter, pensive, fearful steps as I hold her gaze with mine. "I'll be back tomorrow," I mumble, and take off outside. The wheels of my skateboard hit the ground and I hop on, pushing myself farther and farther away from the store. Over my shoulder, I spot Auntie Dara in the doorway, watching me leave.

I sweat so much as I whip through the neighborhood. The air is sticky with the kind of heat that feels like someone is breathing on you. The sun beats down on my head, rising steadily until it's at the highest point in the sky. I don't wear sunscreen so I'm even more conscious of how the rays hit my skin, making my buttered up arms and legs shine in the midday haze.

Sid texts me and tells me to come to the skate park by his house. *Kirsten's not here*, he writes, and I can't lie, I'm excited. I feel like it's been so long since it's just been us, doing random shit without Kirsten's condescending gaze.

The skate park is filled with kids who look like they're in middle school. They give us customary nods when we skate by. I watch as they head to the steps at the front of the park, an indicator that they're going there to grind the rails. Those rails stress me out. Two years ago, I attempted a nosegrind there, and I fell face-first in front of everyone. It's in the top two most embarrassing moments of my life, and it's not number two.

Sid was there for that horrible moment, so of course he points in the distance and is like, "Isn't that where you almost died?"

I flip him off. "Yep. Hate you."

He snickers, "Cool, cool," and picks up speed.

I follow him. My scalp still hurts a little from the way Tanya did my box braids, but at the same time, feeling the thick air against my head is comforting. I love the wind against my knees, too: against my shoulders, pushing the featherlight ends of my braids. It almost makes me forget about Olu, her whole reason for being here, my parents, Auntie Dara . . . everything.

I get so agitated because I didn't ask for any of this. I didn't know my parents were stealing people's money; I didn't expect them to disappear. I don't even know if I want to look for them.

I'm not sure what I was expecting each time I went back to check the mail at my old house. If I was hoping for a sign, isn't this it? A letter with numbers that don't make sense. A cold trail that refuses to be followed in the middle of a lonely summer. Yeah, that sounds about right. It all makes sense now.

Because, really, if Mom and Dad cared, they wouldn't have disappeared the way they did, without a word, without a trace.

Not even a goodbye.

In the height of a . . . beautiful season.

If I'm being real, it used to hurt much more to think about. My parents and everything. With each day that passes, I question how much I really care. Maybe I don't anymore. Maybe my brain is wondering about this letter and piecing together order numbers and fonts that don't exist, and my heart has already moved on. It doesn't ache; my lips don't quiver. When I think about the things I care about, I get excited, like when I first learned to kickflip, or I get passionate, like when Tanya told me about that ex-boyfriend who was mean to her so we planned to run up on him. But when I think about my parents, about everything that happened over the past year, I mean, all I can feel is the wind on my face, the humidity and stickiness against my skin. I don't feel anything else anymore.

This is why I love my skateboard. It takes me wherever I want to go. It lets me escape.

Kinda like that song Olu played for me. Her demo. It transported me so effortlessly to that beach, and I was able to leave my problems behind, if only for a second. As I ride down the pavement, I catch myself wondering what ended up happening with that, but I quickly eject the thought from my head.

I pick up speed as I come up to a curb. I hear Sid behind me, "You gotta be careful on that or you'll end up face-planting—" and I skate faster, fake chuckling as loud as I can, "Ha ha ha!" so I don't have to hear him.

Suddenly, I glance over my shoulder, turning a little with my board so I can see him in my peripheral vision. "Actually, I still have a scar," I tell him, touching my chin.

"I didn't notice. Lemme see, lemme see."

I slow, putting my foot down and kicking my board up before it rolls away. Sid rides over, but he's going way too fast so I grab onto his hands to steady him. While he's in front of me, I tilt my head so he can get a better look at my chin, even though he's way taller than me on the board. I end up having to bend back more than is comfortable.

Sid leans in close, tapping my chin, running his finger along the scar. I stand perfectly still, unsure if breathing too much will distract him. Unsure if it'll distract me. It's not like I haven't ever been this close to Sid before, but it's hot outside and I'm already dizzy because of the skating and everything. I was going too fast—the thing is, I *like* to go fast when the weather is humid because it's the only way I can feel anything. The breeze. But I am hyper-aware of the distance between us now and how I can't feel anything at all.

Sid says, "Dude, it used to be *so* bad," as he retracts his hand. We lock eyes for a moment of deafening silence before he kicks off again, circling back to the park.

I follow. I touch my chin.

CHAPTER ELEVEN

SID INVITES ME BACK TO his house for lunch. I refuse to turn down a free meal, and I'll literally do anything to not go back to Olu's, so I follow him. The front yard, the door, are all so familiar to me but I still wait on the step for him to walk in before me. On impulse, I grab for my phone, pulling it out of the pocket in my dress. No one would be trying to message me, but I've been gone all day and I guess I thought Olu would . . .

Never mind.

Sid comes up beside me, chuckling while he nudges the front door open. "You can go inside, you know. You practically used to live here."

I let out a chuckle much more uneasy than his and trail behind him into the house. Coming back here is surreal. I work on autopilot, taking off my shoes, setting my board by the door, and letting my socked feet glide down the hall to the living room, to my favorite sofa where I used to always chill. I end up there before Sid because he detours through the kitchen to grab waters for both of us. I can't lie, the one thing I don't miss is constantly drinking bottled water. As he hands me a cold bottle, I hear myself thinking, *What's wrong with tap water?* I accept the water and sink further into the sofa, letting the coldness of the plastic anchor me in the now.

Sid sits beside me as he says, "How's the delivery thing been going?" the same time I ask, "Where's Kirsten?"

I don't even know why I asked that, considering I don't actually care.

Still, he shrugs and says, "Visiting her dad. He's buying her and her sister dinner or whatever." Kirsten's parents are divorced, and from my understanding, her dad keeps trying to bribe her and her sister to come live with him in France next summer. She is, very stupidly, still considering the offer.

"Your turn," he says.

I sigh. "Deliveries have been cool, I guess. I get to skate around all day and then I get money. It's chill."

He slouches back, sinking into the sofa. "Not enough for tuition, though."

I snort because I think he's joking. It's hard to tell. "Uh, obviously not," I say, chortling, because it's funny, right, the idea of me ever having enough money for tuition. Which is fine, anyway, because I'm not going to post-secondary. Haven't even thought of York in a minute. And, I don't know . . . My friends are all excited to go to university, so sometimes I feel like maybe I could just suck it up and actually take this seriously, but then I just don't. There's always something else more important.

Sid turns so he's facing me. Okay, I guess he's not joking. "I bet your cousin would help if you asked her, though."

"Well, I don't want to ask her," I say through a tight jaw, and get up to circle around the open concept kitchen.

"Yeah, but why not?" he asks. Frustration colors his words. "I don't get it."

"Because it's not her responsibility," I grumble. "She doesn't have to take care of me."

"She kinda does, though."

"No, she fucking doesn't," I snap. The heat behind my voice startles me. "And she *can't*, anyway, because she's, like, twenty years old and she has her own shit to deal with and she didn't ask for this and she's—" She's probably leaving, too. How can I trust she'd stick around?

They all leave eventually.

Sid doesn't turn away. I'm surprised—I'm ashamed. I usually never get angry around any of my friends, and I'm terrified that he will find this side of me to be too much to deal with. His eyebrow twitches, a sign he is exhausted. A sign he is tired of me, maybe.

My heart beats fast and frantically. I rush to apologize. "Sorry. I—I didn't mean that." My lips purse as my eyes fall to the countertop.

"S'okay," he says softly, and then after a moment, "Listen, no one's asking you to do everything on your own, you know? It doesn't have to be like that anymore. You don't have to keep going back to your old place, pretending that things haven't changed."

I look at him, a jolt of fear rushing up my spine. "I don't—I n-never went back to my old house," I lie.

He tilts his head—he knows I'm not telling the truth.

"I don't go back *often*," I concede.

He shrugs. "I don't know what that feels like, not having your parents and stuff, so I won't judge you. But you can't keep looking backward."

I hate that he's right. He doesn't seem like he would be so wise, because his head is always in the clouds and he skates faster than anyone I know. I thought we were both trying to escape something, but it's times like these that I realize we're not the same at all. He has so much I can't have. He understands so much that I don't.

Suddenly, a large white envelope on the edge of the countertop catches my eye. I don't know how I didn't see it before. Instinctively, I move toward it, letting my eyes wash over the University of Waterloo crest in the corner. My brows furrow, twisting on my face as I try to make sense of why Waterloo is sending letters to my friend. It's August. It's way too late for them to be sending a rejection.

"What's this?" I ask as I reach for the envelope. Sid turns to see what I'm talking about—and then immediately slides down off the sofa until I can't see him anymore from where I'm standing. How suspect! "You're getting letters from Waterloo?"

"Uhh . . ." Eventually, he crawls off the floor and back to the sofa. We lock eyes across the kitchen when he says, "Yeah, it's from Waterloo."

"I *know* that," I grumble, making my way over to the sofa. "What are they sending you?"

He doesn't look at me while he says, "Acceptance package."

"What?" My mouth hangs open in sheer disbelief. I wait for him to explain, but he doesn't. The awkwardness of my ignorance hangs in the air. So I ask, "Acceptance? But what about York? I thought we decided already."

"*We?*" He lets out a humorless, almost mocking laugh. "Bro, you haven't said a thing to me about York. And your tuition situation is kinda sketchy right now, so . . ."

I can't even say anything. Burning with frustration, I stare down at the envelope, flipping it back and forth in my hand. I get that I wasn't serious about York, but at least it's closer than Waterloo. Waterloo is, like, two hours away from here by car! I don't have a car, and there's no way I can swing bus money to go visit. Even if I wasn't going to York, if he had stayed here, I could still hang out with Sid in the evenings and it would've felt like nothing much had changed. It would've felt normal.

"Besides," he cuts in with a simple shrug. "I liked Waterloo's biomed program better."

"When did you even have time to like another program?"

"When I went to their open house with Kirsten," he tells me.

I swallow, hard. "And when was that? It's *August*. When were you going to tell me that you were l-leaving?" The word sounds so heavy on my tongue. I'm so tired of it, so sick of people disappearing on me.

He sighs, his shoulders rising and falling in defeat. "I mean, I *was* gonna tell you . . ."

"Never mind," I utter, setting the envelope down on the counter. This acceptance package is also none of my business. It's like nothing is any of my business these days, and yet here I am, digging myself in deeper, making myself care about things and people I have no influence over.

Sid gives an apologetic smile, a quiet tug at the corner of his lips, but all I can do is shrug. I disappoint myself in so many ways.

"Are you good?" Sid's voice gets me out of my head.

I nod right away, my body obeying a command I didn't give. "Yeah. Why wouldn't I be?"

He tilts his head to the side, examining my face. "Listen, I seriously would've told you sooner," he goes on. His voice is doing that thing where he sounds very sincere and very honest, and I actually hate it so much. I wish he'd just lie or something. "Honestly. But it was a serious wait-list situation and I didn't think I would actually get in."

"But you accepted already, so that's cool." There it is: my sharp, strict tone, right on schedule. I sound like a robot. So unforgiving, so harsh. I don't mean to be, and it bothers me to hear myself be so rigid with Sid because it's really not that deep. He doesn't owe me anything—he's my friend, he's one of my best friends, but it's not like we're dating and we promised to go to the same school and live in the same neighborhood forever. He has his own life. Everyone does.

I just . . .

For once, I wish someone's plans would include me too.

We stare at each other. I am paralyzed with feelings that I don't know how to show anymore.

Quickly, I get to my feet. "I should head to my cousin's place," I say, and make my way back to the foyer for my board.

"Seriously? Summer, wait."

I do not. His footsteps follow behind but he doesn't try and stop me as I wrestle my feet back into my shoes and reach for the front door.

With a deep breath, I swing around to face him, trying my hardest to look sincere when I tell him, "It's cool, I swear. Don't worry about me."

"But I am," he says. Stern, genuine, honest.

"Tch, why? Should *I* be worried?" I mean it as a joke, even though I don't feel in a joking mood. I hope it'll make him laugh, but instead, concern grows on his face. It just makes me angry.

He says, "Listen, you know I care about you, right?"

"Sure."

"Do you think . . . maybe you need to talk to someone?"

"Someone like who?" It's a dumb question and I know it. I know what he means. He's not the first person who's told me maybe I need a therapist, and he probably won't be the last.

Before he can cut in, I grab his wrist and say, "I'm fine." I try to sound as stern as he does, but my voice wavers a little. "Like I said, don't worry about me."

And again, he says, "But I *am*."

I leave Sid after I do a bad job convincing him that I'll be okay. As I ride down the sidewalk, I will the stuffy air to turn into the slightest breeze the faster I go. Please, I need to feel something. I want to be okay.

When I get back to the apartment, I kick off my shoes and drop my board by the door. Olu is at the kitchen table, typing at her laptop. She does a double take and then gets to her feet when she sees me. The sense of purpose with which she stands at the breakfast bar makes me tired. I can practically sense how bad she wants to talk to me.

Before I can manage one whole thought, she says, "Gardenia agreed to this Friday." This is as serious as I've ever heard her. If she's trying to bully me into something, she can forget it. My guard is going all the way up.

I shrug. "Whatever."

Her eyes narrow. Heat radiates from her gaze. "I really am trying, you know. In case you haven't noticed."

It takes everything in me to not roll my eyes or drop dead on the floor. So she's trying and I should do what, exactly? It's not like she's been honest with me. She shows up and says yes to looking after me for no reason—except there *is* a reason, and she's not telling me. She ran away from Japan after ruining people's lives, and now she's trying to use taking care of me as some kind of redemption? Well, fuck that. I'm not her weird babysitting project and I don't need her.

"Yeah, sure," I grunt, and turn to leave. I hear her give a heavy sigh, muttering something under her breath in Japanese while she makes her way to the kitchen table—and something about that sparks a flame in my chest. So she doesn't even have the balls to cuss me in a language I can understand? My hand is barely on my room's doorknob before I spin back around, stomping back to the kitchen space. "What exactly are you doing here?" I ask, my voice sharp, unwavering.

She looks taken aback, shifting her weight from one leg to the other. "What do you mean?"

"I mean, why did you leave Japan?" I cross my arms, tilting my head to the side. She looks terrified the moment I mention it. *Good.* "Why come all the way out here? I asked before and you never told me. You probably haven't told my social worker, either. What did you say to her for her to agree to all this?"

"Sum—"

"Are they giving you money? Is that it? As if you need it," I scoff.

She shakes her head. "It's not the money—I'm not even getting—"

"Well, then what other reason do you have?" I yell. "You stole someone's husband, felt too fucking guilty to stay in Japan, and then ran away back to Canada where no one knows you?"

"What? No, I . . ." Her fear morphs into sorrow so quickly. She clasps her hands together, dropping them in front of her, and her lips begin to tremble. I don't expect to feel anything while I watch the weight of my words sit on her shoulders, but I do. Something twists inside me. Regret, or something like it, tugs at my heartstrings and I want to take it all back. I didn't mean it. I didn't mean to say it like that. I was, I *am* just so . . . *angry.*

She takes a shallow, shaky breath. "Is that what you think of me?" she asks, her voice breaking. "I wasn't—I didn't *run* away. I was forced to leave."

CHAPTER TWELVE

I HAD COME IN WITH so much anger, so much righteousness. The kind I'm afraid to show others for fear they'll judge me. Unflinching. Ugly. I remembered what it was like to be at home, to feel left behind, and I clenched my jaw, narrowed my eyes, you know . . . Tried to protect myself in a way I hadn't done before. But that all comes crashing down the moment the words leave her mouth.

I was forced to leave.

That's not what I was expecting . . .

How is someone just forced to leave? And by who?

When Kirsten was here, she asked where Olu's bodyguards were. Where her security was. I thought it was so rude and nosy of her, but now, I let my eyes roam from corner to corner of the apartment, really taking in the space of it all. The *space*. The loneliness, the emptiness. The lack of protection. Olu begins to sniffle, and the sound echoes throughout the apartment. It claws its way into my ears.

I take one step forward. Then another and another, until I'm standing close enough that she can see me from where she's shielding her face. She doesn't look at me until I mumble, "W-what do you mean 'forced to leave'?"

She lets out a groan, a crass laugh. "You're making fun of me. I don't need this," she spits out, pulling her hands through her hair. Grabbing and tugging and twisting.

I frown. "I'm not . . ."

Suddenly, she folds her arms on top of the table and buries her face in them. Deep measured breaths betray the confidence front she was putting on when I first walked in. I recognize that shakiness, that need to get a hold on things, and I—I can't stop myself from walking over and sitting across from her.

Olu lifts her head, her eyebrows twisting in confusion as she watches me there. She thinks I'm trying to be mean on purpose, but I'm not. With as much sincerity as I can muster, I ask, "Why would they force you to leave?"

Olu runs a hand through her hair again. I wait for my answer.

She eventually gives it. "They thought I was . . . *shameful*," she says. The word "shameful" claws out of her like she's choking on it. Like she's heard it, thought it, felt it so many times.

She tells me, while her eyes dart across the table and tears roll down her cheeks, "They thought I should've been more c-careful, but, um . . . I didn't know he was married." Her voice breaks. "He's older so he—he . . . promised me so many things . . ." She pauses a moment to clear her throat, but the hoarseness doesn't disappear. And her shoulders begin to shake. And the tears continue falling. "I found out about the scandal at the same time as everybody else. In the *papers*. I didn't even know it was a scandal. No one told me a-anything. Just that I should leave, my commercials would be canceled, I couldn't perform anymore . . ."

Olu is full-on sobbing now. Her shoulders tremble; her face contorts with the weight of someone else's decisions. This isn't fair. "But still," I begin. "If he was wrong, too, then why would they only punish you?"

She wipes her cheeks before she grumbles, "He's a politician's son. He is . . . a *man*." This is all the explanation she can give. She holds my gaze for a moment longer, daring me to disagree, daring me to tell her that this situation could've played out any other way.

As I watch her, I shake my head, frustration taking hold. "He took advantage of you," I say without thinking.

"What?" She looks at me through blurry eyes as if I said something weird. I'm guessing not a lot of people in her life would agree with me. They must not, if they sent her here.

So I lean closer across the table, saying, "He's, like, thirty. I read an article, and they said he was thirty and you were nineteen." She nods quickly as I speak. "That's an insane age gap," I go on. "What's a thirty-year-old want with a nineteen-year-old? He's fucked up."

Olu doesn't say anything.

Silence wraps us, filling that emptiness in the apartment. It's become something like a bodyguard now.

Olu looks at her hands, wringing them, giving small nods like she's coming to terms with the thoughts in her mind.

Yeah, I should've kept quiet. Now she probably thinks

I'm nosy or horrible or whatever. I push back against the floor, my chair scraping loudly, and mutter, "I didn't . . . Never mind," while I take off for my room. But I get two steps away before I circle back. "I didn't mean to say that," I tell her awkwardly. "That stuff about the money and stealing husbands. I didn't mean it. I didn't know what I was talking about."

Then I really book it to my room before she can tell me she doesn't want my sympathy. Before she can tell me she doesn't want me here while she deals with this.

The next morning, on Wednesday, I wake up with the resounding knowledge that I might have extremely fucked up by opening my mouth yesterday and saying those things to Olu—first, by implying she's a homewrecker, and second, by saying that guy she was with is a pedo. "Should've just stayed quiet," I grumble to myself while I roll out of bed. Shame won't let me leave my room early. I'm a little bit afraid to run into Olu, but I guess I can't stay in here forever.

I shower and get dressed, tying my long braids up in a high ponytail. My scalp is still a bit tender, but I wince through the dull pain for the sake of beauty.

When I finally tiptoe out of my room, I follow the scent of scrambled eggs and toast to the kitchen. It throws me a little. She's actually cooking? Damn, I must've really offended her yesterday.

Olu dons her robe, humming to herself while she flips eggs in a pan. She jumps a little when she sees me, as if she isn't expecting me to still be here. As a result, I put on my most sincere smile to try and . . . I don't know. I'm being weird.

I just want her to know she doesn't have to run from me; that I know, and I get it, and I won't—I'm not gonna leave her the way others have.

The way I've been left.

"Summer," she greets. She sounds uneasy.

"H-hey . . ." I clear my throat and move to tuck a stray braid behind my ear, except I played myself by tying all my hair up today. There's nothing to hide behind now.

We stare at each other. Something about Olu is different; she watches me with resolve and ease, like I'm someone she knows. That barrier is gone, the one we both used to keep a safe distance. Now, there are no real secrets between us.

I take a step forward, and another and another, until I'm hanging on the side of the breakfast bar. A deep breath shakes out of me. The barrier is gone, but I still can't . . . It's hard for me to—

"I'm making breakfast," she pipes up, gesturing with her spatula toward the pan. "An omelet." Those are scrambled eggs. I'm not sure she knows what an omelet is. "S-so you can just sit and relax . . . or something."

"I—I can help," I say, and clear my throat before repeating again, with more conviction, "I'll help you."

Her eyes light up.

"If you need it," I rush to add.

"I would *love* it." She scoots over so I can join her on the other side of the kitchen island. "You can chop up those peppers a-and, um . . . Toast." She points to the bread loaf on the counter.

"Sure." I work quickly and quietly, keeping my eyes down. I gravitate toward the last few vegetables, navigating around the knife and cutting board with such ease that Olu stops to watch me. This is so embarrassing. "Wh-what?"

"Were you a chef?"

I bite back a snort. "I'm seventeen, so no."

"You chop like—" She mimics the sound, *ch-ch-ch*, the quickness of the knife against the green peppers. "—oh! Like *MasterChef*!"

I finish chopping the peppers before I reach for a tomato, saying, "I cooked a lot at home, so . . ."

"Auntie taught you?" she asks. All it takes is one sideways glance before she gets it, gets *me*, understands that hidden language in my eyes. She nods, somber, while she looks away. "When you were alone, huh . . ."

I nod.

"My . . ." I clear my throat. I don't even want to say anything, so I don't know why the words start forming. "My mom made cooking look painful. Like . . . It was always so chaotic. Took so much time, too. And I hated it. But then, a-after . . ." I gulp. "After everything, I kinda had to learn and it was like, well . . . I guess it doesn't have to be so painful . . . Yeah." Ugh, what am I saying?

But Olu doesn't grimace or turn away. She nods, as if I've told her some elaborate story, when really it was just a bunch of useless words strung together. They don't mean anything.

"I've . . . Sorry, I don't want to talk so much about myself," she begins, nervously. "But I spent so much time alone, too, and I never . . . no one *ever* let me do anything. It's so shameful, actually. I'm twenty, but I'm like a *child*." She sighs against the word, her cheeks turning a slight pink with embarrassment. "When I was sent here, even my parents were like, 'Kari, will you be okay?' And I said, 'Of course, of course' but . . ." She juts her chin toward the pan. "Like, I *know* this isn't an omelet. You know?"

The knife fumbles in my hand as I bite back a laugh.

Olu lets out a tired giggle. "Don't make fun of me, but I can't get the recipe."

"Oh god, okay, um . . ." It's so hard not to chuckle. How sheltered is she that she needs a recipe for omelets? It's literally just eggs and other shit. And you don't even have to add the other shit! "You honestly just gotta put the—like, the vegetables go in the egg mixture before you put it in the pan, so it can all fry together."

She gives an exaggerated gasp like I've said something profound. I know she's faking it but, I don't know, I'm getting all warm now. Hate it. With two thumbs up, she says, "Summer, sai-kou."

"I don't know what that means."

"The best," she says with a coy smile, and moves to dish the eggs onto a plate. "Let's make another one. We can just . . . We don't have to look at this sad attempt anymore," she snorts, inching the plate farther and farther to the corner of the counter.

Okay, I actually laugh this time. Twice in two minutes.

She cracks another two eggs into a small bowl and begins to siphon the chopped vegetables into it. I work quickly chopping an onion while she says, "You have to teach me," in awe.

I say, "You'll probably chop your fingers off." That same jolt of anxiety comes over me because I think I might've said the wrong thing.

But then Olu says, "Are you kidding? Look at my acrylics. Built-in protection," while she shows off her nails.

I crack a smile.

So Olu is funny. Who knew?

She fries the omelet without scrambling it, and I move toward the bread, grabbing two slices and popping them in the toaster. I turn to lean against the counter just as Olu successfully flips the omelet. She gasps and grins, turning the pan so I can see. My lips tug at a smile, a warmth that feels familiar but still so foreign. My mind is reminding me at every turn that we don't know this girl, we don't need to get this close because once I turn eighteen . . .

But for a second, I'm kinda happy. It feels easy.

When the toast pops up, I set one piece down on each dinner plate. The plates are red with an orange rim, and suddenly I start thinking that these plates suit someone like Olu very much. I don't even really know her, but I already think that.

As she divides the omelet between both plates, I ask, "What happened to that song, by the way?"

"Huh?"

"The one you let me listen to." The one that reminded me of the beach.

"Oh . . ." She puts the empty pan in the sink and glances away. "Uh . . ."

I hold a hand out, cautiously. "You don't have to tell me if it's none of my business."

"No, it's fine, it's fine." A creak of a smile appears on her face, but it's flanked with nervousness. "I heard back from my manager and he said another singer got it. I heard back the day we were supposed to have the social worker visit, actually . . ." My mind flashes back to the overturned wine bottle and Olu passed out in her room. It kinda makes sense now. "He thinks it's not the right time for me to record anything."

I scoff with a swift roll of my eyes. "That's bullshit."

"Eh." She shrugs. "It's just how it is. It can't be helped."

"What else do they want from you?" I ask. I sound so naive, as if I believe there's actually an answer to that question.

"I don't know," Olu says. She brings the plates to the kitchen table and I follow. We sit in stilted silence. I'm still waiting for an answer, and I know Olu can tell. She glances at me a few times before she says, begrudgingly, "It's their decision. I can't really do anything about it."

I grumble. "I can't believe it."

"Mmm."

"Who did they give it to?"

"Mmm, a singer named Kokobean."

My hand stops halfway to my fork. "Is that their real name?"

Olu snorts. "No. It's her stage name."

"It's stupid."

"It's because her name is Mariko, so . . . like, 'ko,' 'ko' again, and then 'bean' for some reason." Yeah, her explanation isn't helping. "She's so cute and popular these days, so I get why they chose her. Also, her music is very relatable to women. Every one of my friends likes her songs."

"I bet you sing better," I blurt out. My heart pounds in my chest, the vibration filtering all the way to my fingertips, as I pulse with anxiety. *Why* did I say that? It's not even that deep but I still pause, waiting for the backlash.

My mouth restlessly barrels on. "I mean, I don't know what she sounds like and I don't—I don't care. I was just thinking, like, when you let me listen to the demo at the food court, I remembered . . . my home. I remembered what it was like to have a place to go to." My tone dips. Emptiness pushes through.

When I finally look at Olu, tears decorate the corners of her eyes. Her hands rush to cover her face and wipe away the blossoming tears. "I'm sorry, aahh, this is so embarrassing," she whines. "I'm always crying these days."

I hold a hand out. "No, sorry, it's me. I should've just kept my mouth shut."

"Oh! No, it's not that—"

"I just meant that, like, my old home—it just made me think of my old home," I say with a deflated shrug. "I've never really said that to anyone before. Like, not any of my friends know that I'm so . . . sappy." I cringe at how open I'm being. Each word is like a gaping hole in my chest, and the more I speak, the wider it becomes. "A-and I didn't mean to make you cry. Sometimes I can be kinda . . . uncool."

"You're fine," she says. "Don't worry about me."

I give a small nod and dive back into my food, happy to have that as a distraction.

Olu grabs a tissue and begins to dot her eyes. She asks, "Why don't you share how you're feeling with your friends?"

Oh hell. I scoff right away, but the fire behind it fizzles out quickly. I think of the beach and how I never keep any real secrets from my friends, but I still can't seem to tell them about it. I don't know what I think will happen if I do. Something bad, maybe. That must be the reason.

It takes me a moment to settle on the right words, but then they appear: "I don't know."

She raises an eyebrow. "How come you don't know?"

"I don't know."

Now I feel like an asshole. I don't mean to come off like I just don't care about anything, even though sometimes I don't, but this is kinda hard for me. In case no one has noticed, things are hard.

I eat fast but don't leave the table. Olu is a slow eater, but because of that, it almost seems like she eats less than I do.

I wait until she's done before I ask, "What do you think you'll do about the song? Before, you said you wanted to have a show. Can that still happen now?"

She smirks, though it's sad. "Everything is confusing. I

keep thinking, like . . . can I still do the show if I don't have a reason to? Things like that."

"But you *do* have a reason," I say. "It's your music. You can have a show if you want."

"The label owns the music."

"So you should write something else," I tell her simply. She stares back at me like she didn't hear, so I repeat, "Write your own stuff. Drop a new song. Hold an acoustic show. Set that Kokobean girl on fire, I don't know."

She snickers, waving away my suggestions. "What? *Me?* No, no way. I can't write. Have you ever heard of 'let those who teach'—no, wait, that's not it. 'Let those who—'"

"What?"

"If someone is good at something, they should do it. If they're not good, they should tell someone else to do it," she says. "I can pay someone to write me a good song."

"But if everyone thinks you're trash—no offense—then maybe they won't want to write you a song," I explain. "So then why not do it yourself? Forget those people. They can't treat you like you're nothing. Plus! We're in Toronto. Our artists are dope. You could find a producer easy, I bet."

She flashes a sad smile before gathering up both of our plates and heading to the sink. I know that look: defeated, exhausted. It's so familiar to me because that's my resting pulse. Tired of being asked questions, feeling defeated with the system, out of place, discarded. Olu and I, for people like us, it's not always so obvious what the next step should be. It's easy to feel like we're shepherded from one spot to another, gliding between non-options with nothing but the breeze tickling our knees to remind us that we're still here.

Olu sets the plates in the sink. "Eh . . ." She sighs. "I want to do it, but I don't know where to start."

"We can look online?"

"Yeah. I guess I should find a producer first, right?" She taps her chin while she thinks. "And I can think of the kind of song I want to write."

I nod right away. "Good. You can't let that Koko-girl win."

CHAPTER THIRTEEN

OLU GETS TO WORK CONTACTING producers and sound engineers after breakfast. She keeps saying she doesn't know what she's doing, but she lists off all these job titles of people who help put together a song that I've never heard of. Clearly, she's lying. Olu's a pro, after all. She really should give herself more credit. What's the point of downplaying your strengths like that? I don't get it.

I grab my skateboard and head to Auntie Dara's shop. She left me two text messages about times to come in: *Be here by 1* and *no, by 11*. I barely make it on time.

She stands in the doorway, looking smug with her arms crossed. I hop off my board and shuffle my way closer to her as she outstretches an arm, guiding me into the restaurant. "Summer, how are you?" she asks, her voice sickeningly sweet. Ew.

"Fine," I mumble back and beeline straight for the kitchen counter.

Auntie Dara has been acting strange, full stop. Ever since I asked about my parents and showed her the letter, ever since I asked about those numbers—ever since I noticed them change slightly. More boxy, more practiced.

I'm caught between wanting to keep my distance and being drawn closer. I just can't seem to let it go. And besides, for someone in my position, whatever money she's giving me for deliveries is the difference between a half hour bus ride and an hour on my skateboard. I can't complain, even though I really want to. Hate being stuck like this.

She circles, smiling at me while she packs each order in their separate bags, and makes small talk about the humidity today. "It's nothing like Nigeria," she goes on, scrunching her lips in annoyance. "There, the heat is dry, so it's only when the sun is beating you, you will sweat. Here, the air is what's hot."

I nod along like I care.

She hands me payment, crumpled twenties for each order, and then she stares right in my eyes like a murderer.

She asks again, "Summer, how are you?"

I repeat, "Fine."

She asks, "How is Oluchi?" with the depth of someone who is secretly plotting to kill her.

I almost forgot that they met each other when Olu dropped me off. "She's good," I mumble, averting my eyes. Quickly, I reach forward for each packaged order.

Auntie Dara grabs hold of the second order before I can. Her grip is firm; her gaze is still fixed on me. She furrows her brow, her voice dropping to an eerie volume, as she says, "*Why* did you ask me about your parents?"

I stop. My hand, outstretched on the counter toward the bag, begins to feel awkward and numb—as if she could grab it, too, rooting me in place.

She tilts her head toward me, lowering her eyes, and says again, "Have you been seeing them around somewhere?"

I cringe, shaking my head right away. "No."

"On the news? People are saying they've seen them in Scarborough or Markham, driving—"

"I *haven't*."

"Then why did you ask me that?"

It's a weird thing for her to say, definitely. My parents are my parents—shouldn't I ask about them? I deserve to be curious. That's completely normal. But the way Auntie Dara is staring at me makes me feel as though *I'm* the liar here. That gets me heated.

"Did you find out anything else?" I challenge. "About the numbers. And the note, it said, 'send this to the lawyer.' D-do you know if my parents had a lawyer?"

Auntie Dara frowns, shifting away. "How would I know that?" she spits. "And I didn't find out anything yet. What did I tell you? I said I will fix it. So stop that your worrying."

"I'm not *worrying*," I mumble. "I'm just curious."

"Well, stop that."

Wow, okay.

"Take these and go," she orders, gesturing loosely to the packaged orders. She turns away, calling over her shoulder, "If there's anything else, I'll call you to come back."

Without a word, I grab the second bag and rush my way out of the shop.

I hit the sidewalk running, kicking and pushing against the pavement so I can go faster down the road. My heart is doing leaps; my hands are shaking, restless. I feel like

I skated into a wall. Can't go backward, but the way forward isn't clear. Frustrated tears spring forward and I practically claw at my eyes to get them to stop. This isn't the time for crying.

Well, then, when is? The voice in my head sounds so soft, so caring. I purse my lips harder, push against the pavement faster, eager to make it disappear.

I didn't want to find them. My parents. I didn't care. I still shy away from their faces when I see reports on TV. I still cringe when I think about all those stupid videos from that influencer girl Holly. How people looked at me at school once the news got out. How they cut their eyes or bit back snarky chuckles each time I walked by.

No, I don't care about my parents, but I want all of this to be put to rest. I want closure. Then, I can . . . I can move on. I can really be free.

I push my parents out of my mind while I speed to each delivery location. The second one is a bit far, so I have to hop on the bus to get there. I wonder if Auntie Dara will reimburse me for bus travel. If I do a good enough job, who knows, she might give me a raise. The thought is laughable but it'd be cool to save up and really get out of here once I turn eighteen. Or, pay tuition at York. I don't know why I'm thinking about that. I don't really want to . . . I mean, I'm not really interested . . .

Tanya texts me as I'm walking down the steps of the second house and asks if I want to hang out. *Come to Java Joe's. West Mall location*, she texts. That's Tanya's favorite café because she loves the smoothies there. She always gets me a drink when we go, so I don't have room to complain.

I get on the first of many buses. As I slip into an empty seat in the front of the bus, I mentally calculate how much I have left on my transit card. *Dad used to give me money for the bus,* I think. He'd drop twenty dollars on my dresser or he'd take me to the station to top it up with his credit card—that probably had stolen money on it. Other people's money, that they actually worked hard for. I swallow down the bitter memory and hyper-focus on the depressing number my phone's calculator brings up.

"Is that fifty cents or am I reading it wrong?"

Quickly, I hide my phone and look up at the person trying to get a good look at my screen. Of course it's Jet. He chortles good-naturedly as he moves to sit beside me.

I kiss my teeth. "Why am I always running into you on the bus?"

"Because I don't got a car, bro," he says with a snort. "Why'm I always seeing *you* on the bus?"

"Because you're a stalker," I say. "Where're you headed?" My mind goes to the beach right away. I start feeling like I'd rather be there than on this bus right now.

Jet shrugs. "I don't know. Was supposed to meet up with Ren and them, but they're busy. You?"

"My friend Tanya is at a café." After the slightest hesitation, I say, "Do . . . you wanna come with? She's cool. I don't think she'll mind."

Jet points to himself, like *me?* and I nod. His face lights up with a grin. "Yeah! I'm down."

On the way over, Jet tells me about his mom. She'll be out this weekend, he says, and he's caught between wanting to spend time with her and giving her her space. "Like, what if she just wants to sleep all day, you know? I don't wanna smother her," he rambles on, fidgeting through every scenario. Jet talks a lot. It's cool because I don't really have much to add, but also, I want to listen to everything he has to say about this reunion. I wish I could live in it. I don't let my mind wander past that, but I want to.

Jet and I step into the sticky air once we get to the West Mall. Our boards hit the ground before we skate forward, with me taking the lead toward the café. "Have you met Tanya?" I call over my shoulder toward him.

He shakes his head swiftly. "Nah."

"O-oh." Kick, push. "She went to our school, but she was in my year, o-obviously. Uh, she let me stay at her place every now and then. She's going to Mac in the fall. She did my hair." What am I even saying? I doubt Jet cares about any of this.

I glance back and he's nodding, taking it all in. "Mac in Hamilton?"

"Yup."

"Cool, cool."

We're quiet until we get to the café. When we enter, I find Tanya sitting at her usual table by the window, light shimmering down her flat-ironed hair while she sips on a green smoothie. But I stop, then stumble, once I see she's not alone.

Sid is sitting across from her.

And wherever Sid goes, there is a Kirsten.

If not for the fact I came all the way here, and that I invited Jet to come along, I'd seriously consider turning around and disappearing forever. I haven't said anything to Sid since I found out he was going to Waterloo, and if I never talk to Kirsten again, I literally wouldn't care.

"Come on," I whisper at Jet before walking toward the table. He follows behind. With each step, I remind myself to look alive, be normal, don't say anything stupid. By the time I get to the table, I'm faking the biggest smile. "Hey. You guys know Jet, right?" I say before taking an empty seat beside Tanya. She slides a drink toward me, an herbal tea, and gives me a nod.

Sid and Jet greet each other, the same nod they do each time they're at the skate park, before Jet sits at the end of the table. Kirsten stares at Jet, eyes running over his many piercings, and Tanya gives a slow nod, as if she's trying to match Jet with some other heavily pierced and tattooed Black skater she knows.

"So. How've you been, girl?" Tanya asks as she touches a braid wrapped across my shoulder. "I really went in with these. My best work."

I exaggerate a hair flip. "Honestly."

Kirsten flexes her fingers and stretches them out in front of her—almost touching my teacup. "They look nice," she says, nodding to my head. I expect something snarky, but it doesn't come.

"Thanks," I say.

Sid and I glance at each other, and I'm suddenly too

nervous to say anything. He looks away at the same time I take a slow sip of my drink. By the time I set the cup down, he's cracking his knuckles, eyes dancing around the table, until they finally land on me. My lips pull into a small, apologetic smile. He says, "Hey, so . . . I probably should've told you about Waterloo earlier."

Tanya gasps. "Oh! You—you didn't say?" She presses her hand to her mouth, avoiding my gaze. Well, that confirms it: Everyone knows everything before me. At least her muffled voice sounds apologetic. "Sorry, girl, I could've sworn you knew, or I would've said something too . . ."

I shake my head right away, feeling the awkwardness of having everyone's attention on me. "N-no, it's whatever."

"Because if they're at Waterloo, and I'm at McMaster—"

"It's *fine*," I cut in. "Like, it's not a big deal at all. I'm not even thinking about university like that."

Sid raises an eyebrow. "But it's next month."

"Next month," Kirsten echoes with a swoon, while she probably imagines what it'll be like for her and Sid to be far, far away from here. Tanya, too. I've heard the McMaster campus is so pretty, like its own town or village.

Suddenly, Jet leans back in his seat, crossing his arms. "You guys are *all* going to uni?" he asks, staring around. Nods and shrugs follow. I force myself to shrug so I can fit in. "That's crazy. When I graduated last year, maybe one of my friends was serious about it. It's cool that y'all are going places together."

Kirsten's eyebrows raise in intrigue. Her true, horrible, condescending self is reemerging. "Oh, so you're not in school?" Of course.

Jet doesn't seem bothered by the sharpness in her voice. "Nah," he says simply. "I wanted to go for music, but it wasn't feasible at the time."

"Feasible?"

"Like . . . possible," he explains with a quick glance at me. Kirsten bristles at the idea that he thinks her vocabulary is lacking. I have to scrunch my lips to stop myself from smiling. "Lotta stuff was going on, but things are easier now, so who knows."

"I didn't know you were interested in music," I say.

Jet grins. "Oh, yeah. Producing or engineering is mainly what I'm leaning toward, but I'd do live concerts, too, if I could. I love it all."

"I should introduce you to my cousin," I say. "She's, um, she's a singer." She's a wildly successful singer, but it's too embarrassing to go into all that. "She might have some good advice or whatever."

"Dope."

Kirsten clears her throat. She can't let anyone live, my god. "Oh, well, at least *you'll* be around if we're all gone to other schools," she tells Jet, and then has the audacity to look at me. "Right?"

I shut my eyes on impulse, trying to push away all the ways I want to tell Kirsten to shut up. She's still watching me when I open them. "Mmm," I hum, my lips pursed together. I don't know what to say.

Instead, I turn to Sid. "Listen, you going to Waterloo is chill. I *am* happy for you, contrary to what everyone thinks." I save a glare for Kirsten before I continue. "You know what, I'll even help you pack next week or whenever."

He raises an eyebrow, intrigued but cautious. "Yeah?"

"Yeah." I'm trying so hard for this to not feel like a lie. It's hard for me to admit; it's hard for me to silence that gnawing feeling that tells me I'm being left behind again. *This isn't about me*, I try to tell myself, but the feeling doesn't go away.

I say, "It's just that we've just always been at the same school. Middle school, high school . . ."

Tanya gives a feeble shrug, as if the memories of us all being together aren't enough to keep her in place.

Sid leans forward on his elbows. He says, "I didn't know you were serious," and I force myself to look at him. "You seemed like you were running away from something."

"Me?" I repeat nervously, glancing around the table. I mean, it's true, isn't it? That's what I'm doing; that's what I've been doing since my parents left. Hiding, running, deflecting. Of course Sid noticed. If anyone was going to notice, for sure it'd be him. I feel seen in a way I wasn't prepared for, as if I've been caught in headlights on a stage against my own will. I can feel my temperature rising.

For a moment, when we look at each other, that hidden language comes back and I can see in his eyes what he wants to ask me. Stuff about sadness, stuff about emptiness.

I turn away. He's seeing something that isn't there. I'm *fine*. It's normal to feel a type of way about your friend going to a different school. It's normal to feel a type of way about your parents disappearing. This is *my* normal. My sadness isn't different from anyone else's. I am not that special.

Suddenly, Kirsten's voice booms out, "Yeah, I noticed, too, but I didn't wanna say anything," and the trance is broken. She goes on, whispering, "I mean, it's understandable after what happened with Holly's exposé and your parents."

I narrow my eyes at her. "And what's that, exactly?"

"Nothing—let's just drop it," Tanya cuts in, physically using her arms to slice the tension between us.

Kirsten is relentless, though, and I'm reminded time and time again that she's *just* Sid's girlfriend and not actually *my* friend. She says, rapidly, "I mean, they conned all those people out of their money and Holly was just looking out for the general public—there, sorry, I had to."

Sid groans, throwing his head back in frustration, and says, "Babe. Uncool," at the same time Jet cuts in, "Whoa, did you, though?"

I am the only one who knows about Jet's mom, which means I am the only one who understands why he speaks up, why his words sound more clipped than usual. It's so different from his constant grins and mischievous smiles. Now, his eyebrows are pinched together while he looks at Kirsten. I startle when he says, "That's fucked up. You can't just talk about someone's family like that. You don't know what happened."

Kirsten glances away. "Okay, but *everyone* knows what happened. Holly's, like, famous. And it's on the news—"

"Well, fuck the news," he shoots back. The table goes silent. "They say whatever they want. *They're* just reporting, but *you* forget . . . This is someone's life, my guy. You can't be like that."

She shuts up. The sound of coffee being ground fills the air. I can feel myself starting to sweat. I appreciate Jet stepping in for me, but these are my friends and they've been so good to me—he didn't need to do all that. What if they hate him now? What if they hate *me* by extension? I'm scared to look at them, but . . .

Tanya's lips are sucked in and buttoned up. That means she's trying not to laugh. Sid's eyes dance along the table—classic avoidance. When he notices me looking, I see the smallest nod, the tiniest acknowledgment, that we're good. Some of the tightness in my chest subsides.

Suddenly, Jet gets to his feet. "I'm gonna head out if that's cool with you." He dips to grab his board from under the table.

"W-wait. I'll go with you." I get up, too, earning a shocked gasp from Tanya. I don't turn to look at Sid or scan Kirsten's face for what I figure will be obvious intrigue, or disappointment.

Jet scoffs. "You say that like you know where I'm going."

"I do," I tell him. "It's . . . the beach, right?"

He nods sagely. "The beach."

I know that need to run so intimately that I can sense it a mile away. Maybe Jet and I are the same kind of empty.

CHAPTER
FOURTEEN

JET DOESN'T SAY ANYTHING TO me as we leave the café. My brain can't stop worrying about him judging me, thinking I'm the worst for not inviting my friends—and then I start wondering if he realizes I didn't tell them about the beach at all. If he thinks I'm a liar. Or a fraud.

We ride away, skating down the endless sidewalk under a hazy sky, but none of my shitty thoughts comes to fruition. We sit at the foot of the water, letting the push and pull of the waves tickle our toes as we stare into the sand. The only thing Jet asks me is, "Wait, can you swim?"

I turn to him. "No. Can you?"

"Nah." Then, he laughs. "But one day, I'mma learn."

Jet thinks of the future with a glimmer in his eyes. I see it when we stare out into the great lake, twinkling and tugging at the invisible strings on his face until he's grinning at nothing. I wish I could see what he sees. In my future, I will be eighteen and I will be free, but as the days go on, I realize just how little I know of freedom.

Jet is nineteen. He is carefree and does whatever he wants. I'm almost positive he doesn't have a job, but he does have family who love him. Even though he's dealing with this situation with his mom, he still has his grandma. He still has a home, a place to go to.

And Olu is twenty. I guess I could take a hint from her, but in all honesty, she's not how I expected a twenty-year-old to act. She doesn't have any structure, and sometimes I think it doesn't bother her, but I know it does. It has to. She's been cast aside for optics. That has to hurt.

Man, adulthood feels unstable. What exactly do I have to look forward to? What am I running toward? The future is scary, and once I get that in my head, the thought takes over, putting me on edge.

I stay that way until Gardenia's visit on Friday.

One thing's for sure: She is the kind of adult that I absolutely don't want to be. She's rigid and unflinching; she pretends to care about the kids she works with, for the sake of job security and getting her own children into a cushy private school or something, but she doesn't know anything about what it's like to not have a place. She doesn't know anything about me either, and I hate that she's going to come here and continue pretending.

Like I am pretending.

I've never seen Olu wake up as early as she does on Friday morning. Or, maybe it's me who's never woken up this early on a Friday. Something about her seems manic, too. Almost militant. I'm barely out of bed when she pushes open my door without knocking and leans in past the entrance, a morning vitamin C mask on her face. "We have half an hour! Busy day today," she sings, and disappears to the bathroom.

Being a morning person doesn't suit her. She's way too peppy, and she's been that way for the past two days. I mean, sometimes she gets quiet, like she's thinking long and hard about something, but most of the time, she has this smile on her face like she owns the world and no one knows it. Maybe it's about her song, or maybe she got the go-ahead for that show she wanted to have. I figure she'll tell me when everything is finalized, since we're kinda like friends now and all. Actual cousins.

As I get ready, pulling a short pink summer dress over my head, my mind wanders back to Auntie Dara. I hate that it does, considering she probably isn't thinking of me or how I'm waiting to hear back on what she found out about those numbers. She's hiding something, but what am I going to do? Fight her? The sheer thought of it makes me exhausted. Instead, I busy myself with the day's events. I throw on socks, put on body spray, massage my edges, just anything to keep me distracted.

I come out of my room heavily perfumed and fully lotioned, looking like a tall, greasy baby. The TV buzzes in the background, a newscaster riffing about the weather and humidity, but I follow Olu's voice, a soft chuckle, to the kitchen counter. "We're matching," she says, and gestures to the oversize pink shirt she's wearing over black leggings.

"Y-yeah," I say with an awkward smile.

The TV gets louder behind us. ". . . last seen near the Humber Valley Village area . . ."

Olu's eyes grow wide, first with shock, and then panic.

She stumbles past me, saying, "Ah, no, no, no . . ." toward the TV as the sound grows louder and louder.

I turn. Time seems to slow as my eyes connect with the screen.

". . . any information on the whereabouts of Mabel and Jacob Uzoma—"

"No, no," Olu mutters over and over again. She swipes the remote on the coffee table, nearly fumbling it.

My eyes stare into my reflection: my mom and my dad on the screen. Mugshots—no, these are just pictures. Just stark, harsh photos of two people I look so much like.

". . . call the police tip line at—"

"And nope!" Olu manages to shut off the TV before the number comes up.

My head feels like it's spinning. I'm breathing so loudly that the sound begins to muffle in my ears. I feel cloudy, filled with a lot of nothing. Just *stuff*. Olu turns to face me, clutching the remote, her lips in an apologetic pout. Why is she acting all sorry? She's not responsible for any of this.

She takes hesitant steps toward me. "Forget about all that," she says reassuringly, reaching out to squeeze my forearm. Only when she touches me do I realize that I can't move. I'm still stuck in place, staring at the phantom image of two people who are supposed to be my parents.

Olu sets the remote on the kitchen counter just as the buzzer alarm rings. Gardenia must be downstairs already. "Damn," she clicks her tongue against her teeth. "I wanted to tell you something, actually, before she came here. But we can talk after?"

I blink my way back to attention. "Is . . . it important?"

Olu hides a smile, hides her excitement. "Ehhh." It is. "Something interesting happened. With Kokobean."

"For real?"

She holds a finger to her lip, swaying back and forth like the excitement can't be contained in her body, as she dances to the door. Within a few moments, she pulls it open, stepping aside as Gardenia enters.

Gardenia looks the same, obviously, but she appears to be in better spirits than I've ever seen her. Her eyes look brighter; her skin even looks like it's sun-kissed. "Summer, you're looking well," she tells me, reaching out for a handshake. I return it awkwardly.

"Thanks."

"And, Hikari," she says, finally turning to Olu behind her. "You two are matching."

"It's on purpose," Olu tells her with so much seriousness that it sounds like this somehow proves she's a good caretaker. I snort but disguise it in a cough. "Can I get you tea? Or juice?"

"Just water."

"Ah, right, water."

Olu scurries away to fill a glass. The ten seconds she's gone feels like ten hours because Gardenia is just staring at me, smiling pleasantly with her hands clasped around that folder she brings everywhere with her.

We settle in the living room as Olu comes back with the water, placing it on the coffee table in front of Gardenia. She circles back to sit beside me on the sofa.

I exhale.

"So . . ." Gardenia opens her folder and glances down at it. "We didn't get a chance to do a proper visit the last time. Summer told me you weren't feeling well?"

I can feel Olu's eyes on me for a second before she says, "Y-yes. I was, um, I just had a stomach flu."

Gardenia nods. "Understandable. This time of year can be brutal for that. It's so humid and food expires so quickly . . ." She waits for one of us to jump in and agree, but I'm not sure if Olu is following and I don't care. Eventually, she drops it. "Anyway, let's first talk about any questions or concerns. Let me know if you'd like to talk one-on-one or if this setup is okay."

"It's fine, we're cool," I say right away. From my peripheral view, I can see Olu nod.

"Perfect." Gardenia scribbles something in her folder. "Summer, let's start with you. How have you been adjusting? Talk to me about any concerns you may be having. The more we know, the better we can assist you."

"Uh . . ." What to say?

There's no way I'm telling Gardenia about Auntie Dara or that letter I found. First of all, my parents are back on the news. Again. People are claiming they've seen them. *Again*. If I say anything to Gardenia, about the letter or even the fact I found it in my old mailbox, I might get in trouble. And then second of all, it's none of her business.

Oh, and then, the fact that Olu and I were barely even talking to each other feels like a moot point now. First, it's not that deep, and Olu has a lot of her own shit to deal with, but we're better than we were. Second, it's none of her business.

I'm also not going to tell her I'm still on the fence about university. First, I'm allowed to change my mind. She was the one who told me to just "be a kid," anyway. Going to university is expensive, and I'm not about to take Olu's money for something I'm not 100 percent decided on. Second, none of her business.

Okay, and if that's the case, I'm definitely not telling her that I'm still kinda pressed about Sid not telling me he's going to Waterloo. Knowing that Tanya is already headed to McMaster in Hamilton and, like . . . Things will be so different soon. They'll have places they belong, places they can escape to, and I'll be here by myself. I *know* I could just suck it up and get serious about York, but I just can't seem to visualize it. Me, at a dorm? With a—with a place of my *own*?

Me, with my own place.

I sigh, letting my eyes flash to Gardenia's before settling on the wall behind her.

"I'm good," I say with a noncommittal shrug.

Olu smiles. Gardenia begins to scribble.

"And you, Hikari," she goes on, finishing up her notes before she looks up at Olu. "How are you adjusting? Anything you'd like to share that may be an issue for Summer?"

"Oh, Summer isn't an issue," she says right away.

Gardenia gives a press-on smile. "Right. So, let's see here . . ." She flips through her notes slowly, combing through each thing she wrote down before she finds what she's looking for. "Has the tuition debacle been sorted?"

Olu and I look at each other. It's immediately obvious we aren't on the same page, considering I don't even know what page I'm on half the time. Still, I'm nervous letting Gardenia see my hesitation. We don't really have a choice. We haven't actually talked about school.

But Olu sees something in me that I don't. She watches carefully, the same way Sid does sometimes, and pulls it out before I have a moment to hide it. All I see is a shift in her eyes, a knowing. I barely have time to register before she turns back to Gardenia and says, "We're still in the middle of trying to figure out what's best for Summer."

Clasping my hands together, I nod slowly in agreement with Olu, feeling so tense. Protected. But also so vulnerable. What did she see that made her say that?

Gardenia raises an eyebrow, taken aback. "Well, what's best for her would be post-secondary, of course," she says, even looking to me to agree.

"She's been going through a lot," Olu speaks up. I take deep breaths—one, two, three—while she goes on, way calmer than I am. "I think, for a normal teenager, going to university is so stressful, but for someone like Summer, it may be even worse, so—"

"Her being here means she's, I mean, you're meant to provide financial assistance . . . ," Gardenia rambles. She even begins flipping back and forth between all her notes as if to find her point in there.

Olu's eyes narrow. "I didn't know my *only* job was to pay for her school."

Gardenia huffs. "N-no, of course not." She's so clearly annoyed and she's doing a horrible job hiding it. The me in my mind is laughing, but the me sitting on the sofa feels strange in her own body. She can't move, again. "That's, okay, you know what, that's fine," she says eventually, closing her folder. "This makes sense. Summer has been through a lot."

"I just think we should . . ." Olu sighs, chewing on her bottom lip before she settles on saying, "Pay more attention when stressful things happen to people."

Yes, we should. We should pay more attention.

Gardenia nods with some weird fake enthusiasm. "I couldn't agree more." She probably could.

Olu turns to me, reaches out, squeezes my arm. "Right?" she whispers. The tension I was feeling dissipates; my chest pushes out the last of my anxiety with a breath.

I nod, my voice small when I reply, "Right."

Gardenia writes some more. We sit in silence for a while longer before she says, "We're due for another visit in a month."

In a month, when I'm already eighteen.

And I won't be here anymore.

Right?

"Perfect," Olu says.

Gardenia finishes up her notes and, after a quick walk-around, she makes her way to the door.

"Summer." She turns to me. "You have my number if you need it. I'd also like to give you this so you may reach out directly." She hands me a card for someone named Rayna Cole, a registered psychotherapist. Ugh. How many times do I have to say *no* before it means something? What about today made it seem like I needed psychological help? Because I didn't jump at the idea of going to university? People like Gardenia are always trying to find problems where there aren't any.

"Thanks," I mumble and practically usher her out the door myself.

The moment Gardenia is gone, Olu is eerily silent. With the way things were going, I half expected her to turn to me, wide eyes and jittery fingers, whispering, "Oh my god, can you *believe* that lady?" while we poke fun of Gardenia and all she stands for. But she turns to me, gives me a simple look—it's not angry or emotionally charged at all—and saunters into the kitchen.

I follow, unsure what else to do. It's not like I have plans today, but it's not like Olu needs me around, either.

She reaches for the fridge and pulls out a bottle of water. Cracking it open, she chugs about half before setting it down on the breakfast bar. I'm close enough that it almost feels like she wants me to reach for it and drink the remainder. I don't, though.

She looks at me, her hand on her hip, and says, "Do you even want to go?"

I frown. "Go where?"

"To school. To university," she says with a finality in her voice I haven't heard before. It might just be me, but she sounds so adult right now.

I fidget under her stare. "I'onno."

"Exactly!" she says, exasperated. "This entire time, I

thought maybe you weren't interested because you never said anything about it. But I think knowing something like that would've been good before, I don't know, your social worker shows up."

I grimace. "I mean, there was never any time to say anything."

"What? *How?*"

"A-and you've been busy, and I've been busy, and like I said, I. Don't. Know."

"*Busy?*" She pauses a moment to think, as if she's racking her brain for every instance she's ignored me for work or something. That was a lie. I panicked—I know it's not because she's been busy. It's because I didn't wanna talk about school. Simple.

Olu sighs. I watch her carefully as she crosses her arms, shrugging a little. She says, "I don't know anything about you. Actually, we don't know anything about each other . . . do we?"

Well, maybe that's for the best.

It's hard not to see how her eyes deflate, how defeated she looks, at the realization. "I won't pressure you to do anything you don't want to," she says quietly. "It's—I'm not sure what I'm even asking."

I know.

"I wish I knew you better."

I *know*.

"That's all, I think." The corner of her mouth pulls into an apologetic smile. One blink and it's gone.

I'm so bothered by the disappearance of that glimmer

of hope. For a second, Olu thinks we can really be close, really be friends, and a part of me wants that to be true, too. But I'm not used to this, trying to get to know someone new. I've spent the past year skating around inside four walls I built myself. It's why my friends didn't know that I was hanging out with Jet often. It's why I can't even tell them about the beach.

But Olu, she stuck up for me.

She didn't have to—she could've told Gardenia that I would be enrolling and moving away to some dorm room on campus before September, but she didn't. And even as Olu glides past me down the hall, I don't feel as if she's judging me for being unsure or being reckless. She is giving me my space while I skate back and forth across this man-made cube, trying to find an exit. She makes me feel like maybe I can get out.

My feet follow after her while I try to gather my words.

"Are you going to Dara's today?" she asks over her shoulder.

"Nope," I answer right away. "Actually, hey, listen . . ." She slows, turning to face me just before she crosses into her room. "Are you . . . Do you need help with the song stuff? You said there was something you wanted to tell me about Kokobean, a-and I was wondering, you know, if maybe I could also help with the show? I'm not really doing anything today, so . . ." My voice tapers out. My confidence, too.

That seems to be the exact thing she needs to hear to lift her spirits. That spark comes back to her eyes, albeit slowly, shimmering against the dullness of the hallway.

"Oh, right . . ." She taps her chin, then grasps it with her index and middle finger. "Kokobean, huh? Let me get my computer. One second."

She disappears into her room for her laptop and then gestures for me to follow her into the living room. "So, the weirdest thing happened to me yesterday . . ." She drops onto the sofa and I settle in beside her. At first I'm awkward, sitting with my back straight against the seat, but then we almost curl into each other, as if she's telling me a secret. "Kokobean—Mariko—messaged me online."

My brows furrow. "What's she want?"

"To do a livestream at my event!" she says, her excitement compounding the more she says. "I haven't told my manager yet, but I will—today, I promise, ugh. But she messaged me first just to talk. She says the media is being very harsh back home, but she understands what it's like to be judged like this."

"How? Did she . . ." I bite my tongue, the words *did she also end up with a married guy?* on the tip of it.

Olu seems to know what I meant, and she shakes her head quickly. "I don't know. But we're girls in the entertainment industry, so we've experienced similar things. Not the same, but similar."

"Right."

"And I told her about the show I want to do here, you know, with a new song. I want to do just me and a small band setup. Maybe just a guitarist. Very intimate. Oh, I have so much to show you . . ." She talks fast as she types, pulling up websites and quick notes all in Japanese.

"Mariko will do an introduction for me at the beginning of the event. She wants to say hi and do an interview, or something. But it will just be the two of us talking. Like this format." She pulls up a YouTube tab and shows me a clip of two people having a video interview.

I nod along. "Okay, cool."

"And then I was thinking, like . . . Kari, how can you market this without Mr. Fukuda knowing?"

"I thought you said you'd tell him."

"Ah." She waves away my concern, giggling. "Yeah, but still. My manager is very old-fashioned, so maybe he still won't say yes. But I *want* to do this. So then, I noticed this page here kept commenting on some of my old posts . . ." As she explains, she brings up a social profile of a group called KCTO Fans. I'm confused. After a beat of silence, she says, "Kari-chan Toronto Fans."

"Ah."

"Yeah!"

I'm missing the full picture here. "So . . ." I clear my throat. Olu's enthusiasm spurs me on while I try to piece everything together in my head. "You're doing the show, you're working on the new song, and this Mariko girl, who may or may not be your rival, has agreed to show up as a—a guest host? Or something?"

A fire behind Olu's eyes ignites. "*Yes.*"

"A-and where do I come in?"

"*You* will help me with this." Olu types fervently before arriving at the page of a venue called the Axis Club. I stare at it. Olu watches me, and I can practically feel the heat emanating off her while her excitement grows.

I glance at her. "Wait, what do you want me to do?"

"Finalize the spot, pay them—I'll give you money, of course," she adds with a sheepish grin. "My manager used to do this stuff for me, because I'm not very bold. And also, I don't know how comfortable I am with business English. Emailing is one thing, but speaking is another."

I frown. "Olu, business English isn't even real."

"Yeah, well, it would be nice if Summer could help me with this." She nudges the laptop closer to me until I take it from her and set it on my lap. "I will talk to KCTO and I'll work on the song, but you have a very direct way of speaking. This will be good for you, I think," she says.

"Direct?" I cringe. "Yeah, I don't know . . ."

"I've sent, like, one email already. It was too much pressure. You have to pick a date and finalize everything. You can pretend to be my manager," she snickers. "S. Uzoma."

I snort at that. "No one goes by a first initial."

"Famous people can do whatever they want," she retorts. "Oh, and I'll need to figure out the day-of setup. I need to contact more musicians . . ."

More musicians? I immediately think of Jet. He said at the café that he was interested in music, and I mentioned that Olu would be a good person to ask for advice. "I have a friend who's into music," I tell her, not knowing if that's a sufficient enough answer. Olu's eyebrow raises, a tick of intrigue, as I explain, "His name is Jet. He's a skater friend—or, well, more like acquaintance. I see him around sometimes."

"Does he play guitar? I think I'll need a guitarist," she says.

I shrug. "I can ask?"

"Yeah, ask." She turns back to the laptop. "Maybe he can come to the venue with us."

"We'll see," I tell her. Already, I feel I'm seeing too much of Jet.

CHAPTER FIFTEEN

THE AXIS CLUB SITS NEAR Little Italy in Toronto, amid quaint-looking restaurants with patios and a large grocery store that has paid parking. This is the type of place parking can never be free, because it's pretty close to the downtown core. Streetcars rush by back-to-back. It's so different from the suburbs, from the Port Credit area, where you have to do advanced math to line up a bus trip.

Olu calls us a rideshare from her apartment. "Will your friend come with us?"

I have no intention of telling Jet where I'm currently staying, so I shake my head as I climb into the back seat of a stuffy van, shifting so my legs don't stick on the seats in an awkward position. "No, he'll meet us there."

I don't know how long it takes to get to the venue from wherever Jet lives, but he must be good at advanced math because he's the first thing we see when the driver drops us off. He doesn't stick out here, oddly enough. His many piercings and ripped jeans look right at home in this neighborhood.

"He-ey, Summer!" he calls to me as we approach.

Olu grins when she sees him, sticking out her hand for a shake. "I'm Hikari," she says. "Summer's cousin. She told me a lot about you." What? No, I haven't. "You play the guitar?"

I sigh, "I said he *might*—"

Jet chuckles, waving away my words. "What do you mean 'might'? I've been practicing, you know."

Olu's grin deepens. "Per-fect," she says with the hardest *T* I've ever heard. "Let's go inside and we can talk more about the setup. And then, I guess I should tell you what I'm thinking for the set list . . ."

The inside is dark and sad looking, just like you'd expect of a club space during the day. A man with a face tattoo greets us at the door. He says his name is Chris. I see something go off in Jet's eyes as he watches him, and I bet he's thinking about getting a face tattoo now.

After Olu shakes his hand, she gestures to us. "This is my guitarist . . . Jet!" She says it like she just remembers his name. "And this is my, um, assistant . . . My manager . . .'s assistant, Summer."

I bite my bottom lip so I don't laugh because we so obviously didn't prepare this well. Chris doesn't seem fazed, though. He reaches for my hand and I give it, wincing through the most intense handshake of my life. "Good to meet ya both. You look a bit young, but it's all good."

"I, um. C-can we see the space?" I ask, nodding over his head to the main hall.

"Of course. Come on."

Chris points out a bar to the left—"We check ID at the door and at the bar"—and a VIP area elevated to the right— "If you wanna do an upgraded experience, signings, all of that, then those people there can be shuttled through a second hallway to the green room." He says all this before we get to the stage. He puts his hands on his hips as he nods toward the platform and backdrop. "And here we are. Lights, sound. Usually, we get lighting to operate from back there, but let me know what y'all prefer. I can also get my own sound guys to hook up anything, but that'll be extra, just so you know."

Olu looks at me with stern eyes and I suppose that means that as her manager's assistant, I should say something. I try to gauge what she wants me to say based on the look she's giving me. "We, uh, we can . . . pay that," I say eventually. It isn't like Olu knows any music technicians out here, so I'm guessing we'll need all the help we can get. Not to mention, money isn't an issue for her, so she probably wouldn't mind paying a bit extra. "What's the capacity for this place?"

Chris squints as he thinks. "Eh . . . Maybe five hundred, six hundred people, if you don't want a code violation."

"And do you offer ticketing or do we provide our own people?"

Olu nods fervently at me before both she and Jet turn to Chris.

"We can provide almost everything. Full service," he says with an easy smile.

Olu whispers. "The livestream."

"Oh, right." I clear my throat. "We might have a livestream interview thing before the show. Do we rent our own projector for that or, like . . . ?"

Chris nods behind him. "All good questions. Why don't we talk over here and nail down what you're looking for?"

Instead of leading us to an office, he guides us to an unused bar space where another employee is fiddling with old mixers and headphones that are tangled up on the countertop. Chris pulls out a notepad, starts talking nonstop, "So, Hikari, we got your initial email with some details, but Summer, I just want to go over and reconfirm where we are with scheduling, like I know that you, Hikari, had mentioned, uh, something about an open date sooner rather than later, but that's gonna be a bit hard, as you know, since dates are booked well in advance, but—and there's always a but—we might have a cancellation coming up—*very* short notice, but the singer is *very* sick, and has to rest and then bump up their surgery date—an-ny-way, it's a whole thing, but my point is this: We have a few dates we can run by you for the very end of this month *or* the end of next month, where another event might be canceled for low ticket sales—they haven't decided yet, it's all very up in the air." Deep breath. "Take your pick. We'll see what we can do."

He swings around his notepad on the bar top so I can see the dates he's jotted down. August 23 with doors open at 8:00 P.M., August 24 with doors open at 6:00 P.M., September 21 with doors open at 5:00 P.M. I mean, these are all arbitrary to me. I show the notepad to Olu and she frowns, staring down at them. "It . . . It just can't be next month," she says quietly.

I raise an eyebrow. "Uh, okay. Preference for the others?"

She tilts her head to the side, staring between the dates. "Hmm . . ."

The man, or boy, fiddling with the headphones finally manages to break one away. The more I look at him, the younger he appears. Maybe he's a kid like me. Maybe he's a few years older than Olu.

He pulls another cord free. Then, he pumps his fist in victory while flashing an embarrassed smile. "Need to invest in cord ties, eh?" he chortles.

I give a press-on smile, my best neutral response.

His eyes linger a bit longer before he returns to another set of headphones. It's weird. Even when he looks down, he glances at me, each time taking in more and more of my appearance.

Jet notices, too, because he flashes a shy smirk, a small hint of amusement. How exactly is this amusing to him? I am too nervous, too perceived, to be amused. Usually when people do a double take, it's never a good thing for me. My mind remembers the stares from school, from the skate park, from my old neighborhood . . .

Finally, the boy looks up, stares at me again, and lets out a confused sigh. "I . . ." He snaps his fingers a few times, letting his words come back to him. "Sorry, I thought you looked like someone."

My heart thuds.

"Some . . . one?" I utter.

"Yeah. I swore I saw your face somewhere, like the news or whatever," he answers coolly. But his words feel so targeted, like a heat-seeking missile that has finally found its mark.

The word "News . . ." tumbles out of my mouth. I hear it echo in my ears.

The boy shrugs, then his eyes drop to my cheekbones, suddenly so pointed and harsh. My lips, suddenly too big, too obvious. My eyebrows, suddenly so bushy, so loud. The gauntness in my face, like my mother's. The intensity of my eyes, like my father's. He's scanning a face he must realize he's seen so often before on the news, on social media, in the papers.

I can't . . .

"I have to, um . . ." My throat grows drier by the second and I look around, desperately searching for the exit. Inhale, exhale. Inhale. Inhale. Exhale. I catch a glimpse of Olu and her furrowed brows, pouty lips, her confusion—and Jet and his narrowed eyes, tilted head, his concern, and—I don't need it. I don't need this.

Fucking *run*, Summer.

As fast as you can.

As far as you can.

I stumble and then take off, retracing my steps through the venue. The floor feels stickier than it did when I first got here. My feet drag heavily across the hall; my legs shake, then slow, as I approach the door. I hear Olu's voice behind me: "Summer, what happened?" Jet's voice, too: "Wait, where are you going?" But I'm too scared to turn around. I've gotten so far ahead already.

The sun hits my face, making me squint the moment

I get outside, and it's then I realize that my breathing is stilted. My god, I am *shaking*. I feel around my pockets, tapping my chest, my hips, what am I looking for, my keys? Where am I going? Where's my skateboard? A whine escapes my lips and I press my hands to my mouth frantically. Just breathe, Summer.

A hand grabs me by the arm and I scream. Passersby on the street pause, cast a wary glance over their shoulders, but they don't bother stopping.

Jet loosens his grip. "Hey, sorry, I was—*we* were . . ." He gestures to Olu, who stands beside him, flustered and frantic. We lock eyes for a moment. I don't know what to tell her, what side of myself to show. She's never seen me like this before. *No one* has. I can usually keep it together, but I just . . . This time, I don't know why I can't.

When I turn back to Jet, he asks quietly, "What happened? You just took off."

"Is it . . ." Olu shakes her head, rife with worry. She watches me, the uneasy way I shift my weight from leg to leg. The way I avoid her stare. I know she sees it, the secret thoughts and words I can't say. She can see it the same way my friends can, but she's not like them—she's going to call it out. I can feel it as the small hairs on my arms lift. As my temperature rises. Just like when Gardenia was over and Olu looked at me and she just *knew*. How can she? We don't know each other like that. And then I remember: We are a little bit alike, the two of us. All this running.

She opens her mouth, "You—"

I cut in. "I wanna go somewhere else."

She furrows her brow. Have I thrown her off? No, the way she purses her lips and homes in on my words . . . She sees me.

She says, her tone flat, "You want to be alone."

My gut twists. The answer is usually yes, of course, but for some reason, that doesn't feel right this time. "Hmmm . . ." I tilt my head, think. I inhale, think. "I don't know . . ."

Jet gasps and nods, "Aaahh! I know where we can go."

We?

"The beach."

But I wanted to be by myself. Right?

Olu frowns. "The beach?"

Jet is still nodding. "It's this dope spot off Lakeshore. Kinda secluded, but not too secluded that it's weird."

"Oh! I live off Lakeshore," Olu says, and then looks at me, her gaze softening. "Do you go there often?"

"Sometimes," I mumble, my voice a hoarse whisper. "When I'm not feeling too good or when I just wanna . . ." Be alone. "Breathe."

A hint of a smile comes to Olu's lips and she reaches out, both her hands clasped onto my forearms. She looks me right in the eye. "We can go together," she says calmly. "Do you want to?"

How does she do that? Make me feel like I can just stop and stay still. My uneasiness, the twisting in my gut, begins to subside. I nod right away. "Yeah."

It's a weird thing to have people know you. To be seen like this.

Olu calls a rideshare to take us to the beach. We don't talk in the back of the car as the air from outside whooshes past our faces. The driver has all the windows rolled down. "Summer in the city, eh?" he chuckles, glancing at us in the rearview mirror. "Always stuffy, always smoggy."

Jet shrugs. "I mean, sometimes it's all right."

The driver *tsk*s like Jet isn't old enough to really get what he's saying and roots his eyes on the road. He gets on the highway and speeds as best he can through stop-and-go traffic. Olu leans toward her side of the window, staring at every car that pulls up beside us. I want to ask what's so interesting about the inside of someone else's car, but I catch myself doing it, too. It's less awkward because when people catch us staring, they usually look away first. She flashes me a small smile as our current target speeds up a little. Then, she squeezes my forearm again. Softly, securely.

The car drops us off at the same crosswalk the bus usually would. I'm used to dropping my board and hitting the pavement as I skate down the path toward the beachfront, but this time, we climb out of the car and take the walk together.

Jet is hyping up the beach so much: "It's not like some of those other trash ass beaches around the city. I've never even *seen* a bottle cap in the sand here!" Olu laughs along, probably imagining clear skies and white sand. But he leaves out so much. He doesn't talk about how the waves dance to the shoreline, or how you can whisper a word and hear it carried down the lake, or how the sand is never too hot or too cool, or how you can be there and always feel like you're everywhere at the same time. He doesn't talk about any of the important stuff.

We break through the last stretch of the path and there it is.

Olu gasps in an animated way that leads me to believe whatever Jet was describing was nothing like what she's seeing. "*What?* Wait, wait, this place is so close to my house and I didn't know? Oh, no, no, no . . ." She takes a few steps forward before her feet hit the sand. I swallow a laugh while I watch her take it all in. Jet snickers and we glance at each other. He looks proud of himself.

Olu spins around. "This is *beautiful*. Can you swim?" She points to me. I shake my head, and she turns to Jet. "What about you?" He shakes his head, too. Defeated, she turns back to the water. "I wanna go in but I don't wanna go alone."

"Oh," Jet snorts. "I said I *couldn't* swim. I didn't say I *wouldn't* go in the water."

Uh. "Wait, that's dangerous," I cut in as Jet bends to take off his shoes. "I can't save you if you drown."

Olu shoots up a hand. "I'll do it."

"You can't carry him. He's taller than you!"

"I'm not gonna drown, relax," Jet chortles, as if drowning isn't a real thing that could happen. He tosses his shoes a few feet away and eyes the water like it's a prize. Olu, too. They're sizing it up.

"Okay, but still," I protest, holding a hand out—

The two of them run at full speed toward the water and

dive in. I scream because I don't know what else to do. Jet might drown, like straight up *drown*. His mom just got out of jail and they're rebuilding their life. What will she do without him? And Olu doesn't have another change of clothes, which isn't the worst thing, but what if Gardenia shows up at the apartment and thinks Olu is unfit to look after me? What if they separate us? What if—I mean, what if . . .

But then, the two of them emerge from the water. They're laughing.

I realize they're not in far enough for Jet to drown.

And I should know by now that Olu can be so carefree it hurts.

They stand chuckling and shivering, waist- and chest-deep in the water. I kick off my shoes and approach the shoreline slowly, feeling the sand dampen under my feet as I go.

Jet wipes water from his face just as Olu splashes him. "Hey!" he cries out, laughing boisterously. She cackles. I've never seen either of them like this before. I inch closer and closer to the shore. I let the water tickle my toes.

Olu beckons me forward. "Come in!" she says with a wide smile.

I close my eyes, take a deep breath, and take a running jump into the cold lake water. Before I'm fully submerged, I hear Olu laugh and Jet shriek. And then, there is nothing. For a split second, all I can hear is the muffled sound of water swishing all around me. It's peaceful being down here.

When I push my way back up, the hazy air clings to my

skin like it never left. Jet splashes water in my direction and I put up my hands to shield it. "Acting like you weren't gonna come in," he teases, to which I splash him back.

Olu is grinning as she wipes water from her eyes.

I look at her. My cousin. She's almost my age, or I'm almost her age, and I guess I thought that meant something. But Olu has something I don't. I'm not sure what it is. If I stare at her long enough, I think I can describe it. It's like . . .

When the wind hits your face on the hottest day of the year.

When you never have to squint outside, no matter how bright it is.

When each break in the sidewalk taps out a beat as you skate by on your board.

It's knowing that you are not wrong, even when everyone says you are. It is deservingness, the feeling that you belong.

I don't have that.

But at least in this moment, I'm here and my hair is wet and there's lake water in my mouth and it's salty so I may die—but I'm laughing. *So* hard. Harder than I have in years.

Maybe this is belonging.

CHAPTER SIXTEEN

THE SUN REFUSES TO SET, which is perfect because its warmth dries us off as we sit on the beach. I don't know how long we've been sitting here, but I don't want to leave. The hot air whips moisture out of my hair way faster than a towel would. Plus, I love it out here. I glance to my right where both Olu and Jet are lounging beside me, and for a split second, I don't think about anything else. My mind is empty, calm.

Olu tries her hardest to dust sand from her bare legs, but it doesn't seem to be working. Eventually, she gives up and reaches for her phone. "Should we order food?" she asks.

Jet shakes his head, *I'unno*, while he uses the neck of his damp shirt to dry off his damp hair. "I should head back home, though. My, uh . . ." He goes silent for long enough that even Olu stops her scrolling. We watch as he wipes his hair, wipes his forehead, squeezes his shirt dry again. When he clues into our silence, he laughs, shifting away from the intensity of our stares. "Whoa, sorry, I meant to say, like, my mom is home, so . . . yeah."

My throat goes dry. "Your mom's back?"

He nods, glancing away, but says nothing else.

After a moment, Olu looks at the both of us, her voice hesitant when she asks, "That's cool. Right?" She doesn't know about his mom. It's not my business to explain Jet's situation, but a part of me is hoping he trusts Olu enough to do it himself because I really, *really* want to hear more about it.

Jet wipes his forehead again when a drop of water breaks free from his hair.

Olu chews her bottom lip.

I take a deep breath and exhale into the hazy summer air.

And I ask, "What's it like?"

Jet shifts so he can see me better from beside Olu. "What's what?"

"Your . . ." I clear my throat and face him. My mouth almost doesn't want to form the words. "Your . . . mom being out of jail." Olu's eyes go wide at the admission and she shifts to face Jet, too.

He doesn't look too bothered at me bringing it up. In typical Jet fashion, he kinda gives an awkward chuckle and leans back onto his hands. "Yeah, what's that like?" He sighs, a great big exhale, and squints up at the sky, as if there's an answer there for him. "It's weird. She's back and, like, asking me questions about stuff my grandma already knows. 'Whose is this?' or 'What happened to that thing you were doing last time I saw you?' So sometimes, I'm sitting there frustrated, thinking, like, 'I already said this. We already *been* over this.' And I can feel myself getting mad because if she was just *here*, she'd know, you know?"

I nod fervently. I want him to see that I get it.

"And sometimes," he goes on, "I can see her slipping away. She's trying, though, to stay present and make it up to everyone, but then she gets distant and I don't know what to do. I get mad at myself for getting mad. I missed her too, and when I'm angry, I forget."

"That sounds hard," Olu says softly through a sympathetic smile.

Jet nods, shying away from our gaze. "Yeah, it's a struggle, I can't lie."

"Is it . . ." I clear my throat again and again. "Do you forgive her?"

My question is like a fire that barely has the space to burn. The moment I ask it, I feel it gets shut out by the wind, by the heat and the haze around us. It's swallowed. It's awkward. Jet looks away as if he's thinking. Olu freezes in place; she barely looks like she's breathing.

But I really want to know what Jet is feeling. I want to know if I'm meant to feel the same things if—*when* I have to face something similar. His reality looks so much like what mine could be like. Maybe one day I'll have to deal with my parents being taken away and never coming back. Or, maybe they will come back, and then I'll have to fill them in about what they missed during the year they were gone. I'd be angry, like Jet. I'd try to laugh it off, like Jet. I wouldn't tell anyone.

"Uh . . ." Jet scratches his head. "Forgiveness is hard."

I nod as I shift closer on the sand. "Yeah, honestly."

"They always say it's for you," he tells me. "Like, 'forgive them so you can move on,' but they make it sound so easy. It's hard to really move on. Even if you forgive. It's like being alive is the reminder."

I shiver. Being alive is the reminder. Every day is the reminder.

Olu sighs, "Wow," and curls into herself, sitting cross-legged and leaning her elbows on her knees. Her eyes trail the wisps of sand at our feet. The more she stares, the more she frowns. I wonder what she's thinking about. If she has someone she has to forgive, if she has something she has to do before she can. When I nudge her, tapping her leg closest to me, she glances over. I wait for her typical smile, but it doesn't come. All I see is sadness reflected back at me.

We leave the beach and I leave my thoughts there. Putting everything out of my mind is for the best. I'm so busy now that I can't keep everything together in my head.

I still have to help Olu with her show. She prefers the end of this month, and even though she won't say why, I kinda prefer it, too. It's a nice distraction for me while my friends start getting ready for the long drives to their dorms and residences in different cities.

Then, I still have to help Auntie Dara with deliveries—like, I'm two seconds away from asking for a raise. And I need to get her to talk about that letter and those numbers, too. I'm tired of this. Either she's gonna tell me the truth or she won't, but I want it to be done so *I* can move on. So I can try and forgive.

And, oh, I promised Sid I would help him pack. I was so

bold, telling him, Tanya, and Kirsten that I'm completely chill and there's nothing I'd rather do than help one of my best friends shove his life into a suitcase so he can go to school two hours away from me.

By Monday, I'm regretting that decision.

I'm at Sid's place bright and early. We're in his room, sorting through mounds of games and comics so he can decide which to take with him to Waterloo. I bite my tongue and show the most enthusiasm I can. I want him to believe I'll be okay after he goes, and that means sorting through his old *Assassin's Creed* game collection with a smile.

I look down at the cases. "Are you taking these?"

"No. You can keep them." Sid shrugs, and then crouches down to pull whatever else out from under his bed. "I already have the digital remastered versions. Also, I figure my roommate would bring stuff, and I don't want double copies getting mixed up."

Today's the first time I heard Sid mention his roommate. One day, he's completely quiet about the Waterloo thing, and suddenly the next, he has a roommate. If he's talking about Kirsten, he can just say it's her. Although she doesn't even game, so it probably isn't.

"You sure about this?" I ask, eyeing the games. "It's not like I have anywhere to keep them. Plus, you might need a distraction from biomed. Or Waterloo, in general. I hear they don't season their food out there."

I hear how bitter I sound and cringe. Sid notices, obviously, and pops up from under his bed. "I told you I'd come back and visit," he says. "Waterloo isn't even that far."

"Yeah, it's cool," I tell him, waving away his concern. I practically hide my face behind the game case so he doesn't see the guilt in my eyes. "I'm happy for you. I said that already, right?"

"Can't remember."

"Well, I am."

"I'm happy for you too."

I frown. "Meaning?"

"Jet seems cool," he says simply, shrugs, and disappears to grab more stuff under his bed.

Okay, hold up.

"What does that mean . . . 'Jet seems cool'?" I ask.

"He's got, like, piercings," Sid calls out. "And he's a pretty dope skater. Also, he's a good guy. I don't know."

My skin crawls with unease at the assumption. "Jet's my *friend*," I say, pressing into the word.

Sid pops up again, a bemused look on his face, and chuckles, "Yes, and? He's a pretty dope skater. He's cool, he's got a million piercings. Relax."

"*You* relax."

"And you guys apparently have secret hangout spots and stuff, so that's, uh, that's whatever."

That was a dig. It felt like a dig, sounded like a dig. He's talking about the beach. I've been wanting to show Sid and Tanya, but the timing hasn't been right . . .

I let my eyes drop to the pile of games on my lap. I can't think of anything else to say except for, "We don't have secret hangout spots," which is clearly a lie at this point. Even Olu knows about the beach. Why can't I just tell Sid?

"Like I said, it's whatever," Sid says with another shrug and disappears under his bed again.

It's obviously not just whatever.

I set down the games. There's no way I can take them with me. I'm not trying to fill up Olu's apartment with a bunch of extra stuff. She has enough shit as is.

I get up and find my way to his window. The street looks so welcoming—empty and peaceful, waiting for the rumble of my board's wheels against the road. Sid comes up beside me, gazing out through the window to see what I must be looking at.

I say, "Let's go for a ride around the block."

He chews on his lip. "Packing, though."

"I'll help you after," I tell him. "Come on, please? Literally just up the block that way and then back around this way." As I talk, I point in each direction, tracing my hands around an invisible track. "We'll skip the park this time. Besides, you have a shit-ton of things—no way we'd be done today, anyway."

He looks over his room, a tornado of clothes and old notebooks and games thrown everywhere, and in a second, I know he agrees with me. "Just once around the block?"

"Just once."

We head downstairs and throw on our shoes before stepping onto the porch. By the time we make it to the sidewalk, the sun is creeping farther and farther into the sky and its warmth on my skin is making me forget about everything that's bothering me. My parents, Auntie Dara, Olu's show, how sad Olu looked at the beach right before we left . . . She must be thinking about her situation back home. Maybe she's starting to feel the weight of being displaced. I could talk to her about it, or something. I could be a listening ear for her, find that secret language in her eyes and draw out her thoughts, just like she does for me.

"Freedom!" Sid exclaims, then drops his board and pushes off from the sidewalk. I do the same.

"Your mom really expects you to be fully packed by the end of this week?" I ask, trailing behind him.

He glances back at me and groans. "Yeah. It's ridiculous. Plus, she went to Waterloo back in the day and she's being way too intense with the moving situation."

"Why the rush? Does she wanna turn your room into a studio or something?" I snicker.

"What?" he laughs. "Then where would I stay when I come home?"

"Nowhere," I say with a smug smile. "You'll be a nomad. Like me."

He slows, trying to match my pace. We hang a right around the corner toward the street opposite his. Once we loop through here, we'll circle back to his house, but I'm wondering if he'd be down to head to the next street. And the next. We don't need to pack everything today, anyway. There's still time.

Sid says, "You have a place to live now, though."

"Huh?"

"You're not a nomad. You're not cool enough to be

one," he teases. "You're staying with your cousin. What, is she gonna kick you out or something?"

"She has her own life," I say, my eyes set on the path in front of me. I don't bother looking over at him, even though I can feel his eyes on me. Olu is a celebrity; *I* am the pleb doing volunteer hours on her show. She will always have a safe place to land. I might think Olu and I are a bit alike, but not *that* much. There are some differences that can't be wiped out by one omelet and a day at the beach.

But! I'll be eighteen soon. It might be the bare minimum, but at least I'll have that going for me.

"After my birthday, I'll figure out where I want to live," I tell Sid to lighten the mood. "Port Credit is nice, but way too expensive for me. I like the area around Sherway Gardens. Could even do North York."

He shrugs, breezing past me with that casual, lazy confidence he always has. "You don't have any money, bro."

Okay, that hurts. Like I *know* that, but damn. "I—I mean, obviously."

"And it feels like you're avoiding the York thing on purpose, so."

"Again with school?" I groan, indignation bolstering words. He stops mid-push, slowing until he's able to put his foot down. I do the same, though I'm anxious because I'm sure I don't want to hear what he has to say. I blurt out, "Listen, I'm fine. I don't know why you're so fucking worried," before he can bring it up again.

He raises an eyebrow, tilts his head, examines me. "Are you? Because the average person wouldn't be."

"Well, I *am*, so drop it—"

"Your parents disappeared right before your senior year," he says, counting off on his fingers. "You technically got evicted. You were technically homeless. Now, you're less than a month away from supposedly starting university, and you don't seem to care about orientation, or registration, or tuition payment plans, or any of that shit. And you're gonna lie to me and tell me you're 'okay'?"

I inhale sharply. "I *am* okay. I'll be fine. Once I'm eighteen—"

"Holy shit," he groans, rubbing a hand down his face. "Being eighteen doesn't mean anything. It's not gonna solve all your problems. *I'm* fucking eighteen." Quickly, he sweeps a hand from his head to his toes, a grand gesture that makes me feel small.

"S-so?" I mumble, glancing away. "We're not the same."

"I'm not saying we are," he tells me with a sigh. "But I don't want you to wake up on your birthday and realize nothing has changed. I just don't want you to run anymore."

I twitch at the sound of his words, the truth behind them. "Running? Y-you think I'm running?" So what if I am? How *dare* he see that?

A burst of anger surges through me, a kind that I've never dared to feel in front of any of my friends. Fists clenched, voice shaky, I tell him, "Why's the issue me running, but not other people running *from* me? Don't I deserve to run? I don't belong anywhere. You can say whatever you want about the future, but at least you know what it'll look like. I don't."

Shame grips me at once. Was that too much? My body is heavy, almost immovable. I can't look at him. No matter what he thinks, he has no idea what things have been like for me. I'm not even sure I do. I'm so used to ignoring and pushing things away, that being confronted by my own anger, by my own situation, is like being slapped in the face again and again and again. And I'm so tired.

He tells me, "Why're you saying that like you don't have people who can help you?"

"I don't need help," I bite back. It's a lie. I want help, desperately. But my mouth just can't form the words. Why would I, when everyone who's ever promised to help me, to be there for me, just hasn't? Family, friends, everyone.

Everyone leaves eventually.

Everyone.

"I'll meet you back at the house," I grumble as I get onto my board and push off. The air whizzes past my ears, blocking me from anything he might be saying. I kick farther, push faster, just to pick up speed and get away. Ironically enough, to run.

I don't go back to Sid's place. Instead, I ride past his street on my way to the bus stop while I text Auntie Dara. *I have some free time to help with deliveries*, I type out. I'm already at her shop by the time she tells me to come over.

CHAPTER SEVENTEEN

KICK, PUSH, FARTHER.

The wind whips against my face as I race down the street on my board, packed food tumbling awkwardly in my backpack. Luckily they're mostly snacks, like meat pie or chin-chin, so if it gets jostled, that's fine. My head is empty: no thoughts, no time to think, just my destination.

Each time I get to a house with a package in hand, the person who answers the door—always Nigerian, always old—pauses to ask, "Did you drive?" while they crane their neck around me for a waiting vehicle.

"Nope," I say. Their eyes fall to the way my hand tiredly clutches my skateboard, clinging to it like the wrong breeze will push it to the ground. By then, they've probably figured out that an unholy combination of skateboarding and running for the bus got me here, and they slip me an extra five dollars if they have it.

After I leave my second house, I stop at the bus station's convenience store to top up my phone and transit card. Fifty dollars gone, just like that. It's hard to hold on to money like it's hard to hold on to anything else, I guess. *At least you had the fifty dollars to pay, Summer,* I tell myself, swallowing down my discomfort as I leave the store. Imagine being stranded without transit money. Well, I guess I don't really have to imagine, since it's happened before.

Ugh, Summer, no thinking. Just—kick, push, farther.

Skating is my refuge. Soon, the sound from the rumbling of the wheels beneath me, the wind whizzing past my ears, the cars honking around me, the chatter—it all drowns out my thoughts.

Auntie Dara says she'll text me if there's anything else to deliver, but after my last drop-off, I contact her first. Can't really rely on her for a useful response these days, especially when she's so sketchy. Still, her reply comes quickly: *Go home for today.*

I groan until my throat starts to hurt.

The next morning, with Olu off at the venue to sign some paperwork, I nudge Auntie again: *Do you need anything?* I ask. The desperation bleeds through each word. If she saw the pleading look on my face while I sent the text, the whine that threatens to break free of my throat, she'd pity me. Maybe, if she was even capable of it.

I almost send, "Also, any updates with the numbers?" but her response to my first query lands on my screen before I can. *Come later. Afternoon,* she tells me.

"Afternoon?" I look at the time. That's at least four hours until she needs me—which means four hours for my thoughts to take over.

The apartment is noticeably empty without Olu. I didn't realize how much of the space was just her weird personality, her singing, or her stack of empty wine bottles. It's been a while since I've seen them, so I'm shocked to find one hidden at the back of the counter, closest to the sink. When did she even have time to drink this? It feels like we've spent so much time together this past week that if she was really wasted, I would've noticed. I mean, when we were at the beach, she seemed normal for a while, and then she got kinda weird. Somber. I bet it's about the show. I bet she's nervous being in front of people after what happened to her back home. I should . . . I should've said something. Like, *sorry you're going through that* or whatever.

I stuff my phone in my pocket, grab my skateboard, and lock up before heading down to the venue. There's a text on my phone from Olu asking me to meet her there when I can. I wish I'd just gone with her when she woke up, partially because then I could've had the luxury of sitting in an air-conditioned car all the way down, but also partially because I'm the one who volunteered to help her in the first place. "Well, if you were supposed to be helping, then maybe *you* should've offered to go before she asked," I grumble to myself. It's just that I was so distracted with Sid and the packing and my parents on the news and, and, and.

It's always about me. I can't make Olu's show about me, too.

I get to the venue, sweating. Toronto smog is no joke. One tug on the front door tells me it's locked. Makes sense, since it's way too early for a music club to be open for patrons. I slip around the accessible ramp and hang a left at the building to get to the back door. I've never seen it, but I assume it exists. All venues like this would need to have one for performers and musicians to get in without being watched.

The door is propped open. "Yes!" I breathe a sigh of relief as I tiptoe closer to it. There's no one in the immediate vicinity, though I can hear voices farther down the hall when I poke my head through. Carefully, I slip in, mentally rehearsing answers in case someone asks me what I'm doing here.

I get my first opportunity to show off an answer when someone pops their head out of an office to stare at me. He is white, bald, and has strong, judgmental eyes. "Front door" is all he says, in a voice that tells me he's had to shoo people off before.

"I'm, um, my cousin—I'm here to see my cousin," I blurt out, feeling my body grow warm with anxiety. The man cocks his head at me, and then takes one last look from my head to my toes to my skateboard. I know what I look like; I know what he's thinking.

"Kid, we don't do handouts here," he grunts, taking a few steps forward. I step back. "You're gonna have to—"

"I *swear*, my cousin is here," I tell him. "Olu? Oluchi? Hikari? I'm supposed to help her with planning her show."

He shakes his head. "I don't know who that is."

"She's, like, she's this tall." I hold up a hand a bit shorter than me. "She has curly hair. She's a singer. She should be here to talk about setting up for her show, probably on the twenty-third. Or was it the twenty-fourth . . ."

He sighs, crossing his arms. I can tell he's two seconds away from literally kicking me out. When he steps forward again, I brace for the worst. But then he grumbles, "Come on" and gestures for me to follow him farther down the long corridor. I skip to keep up.

We pass three more offices, most of them empty, some with equipment and some badly lit, before we land at what looks like the backstage area filled with unused props. He stops at the threshold and points forward, over the stage and toward the venue floor. "Take a lap around and look for her. I'll be here, watching."

Creepy, but sure. "Yeah, thanks."

The lights above the stage are on for some reason. I step onto the platform, squinting through the space, and turn in time to see a giant projector hanging to my left. It faces the crowd and is big enough to be seen from the back. It's practically the same width as the stage.

"Oh, the livestream," I gasp, gazing at it. If this is up, Olu is definitely around here somewhere, probably trying to make sure it'll work on the day of. "O-Olu? Olu, are you here?" I call softly as I walk farther down the stage. No response. "Olu?"

I might as well be the only person here. This is so weird.

When I turn back around, the bald man has fully stepped onto the stage. His arms are crossed and he's still staring at me, rigid like a statue. I hold up my phone. "Lemme just call her."

"Should've done that first."

I turn so he doesn't see me roll my eyes. The phone rings once, twice, three times, four times. She doesn't answer.

"I gotta get back to work, kid," the bald man calls as I look his way. "Your cousin isn't here. You gotta leave."

"Do you know Chris?"

"*Chris?*" he repeats like he didn't hear me the first time. After a moment, he nods. "Well, yeah."

"Is he—"

"He's not here today. Come on, let's go." He beckons me forward.

"I—" There are voices in the distance somewhere. I stop, hold my breath, and strain to listen. One is definitely a lighter voice, a female voice. "I think I hear her."

"How convenient for you."

This guy really doesn't need to be like this, and yet, here he is.

"Can I check the front?" I ask, pointing to the doors that lead to the lobby. "It's really important that I find her. I *promise* I'll just look quick and come back."

He lets out another sigh. "Just stay where I can see you."

Quickly, I take off toward the voices. They become clearer with each step. That's definitely Olu's voice, but then there's a male voice I can't really recognize. He sounds a bit like that employee who was untangling cords the last time I was here. The one who said I reminded him of someone.

The doors leading to the lobby are slightly ajar. I reach forward to push them open, step through and apologize to Olu, but then I hear: ". . . as a comeback show."

I hesitate. I'm not sure why. *They're in a private conversation*, I tell myself. *So just listen.*

Listen.

My hand stays frozen on the door for a few moments until it slowly drifts back to my side. I take another uneasy step, straining to hear Olu's voice and what she'll say next. There is a sigh, and then the familiar tempo of her words: *Yes, but that's why it has to be before I leave.*

Before she leaves? I frown immediately. What's she . . . What's she talking about?

Olu never explicitly said anything about leaving. We were just together, jumping into the water and laughing like nothing else mattered, and she never brought up the topic of going anywhere. She talked about her show, and how unsure she was about writing her own song, and that her manager might not believe in her, and how the media has been cussing her since the scandal broke—about how she doesn't feel like she has anyone on her side.

About how she wishes she knew more about me.

And how she agreed to look after me—she *said* she would. She said she'd be there for me.

My ears are buzzing; my chest rises and falls with frustration and anger and that restlessness that makes me want to run. Catapult myself onto my board and skate away. Fly somewhere that only I know. The beach. My old house.

Olu's voice comes through again. "Now that I'm doing this on my own, I don't have a lot of time. I'm like . . . what do they call it? Like, an 'independent artist,' right?"

"Right, right," comes the man's response.

My heartbeat thuds in my chest. Since when is she an independent artist? I thought she had a label and a manager and all these people looking after her. She did a car commercial, for fuck's sake!

I hear rustling, as if someone is shifting to another

corner of the hall. The man's voice is muffled as he asks, "And when are you leaving again?"

"Yeah," I whisper, leaning in close. "When *is* that?" Bitterness creeps into my throat. I want to spit it out, cough it out of my chest.

The silence cloaks me. I hear nothing but the *thud-thud-thud* of my heart. Anticipating her answer. Dreading it.

Olu tells him, "End of August."

The end of August.

Her voice echoes in my mind—*It just can't be next month . . .*

"Is that why?" I murmur.

She's leaving. Olu is leaving at the end of August, in two weeks, and I will be alone. Again. I'll have no one and nothing—*again*—and she couldn't even tell me. She knew she wouldn't be here past August, past my eighteenth birthday—when I will be an adult, when I will finally be free to do whatever I want, whenever I want, not bound by other people's expectations. That's right. Sid will be at Waterloo, Tanya will be at McMaster, Olu will be back in Japan, and I will be free. And that's exactly what I wanted, isn't it?

Isn't it?

My throat tightens. I think I'm going to throw up, or worse: cry.

Quickly, I turn away as I hear the man's reply: "Well, we gotta figure this out fast, then. So I guess the livestream with this Mariko girl will be up first . . ."

I stumble back, my shoes squeaking against the floor. Shit. The air thickens with my own unease as the man's voice halts. "Uh . . . Anyone there?" he calls. Footsteps approach the door from the other side. Whether it's Olu or that stranger she's talking to, it doesn't matter. I turn and run, my jaw clenched, my breathing heightened. She's leaving, she's leaving, she's leaving. She's leaving, and she hid it from me.

I make it back to the bald man on the stage. He starts speaking, "Did you find—"

I push past him, running backstage. He calls after, "Hey!"

She's leaving, she's leaving.

Quickly, I race through the corridor to the back door that's still propped open. Fresh air, bright sun, summer sadness. My wheels hit the pavement. I kick off the ground and speed down the street, as far away from the venue as possible. The breeze on my face makes my eyes water. Makes my tears fall faster.

I push harder as I wipe my face, hiding my disappointment and shame. *God, Summer, just shut up, okay? Just shut the* fuck *up.* It wasn't like Olu and I were best friends or anything. I guess I just thought . . . I guess I thought when she said she'd be here that she was telling the truth. That she wouldn't lie to me.

The farther I get, the more the side streets start to look like my old neighborhood. This feels the same: the final departure, the stark realization that no one is coming after you.

It's fucking ugly to have to leave a place twice.

CHAPTER EIGHTEEN

MY LEGS FEEL LIKE JELLY by the time I get back to Port Credit. I'm too afraid to stay here, though. What if Olu comes back and tries to talk to me? Tries to explain, in not so many words, why I am not worth staying for? No, not that. What if she tries to explain why I wasn't worth even *telling*?

With a swift shake of my head, I push out all thoughts about Olu, her concert, her being here. I was right the first time: I didn't need anyone to look after me then, and I don't need anyone now. I am almost eighteen. Just a few more weeks and I can do everything my way, like I wanted to from the beginning.

I don't need her.

My only hope now is to save up some more money and get the hell out of here. Auntie Dara told me to text her in the afternoon, and it's still pretty early, but I don't care. *I'm free from now*, I type, my fingers dampened with sweat and tears. My face is the same. No one passing me on the street can tell what I'm drenched with until they take a closer look at my eyes. Puffy, red, tired.

Even without a response, I begin the long trek to Auntie Dara's—although it really doesn't make sense to go to her restaurant if she won't be there yet. *Think, Summer.* Where does she live again? We used to visit her, back when she and my parents weren't fighting, and I think she lived around . . . Did she live around the mall? *A* mall? Cloverdale? I pace back and forth in front of Olu's building as I dig through my memories. I can picture her house, a bungalow on an older street, a park that was two streets down with a broken swing set . . . um, and a STOP sign that someone graffitied with *Break It Down* underneath. None of these clues are helping. In the west end, every bungalow is an old bungalow on a street that has parks and broken swings.

Frustrated, I shut my eyes and try to piece the picture together in my mind. The first thing I see is the beach. "No, go away," I grunt. I don't need that place right now. The sand, the waves, the solitude, none of it will help me save money to escape. I went there for so long, pretending. Well, now I know for sure that pretending is useless. In my reality, I'm still trapped.

I backtrack from the image of Auntie Dara's house in my mind, as if I'm rewinding a video. From the house, I see the long driveway, cracked and uneven. Then, the lawn, the road, the grocery store closest to her house. The highway closest to the grocery store. My parents' car, and me inside it, when we used to visit. I remember when we'd turn right, left, left, left, and hit the highway from our house. Then we'd turn right, right, right, left past the grocery store, and left again onto Auntie Dara's street. I open my eyes, blinking into the brightness. I think I can get there from here.

Never mind, I text Auntie, before hopping back on my skateboard and racing to the bus stop. All these extra trips are eating into the amount on my transit card, but I bet if I swallow my pride and ask, Auntie wouldn't mind spotting me a bit extra. I gotta talk to her about maybe working more hours, or having a set schedule, or finally telling me what she's managed to find about this letter thing so I can just get out of here once and for all. I could get a real job somewhere else. A place with benefits. A store with a back office I could sleep in every now and then.

The first bus is crowded. I expect to see Jet on there, and I find myself staring around, looking for a glimpse of his many piercings or his high-top. I bet hearing more about his mom's return would be a good distraction right about now. And he always has such an easy way of talking. I catch myself hoping I could hear it now.

The second bus is standing room only. My feet are too numb for me to care.

The third bus has more room to sit since it's ahead of schedule, trailing behind another bus for the same route. The emptiness reflects the space in my mind, and soon, without warning, I am thinking about Olu. How she . . . How she's . . .

I pinch myself, hard. My brows furrow, my mouth pulls into a frown. Sitting at the back of the bus, I hug my bag close to my chest. I can barely see past my own anger. My own frustration. I drop my head onto my bag, groaning, whispering, pleading, "Stop thinking. Just stop thinking. Don't wanna think about . . . anything."

About the end of August.

Having to say goodbye.

At the end of a beautiful season.

The bus slows down. Finally, it's my stop.

I utter, "Thanks," to the driver as I head out the front doors. It takes me a second to situate myself. I recognize the park with the broken swing set. Okay, so then . . . "She lives down here?" I mumble, staring around. The scenery is slightly different from what I remember, but there's the STOP sign from my memories. I turn until I see the beginning of Auntie Dara's street, or what I think is her street, anyway.

There's a car in the driveway.

I think that's Auntie Dara's house, but there's a different car in the driveway.

Kinda like a tacky purple . . . A sedan. It's faded. From this angle, it looks like the license plates are so eroded that the numbers and letters barely stick out.

My feet shuffle forward, slow at first, and then faster. I want to get closer to make sure I'm not imagining this faded purple sedan in the driveway.

"M . . ."

My lips press together. They are unable to open, almost shaking at the resistance. Closer, closer.

"My . . ."

And the street is so fucking quiet, too. No birds, no neighbors, no cars whizzing by—except *this* car, this car in Auntie Dara's driveway.

Closer, closer, closer.

My heart is pounding, like bricks to the chest over and

over again, each beat threatening to push me back. Still, my feet gravitate forward until I reach out to touch the body of the car. It's burning hot, just like everything else in this city. The temperature, the humidity—it's too much. It's almost . . . I swear it's making me see things.

But I touch the car again, ignoring the sensation on my fingertips that tells me to pull my hand away. No, it's real. This car is really here.

"Mom's car?"

I stare into the windows, peering into a back seat I've seen a million times—*been* in a million times. The stale smell of old car. No matter what, that stuffiness would never disappear. I think it's because Mom never replaced the air filter. She never maintained her car the way Dad did. Or, maybe they both didn't . . . I can't remember. I don't know. I touch the car door again—yes, it's hot. Yes, it's actually here.

So where is . . . my mom?

My chest heaves with the weight of what this means.

She's—Auntie Dara—she's here, at Auntie Dara's house.

Auntie Dara, who has been lying to me about that letter.

Auntie Dara, who looked at me with pity.

Auntie, who said she would help me.

I turn and press a hand to my mouth, swallowing down the urge to throw up. I'm light-headed and nothing feels real, but then I hear the front door, Auntie's front door, and I realize, no, I'm just stuck, that's all, stuck in this time warp where everything has slowed. From the moment I hear the click, my head swings over. My gaze focuses.

And I'm hit with it. *All* of it.

Everything I've been trying not to feel for a year resurfaces the moment I see her on the front step, walking out of Auntie Dara's place.

Memory is so fucked up. The person I remember, who always gazed at me with warm eyes and laughed when I laughed, the person who used to buy extra snacks from the store when I asked, is replaced so easily with one look. Suddenly, the mother in my memories is painted over with one swoosh of a brush. I blink, I dare to shift my focus for one minute, and she's gone.

This mother, the one before me, is slouched. She is thinner; she is anxious. Her oversize clothes fall off her frail body, and I'm not sure if it's meant to be a disguise or what, but she looks smaller than I remember. As if she's been trying to disappear, too.

Her eyes skirt around my face without any warmth. I buckle under her gaze. Tears hit my collarbone before I realize I've been crying.

"M-mom," I utter.

She becomes even more still. Trying to disappear more and more into the heat haze.

It's infuriating. Quickly, I wipe my tears and toss my board on the grass. Mom startles, holds my gaze, doesn't move. Then, she shifts her weight forward onto her right foot. Back again. Forward. I know this as well as I know myself: She's going to run.

I take one step and she beelines for the car door, muttering, speaking frantically, "Ah ah, what's all this, na? What are you doing here?" The harshness in her words knocks me off balance. Not a "hi," not a "how have you been?"

"W-what am *I* doing here?" I repeat through tears. "Mom, what—*what*?" She gets to the car door and reaches to pull it open, but I slam my hand against the door so it won't budge. She tries to pull it again and again, her eyes so focused on the door handle. She glares at it so hard that within seconds I realize it's less about what she's looking at and more about what she doesn't want to see. Me, her daughter. "Mom," I start. She gives the door one final yank and I press against it with all my weight so it won't open. "Mom, why won't you look at me?" I snap.

She bristles, kissing her teeth in annoyance. "Oya, what, na?" she exclaims, throwing her arms up. Her face hardens when she looks at me. She jumps back and I can see she's shuddering, shivering, even in this weather.

I step forward. She shifts back again.

"M-mom . . . ," I whimper.

She won't stop moving backward, trying to get away from me. From *me*.

"D-don't you . . ." I gulp. "Wh-what's going on? Have you . . . have you been here this e-entire time?" I look at Auntie Dara's house, how ominous it looks now. How it takes up more room, more air, than it's allotted.

Mom shakes her head, then sticks out her ear like she didn't hear me the first time. "Summer, listen to yourself. *Me*, stay *here*?"

"I'm just—I'm *so* confused . . ."

"Not when everybody out there is looking for us," she

goes on, gruff and bothered. "Not when lawyers and those people on the internet have been trying to find us."

A beat passes between us. Silence. I'm desperate to fill it. "So where have you been?" I ask.

She buttons up, turning away, her nose high in the air. God, who *is* this person? Why's she being like this? She's acting like—like I'm just some stranger. I'm her fucking *kid*!

Mom doesn't answer me. My stomach churns with anger and unease. "Fine," I bite back, turning my nose up, too. "Take me with you."

Her mask breaks for a moment, slipping, before she reassembles it with a quickness. In the blink of an eye, she scrunches up her nose, gazing at me with disgust. "*What?*"

"I have nowhere to go." My voice sounds as pathetic as I've ever heard it. I am as pathetic as I've ever been. "I—I have . . . n-nothing." Even as I cry, hearing the words echoing in my mind, I know that's not true. What about Olu? And Sid and Tanya? They're my people. *But they're leaving.* I'm quick to push away any hope. *They're all leaving you.*

I press my hands into my eyes, wiping away tears with enough force to rub my eyelashes loose.

"I don't understand . . ."

"What?" she says again.

"I said, I don't understand," I tell her. "I don't get why you left me. Where's Dad? Why did you both leave? What the f-fuck?" My voice is breaking. I'm sobbing, openly and painfully, begging for answers from a woman who stares back at me like I'm someone else's child. Someone else's problem.

Her brows furrow. She kisses her teeth again, the sound seeming to echo in the open air, before she waves me off. "Summer, please, I don't have time for this. Please. I have to be going, I have to be going . . ." Mom repeats it over and over as she steps back toward the car. This time, though—this time, she gets to the door before me and pries it open. I shriek—"Mom, *please!*"—as she jumps into the driver's seat and locks the door.

I reach for the handle, yanking it with all my strength but it won't open.

She sits inside, watching. That pride, that annoyance from a moment ago, softens once she's safe in the car. In her eyes, I see a flash of familiarity, something that shows me that she's not completely lost, that she's still mine. But that can't be true, because the mother who lives deep in my memories, the mother who raised me, fed me, clothed me, kept me sheltered from the reality of what she and my dad were doing—that mother wouldn't do all this to me.

I try the handle again. "Can't I come with you?"

Again. "*Please*, I'll be good, I promise!"

Again, with a groan.

And again.

And again.

When her face swells with pity, Mom turns away from me so I don't see the emotions she's really feeling. Sadness, maybe. Regret. Remorse for someone she never intended to see after the day she walked out on her. On me.

This was no accident.

I don't . . . I think . . .

This entire time, I thought maybe if my parents had just . . . if they had just *seen* me. Looked in my face and saw that I, I don't know—I don't *know*. Maybe they would've stayed. It's embarrassing to admit now, but deep down, that's what I believed. I could've changed their minds. They could've turned back, told me what was going on, made a stronger case to stay together through an arrest and a trial, or public scrutiny. But as I watch my mom's shoulders tremble with the onset of tears, as I panic at the growing distance between us, I realize none of that is true. Mom has seen me. She knows who I am, and still that wasn't enough for her or Dad to stay.

I'm never enough for anyone to stay.

Her shoulders hunch as she starts the engine. I smack my open palm into the window, startling her. Fucking *good*, I wanna see exactly how much she's crying. She doesn't wipe her tears like I do, but her glossy eyes feel like such a slap in the face now.

I'm the only one who deserves to cry.

Anger builds in my feet like a current, pulsing through my legs, through my stomach, through my arms, up to my cheeks. My jaw tightens with that burning sensation and I have to bite my lip, pressing down on it until it goes numb, just so I don't say something I shouldn't. Things like *you're a shitty mom* and *I never needed you*, things like *you're dead to me*—

Things like *what did I ever do to you?*

I swallow all of it, but it's threatening to burst out, anyway.

As the car switches into reverse, I reach for my phone and throw it with all my strength toward her car. It barely dents the driver's side window. She jerks to a stop, gawking at my audacity, and I see on the inside, she's screaming and crying, *pleading*, saying all kinds of things I can't really hear from out here. Can't hear past the sound of blood pumping in my ears. But she doesn't stop driving. She continues to reverse, crushing my phone as she goes.

A growl so guttural and primal escapes from within me, and I yell, "Fuck this, fuck this!" Quickly, I rush over to the grass for my skateboard, and as she shifts gears to drive away, I hurl the board at her fleeing car. It dents the back bumper, but it's not nearly satisfying enough, because she's driving away again, and here I am, left behind, waiting for an explanation that I don't think will ever come.

"No," I say to myself and run for my board. It's decent enough to skate on, so I break fast against the ground, chasing after the fleeing car. "Where are you going?" I scream as I skate faster and faster.

It's so funny. Normally, this feels like flying, like freedom. Normally, when the wind catches me, I blend in with the scenery and I can go anywhere on my board. Time becomes nothing. But right now, I feel trapped in an endless cycle of departure. Mom speeds up. My feet can't work like this; the board can't carry me fast enough to catch up with her. She turns a corner and burns down the road.

I slow to a stop, watching the air in front of me where I *swear* I could've reached out and touched her. I swear it.

Then, I scream.

My legs give way and I fall to the ground, sobbing, holding my board to my chest in the middle of the road. In the middle of the day. In the middle of Auntie Dara's street.

Mom isn't the only liar around here. Auntie Dara, she lied to me—she fucking *lied* to my face.

She knew how much this meant to me. She knew that she could give me the one thing I wanted, and she refused to do it. Instead, like some sort of sick, deranged bitch, she strung me along and, what, did she think I'd never find out? Did she think she could hide this from me forever while she underpaid me to run up and down the city?

I get to my feet, my throat hoarse from all the crying, and I get back on my board. Auntie Dara has to tell me *something*. She owes me.

By the time I skate back to her house, Auntie has moved a car from her garage to her driveway. She startles when she hears my wheels coming down the road, and I see her stick her neck out to get a good look at me. Once she sees it's me and not some other skater, she tries to scurry back into her house like the rat she is.

"Don't go anywhere!" I yell, and skate right onto the grass, stumbling off my board into a jog. She brisk-walks to her door but I beat her to it, sticking out my hand to trap her from going inside.

Suddenly, she whines, rubbing her hands together in apology. "Okay, Summer, pele o," she tells me with a pout.

I shove her, both hands pressing into her chest, and she stumbles back on the porch. "Ah!" she gasps and gawks at me. "*What?* You dare lay your hands on *me*—?"

"Why didn't you tell me?" I growl. "This entire time, you've been, what, *helping* my mom? Helping my dad?"

"Helping?"

"Yes, helping," I say through gritted teeth. Didn't she hear me the first time? She frowns like something about the word is off. It pisses me off so, so much. I erupt. "So you've been giving them money or something? So they can run away? And you never told me?"

"No, no, I didn't give them anything. Summer, listen." She rubs her hands together again and makes like she's going to kneel down or something. Begging for my forgiveness. "Please. Ah ah. It's not what you're thinking."

"You don't even know what I'm thinking—"

"It's them who have been helping me," she says.

I shut up. My anger, the anxious rumbling in my chest, the restlessness in my fingers, all of it shuts down. My brain can't process this. I stutter out, "S-sorry, what?" because now it's me who didn't hear well the first time. "How . . . What?"

Auntie Dara pouts again, her lips drawn like she's about to cry. "Yes, o, it's true."

I can't speak.

"The restaurant. They've been helping me with money for years."

I can't.

"If not for them, eh? If not for them, that restaurant

would have closed a looooong, long time ago." She snaps her finger above her head to deepen the story, to deepen the length. A looooong time isn't just a long time. This has been going on for more than a few months. This has been years.

I blink like someone rebooted my system. "Sorry?" It's the only thing I can say. Maybe if I repeat it enough, something here will start to make sense.

"Yes, it's true. On the news and online, they're talking, 'oh, Mabel is this, Jacob is that, they stole all this money,' but to me, they're my saviors. They are!" She holds a hand to her chest, as if she's proud of the money she's been getting from them. She circles past me to the front door. I'm so out of it that I forget to hold my arm out to stop her. And she is so engulfed in this idea of my parents being righteous and good that she's forgotten it's me who she's talking to. *Me*. The daughter they left behind.

I snap back to attention, my gaze turning into a frown. "So where are they?"

She falters, glancing away. "Summer, that's enough, na. I'm busy."

My heartbeat thuds in my chest, echoing in my ears. I ask again, "Auntie, where are they staying? You have to know—"

"Is it because I said I should give you money for small-small deliveries here and there that you think you can be asking me all these questions?" she snaps, throwing her arms up. I jump, thinking she's going to hit me. "Ah-beg, leave my—my—my—leave my house, na!"

"W-wait!" I rush forward for her arm, to yank her back before she gets inside, but it's too late. My fingers narrowly miss being crushed by her door slam. I pound on the door, calling, "Auntie! Auntie, please!"

No answer.

The sting of tears peppers my eyes again. "Can't you just tell me where they are?"

"No!" she yells back. When I pound on the door again, she shrieks, "Stop that! Stop it right now!"

"Auntie—"

"If they wanted you to know, then you would know," she shoots back.

I feel myself deflate, because she is right.

If they wanted me to know, I would. Mom could've told me just now, she could've changed her mind and chose *me* this time—but she didn't.

"Please, don't come back here again," Auntie's voice comes softer, and after a moment or two, I know she's really gone this time. They're really gone.

If they wanted to tell me, they would have.

Summer, you're so fucking . . . You're so stupid. Having these hopes. Pretending. Wanting.

After a year, can I really still be crying like this? I can't help it. My knees buckle and I'm on the ground, curled into myself. I try to steady my breathing, but it's not working. No matter how many times I inhale and exhale, it's more painful, more rushed, than the last breath.

Like an engine, my insides are all fired up. I get it in my head that I can smash my board into Auntie Dara's front door, but there's no point because it's my main mode of transportation. It's the only way I can get out of here. It's all I have left.

I stand up, wipe my face one final time, and get on my skateboard. The scenery fades around me as I kick, push my way down the road, gaining speed the farther away I get.

It's just that . . . I need somewhere quiet. A place I can go to with a soft landing instead of these harsh, ugly edges.

CHAPTER NINETEEN

I CAME HERE, TO THIS place, with my eyes closed.

I should wear sunscreen, really.

I should leave.

But the sun is so hot, burning my knees as I sit here on this curb, board hidden away under my legs, staring out at nothing. Well, that's not true. I'm staring at my knees, watching them and imagining them changing pigment in real time. I came back to a place I've always known, and I've been sitting here, still and quiet, for so long. I want to believe my knees are a different shade of brown now.

How long has it been?

"I can't stay here forever," I murmur to myself. "I can't even *stay* here."

At some point, I will have to leave this place, run away and never look back, but for now, I just want to take it in. I want to run my board along the street; I want to hear my shoes scratch against the pavement. I want to jump over every crack in the sidewalk, every patch of grass—I want to hang off every tree in the neighborhood and pretend I can climb them, even though I've never been good at climbing trees.

One time, when I was maybe eight, Mom freaked out when she saw me trudging home with a bloody knee. She cried so loud down the street, kinda like a shriek, a high-pitched "hey!" My god, it was so dramatic. I tried to walk faster so she wouldn't have a reason to be crying outside. When I got close enough, her concern turned to anger. "What happened? Why did you do this?" All that kinda stuff. I told her about the tree, how I tried to climb it and failed. She didn't ask any questions after that. Just turned up her nose and beckoned me inside.

Even sitting here thinking back on it, why didn't she ask anything else?

The answer comes to me quickly. "Because she didn't care," I grunt, pressing my chin into my knees. "She didn't care about me. She never has."

That must've been it.

But then, she did still help me clean my leg and bandage the cut. She did so many things for me that were kind—things that were motherly.

I groan and shift so my forehead is pressed into my knees instead. I don't get it. None of this makes sense to me. I've been sitting here for what feels like hours, letting the sun, the smog, the humidity wash over me, and I'm not any more secure in my answer than I was when I got here. Did my parents love me or not? Did they care about me or not? And how can I prove it, now that I can't find them?

My chest tightens. I might cry again. I hate feeling this way.

I could just go back to Olu's place, but then I'll have to

confront her about leaving. Grief keeps me on the curb. Shame keeps me quiet.

I let myself cry a little bit, my face hidden. Sometimes I hear footsteps from people in the neighborhood taking a walk or heading to the mailbox, and I wonder if they remember me. The girl who used to skate up and down the sidewalk going way too fast as the wind brushed her face. It's only been a year since my parents left—it's only been months since I last lived here.

I pull my head up, my eyes blurry and face splashed with tears, squinting ahead to see the house I grew up in. It sits across from me, looking as unassuming as ever. The only difference now is that there are people in there. They can probably see me out here crying, if they're home. There's a car in the driveway, an older Volvo that looks like it may have trouble starting in the winter, and a set of Christmas lights strung around the garage that were never here when I was a kid. They must belong to the new owners, and what's even weirder is that I was definitely out of here after Christmas, so that means they probably put them up in the middle of spring. My old house is filled with the kinds of people who put up Christmas decorations out of season. Somehow, that makes me angry. They're probably horrible people. They probably hate the summer.

I wipe my face in one jagged motion and get to my feet. One ride around the block will help me figure out what to do.

As I glide down the sidewalk, feeling the air warm the

tears matted to my face, I think of my friends. And Olu. Every one of them has something else—they don't need me. It's liberating. Fuck! It's a good thing, you know, realizing that I'm not needed here. I can do whatever I want.

Don't I get it? I'm free now.

I try to smile, try to really feel the elation here, but it's not coming. *Come on, Summer, don't be dumb. Isn't this what you wanted?* Now it's confirmed Mom and Dad abandoned me—*great*. No strings. Just air, just the wind on my knees and shoulders.

By the time I circle back to my spot on the curb across from my old house, I've stopped crying.

And there's a woman standing on my porch.

Or, the porch of my old house.

I nearly trip getting off my board because her gaze is so strong. In a way, she looks like my mom, brown skin shimmering in the sun with her hair tied in a bun. She watches me, hands on her hips. When I move, her eyes move, tracking my every choice. A part of me wants to run away, skate as fast I can out of here, but I'm paralyzed under her eyes.

She takes a step forward off the porch. I take a step back, feeling the grass under my feet. If I back up any farther, I'll hit the community mailbox.

What am I doing? This lady has nothing to say to me. She probably wants to call the cops.

I immediately hop on my board—

"Wait, wait!" she calls—and jogs toward me. My foot fumbles the push and I'm late getting away. She boldly grabs on to my forearm, holding me in place. I swing around her as if she's the center of a pendulum. "Wait, wait, wait," she keeps saying.

"G-get off me!" I snap. Panic sets in. I pull my arm away from her, breathing heavily, but she doesn't let go. "I said—"

"I just want to talk. Please, don't run," she says. Her voice is so soft and smooth. It's not intimidating at all, but still, I don't know her like that, so it takes me a second to stop fighting. She loosens her grip when it's obvious I'm not going to skate away. "If you could step off the board, too," she offers.

I narrow my eyes. "Why?"

"Well, it's hard to have a conversation like this," she tells me bluntly.

I'm taller than her on the board, but when I step off, we're about the same height. Her eyes are light, like some kind of hazel, and when she smiles, they seem to shine. It might just be the sun, though.

We stare at each other, neither of us saying a word. My uneasiness grows and I take a small step back. "Who are you?" I utter.

"Tuh!" She clicks her tongue against her teeth and crosses her arms. "I should be asking you the same question. This isn't the first time I've seen you around, staring at my house. Going through my mail."

"O-oh." I grow cold with fear. Is she going to call the police? "I'm, um, I'm so sorry. I just—I come back here sometimes, a-and—"

"Uh huh, uh huh." She nods quickly. "Child, who are you? What's your name?"

"Summer," I say.

A genuine, surprised smile stretches across her face. "Your parents gave you that name? It's a pretty one."

I shrug, letting my eyes fall to the ground. "I guess." Then, I sigh, "Listen, if you're gonna call the police, I'm cool with that. I don't care."

Her smile deepens. "Why would I call those idiots?" The way she says it makes me feel like we're sharing an inside joke, but I feel too threatened, too uncomfortable, to laugh. "You look hungry. Are you hungry? Are you always this skinny?"

I don't think I'm *that* skinny. I also don't understand what she's saying.

When I don't reply, she says again, "You hungry?"

I chew on my lip. "I don't know."

"You wanna come inside? I don't bite," she tells me, gesturing toward her house. My house.

Without thinking, I take a step backward. "Oh, no, I couldn't go in there."

"And why not?"

"I used to live here," I blurt out. The words don't sound right. I sound like a loser. "I should just go. I shouldn't have come here. I'm sorry."

She latches on to my arm again like she knows I'm trying to run, but her grip isn't at all tight. It's way more comforting, like her voice. We lock eyes. "So, then," she begins softly. "It's as much your house as it is mine."

I bite my lower lip, feeling heaviness and sadness wash over me. "N-no, it's not."

"It *is*," she says firmly, and gestures again to the front door. "I don't know if you like fried rice, but I got that. And I have some chicken I can roast. Come on." She doesn't even wait for me to say yes or no before she ushers me toward the front door.

It's strange being in someone else's space, especially when that space used to be yours. From the moment I walk in through the door, I notice everything: It smells different in here, Mom never cooked food that smelled like this, that place is where we hung a mirror instead of a picture, this closet had more shoes than jackets, the sofa was facing the wall not the window, and more, and more, and more.

I take off my shoes by the door and set my board down while I take in all the details. They repainted—of course they repainted. The walls were that dull off-white that scuffs easily. Mom and Dad never really were into home maintenance. Now, the walls are a soft blue, the kind that reminds me of the sky but isn't too gaudy inside a house. I reach out to touch it, just because.

The woman smiles at me. "You can call me Marlene, by the way," she says, placing a hand on her chest. "Come in, come this way." It's awkward when she leads me toward the kitchen because I already know where it is.

I sit at the table before she asks me to. It feels kinda rude, but I only realize it after I'm sitting. She doesn't seem bothered, though. Instead, she lowers the fire on the stove and dances over to the fridge where she gets a whole chicken. "It will take a while," she says with a chuckle. "But you can't eat rice without meat, so I hope you're okay to wait."

That sounds like something my mom would've said, as if vegetarians don't exist. I feel weird thinking of Mom, sitting in the same kitchen where I know she wasn't thinking about me before she walked out the door.

Marlene works quickly (just like Mom), grabbing her large butcher's knife (just like Mom) and hacking the chicken into uneven pieces (just like Mom). But then she fumbles the knife a little, flashing me an exaggerated grimace, and that's when she reminds me of Olu. "It's better to cut chicken when it's almost frozen," she says gingerly, casting a look over her shoulder at me. "Because then you can just cut through the skin and the meat without the knife going all wishy-washy like that. You wanna come see?"

"I'm okay," I mumble.

She smiles. "You're a quiet girl."

I say nothing.

"Well, I live here with my husband. My girl just went to university last year. She's at Oxford, in England," she tells me with a twinkle in her eye. "Her dad is from England. He grew up in London. We went once when she was young . . ."

Marlene goes on and on about her daughter, how much her daughter loved watching Premier League soccer with her dad, and how they always thought she'd go to a local university, like University of Toronto or York.

I don't know what compels me to say it, but I do: "I'm thinking about . . . *maybe* going to York."

Marlene's eyes bug out. The genuine joy on her face is almost painful for me to see. "Wow, congratulations! That's a good place to be, you know. Close to home."

I don't tell her that I don't have one.

"Will you be in the dormitories?" she asks.

"I . . ." I swallow. Dorms are expensive, but they're specifically made for kids like me. Kids who don't have anywhere else to go, except maybe at the holidays. So, I guess, not for kids like me.

But still. A dorm. My own place. Sounds good right about now.

"I have a friend who stayed in, um, what was it? Calumet." She tilts her head. "I think that's what it was called. Do you have a preference?"

I shake my head quickly. I didn't read up too much on it, but I'm compelled to do so now. Marlene is so into it that I feel kinda stupid for not giving better answers. Someone like Tanya, who's researched everything there is to know about Mac, would give the best responses. Sid, too, since he's moving into the dorms soon. They'd know which ones had the best showers or the best view, or which ones were closest to the arts buildings or the science labs. And they'd know because they've been honest this whole time about wanting to go. They're excited. They have something to look forward to.

I feel my jaw tense up with frustration. That could've been *me* too. I was so preoccupied with how far I could run that I shut out every possibility that didn't look like freedom. True freedom. But maybe my idea of freedom was missing something. I guess it isn't always about running fast and being the first. Maybe it's about choice. Choosing which school you wanna go to, choosing which friends you wanna keep around. Choosing to stay.

Marlene watches as I shake my head, finally confirming that I'm probably the one person who got accepted to university and isn't excited. She just smiles at me, very matronly. "Well, no worries. There's time to decide. Besides, it's still a reason to celebrate. I know it's not easy to get into post-secondary these days."

It was kinda easy, but I don't need to tell her that. Her daughter got into Oxford.

"I bet you must be relieved," she says with another twinkle in her eyes.

I sit still.

Marlene is talkative enough for both of us. I watch as she effortlessly seasons the chicken, pulling spices and lemon and whole Scotch bonnet peppers to slice. Then, she pokes holes in each piece of chicken with a fork (just like Mom) and covers the bowl to set in the fridge (just like Mom). I hold my hands together under the table, desperate to stop my fidgeting. Seeing her do everything just the way I was taught, in a room where I spent the majority of my life—I need to get out of here. I don't think I should have come.

Slowly, I push my chair back, getting to my feet. "I'm really sorry. I have to go."

"Oh? Oh no." Marlene frowns. She eyes the fridge and then the pot on the stove. "I can give you some to go. At least just the rice. Hold on one second . . ." She turns and rifles through her cabinet for a stack of takeaway containers. "I wouldn't want your parents to worry. You been out there awhile, so I guess it makes sense you'd want to be getting back home."

Oh, but this is my home. This is my house, this is where I was supposed to still be living if my parents—if Mom and Dad didn't . . .

I take a deep breath. Deep, steady . . .

And I cry.

The sob overtakes me, shattering my defenses, and I'm so shocked that it takes me a few seconds to realize I'm crying. I'm openly sobbing in front of this stranger who can't possibly know how awkward, how weird, how painful it is to come back here.

Because this proves it now: I don't belong here anymore.

I need to let it go.

Suddenly, I press my hands into my eyes and I wail, "I n-need to move on, but I don't know h-how." My voice comes out garbled. It hurts to speak. But for the first time in such a long time, I am telling the truth. I'm so honest, I can feel it in my gut when I draw up the words. I'm speaking life to the feelings I've been trying so hard to ignore. Sid was right; everyone was right. I am sad. That sadness has become so integral to who I've become this past year that I didn't even realize it. It seeped into my thoughts, it dictated my actions, it made me into someone else completely. This sad, sad girl who's been living in her head, skating through the wind to distract herself.

"Oh, baby." Marlene's hand is on my shoulder and I feel her guiding me to the living room. I sit beside her, letting myself cry loud and open into her shoulder. She wraps her arm around me, rests her head close to mine. And she lets me cry, shamelessly, endlessly, in a way Mom or Auntie Dara never allowed. I feel like the tears will never dry up.

I'm still crying when Marlene says, "You should stay and eat at least."

I nod against her shoulder and move to wipe my face for the millionth time. A fresh set of tears trickles down, blanketing my cheeks.

"Cry for as long as you need to," she tells me calmly. "I know, soon as I seen you out there, that something must have been up. Is that something you want to talk about?"

I push myself up, peeling my head off her shoulder so I can look her in the eyes. There's nothing malicious there. Marlene wouldn't judge me, but still, I'm too scared. "I don't know if I can," I whisper.

She holds her hands up in surrender. "No problem. Everything moves at its own pace. Come eat something."

Wiping my face, I get up and follow her to the counter-top. She grabs the bowl of chicken from the fridge, grimacing down at it. "It won't be seasoned as well as I'd like, but let's try cooking it anyway."

She pulls out a baking tray, lines it with foil, and sets each piece of chicken on it, separate from one another. Once the oven is done preheating, she pops the tray in. "And now, we wait," she says with a sigh, and joins me at the table.

"Thank you," I tell her. My voice is still shaky, but this is as clear as it's going to get right now. "I really appreciate this."

She waves away my gratitude. "It's no problem. I like the company. Husband's at work, daughter is gone, freelance project is over. You're doing *me* a favor."

An apologetic smile tugs at the corner of my lips. "Not really . . ."

"Of course you are," she insists. "Don't you know sometimes just being there, being physically present, is enough for some people? I'm one of those people, much to my family's dismay." She chuckles. "Always needing to be around someone, always needing to talk. So, really, thank *you*."

I nod, unsure what else to say.

"So, you wanna tell me when you used to live here?" she asks, looking around the kitchen. "It's such a nice house. I bet you have, uh, a big family. Any siblings? There's only one room that faces the backyard and, if you ask me, it has the best view."

"I . . ." My throat clams up again. Even thinking about family is making me emotional. Quickly, I shake my head. She doesn't look disappointed, but I still apologize, a timid "Sorry" pushing past my lips.

"It's fine," Marlene says with a shrug. "Let me tell you about me, then. We have some time before the chicken is done, anyway."

Her name is Marlene Glass. Her last name before she got married was Lebeau. She was born in Haiti but moved when she was really young and hadn't been there to visit until she turned thirty. "Spent a lot of years hating where I'm from," she tells me with a sour look on her face. "It was a waste. Because no matter where I went, it was right there with me. *I* was right there with me." When she speaks, she sounds sage and wise, though she's probably no older than my mom. She has a way of getting into your head. Her voice pulls me into her story.

Even when the chicken is done and she's serving it alongside a plate full of rice, she goes on about the time she traveled to Thailand. "The *best* food," she tells me with a nostalgic sigh. "Have you ever traveled? You have to. Travel is how we become closer with our humanity, and closer with God. We realize that we're all here to share the earth, you know? It's miraculous. It's a wonderful thing."

She gives me way too much rice and I know right away it's because she thinks I'm too skinny. She even gives me two pieces of chicken—two! There's no way I can finish all this.

"Any allergies?" she asks. I shake my head no. "I know, I should've asked earlier. My daughter is allergic to nuts. All kinds, any type. She won't even come into the same room as a cashew. And cashew is my favorite nut!"

I press on a smile, though it doesn't really reach my eyes. That seems to be good enough for Marlene. She grins. "Tap water or lemon water from the fridge? I don't do bottled water. It's wasteful and climate change is real."

"Tap water is fine."

She grabs a glass for me. "Ice?"

"Yes, please."

"Oooh, she does talk," she teases, and wiggles her eyebrows at me before filling my glass from the tap.

My face burns warm with embarrassment, but also familiarity. Marlene is talking to me like she knows me and it doesn't bother me at all. Actually, it makes me feel seen, like I actually exist.

When she brings my water over, she starts in on another story. "Oh, and then my husband, George, I met him in university." She serves herself a small bowl of rice with only one piece of chicken before joining me at the table. Only after she watches me carefully take a forkful of rice does she settle in enough to continue. "I was minding my business in Psychology 101 and, all of a sudden, to my absolute surprise, there's this white boy who starts hanging around me, sitting beside me in all the lectures, asking to swap papers for editing." She chuckles. "I couldn't believe it! George had come here for school and so his parents were still in England. And I kept thinking to myself, 'well, if his parents were here, would he be spending all his time with me?' I always thought the worst. But then I met them eventually and I figured out the answer was yes, he still would." She gives a sharp laugh. "His parents are—you know the kind, girl—*very* interested in my culture. They only want to eat Haitian food when they come here. Well, I can't really cook Haitian food too well. My mom was from Guyana, so, you know. Anyway . . ."

I eat fast, hanging on every word of Marlene's story. Her husband sounds cool. When she gets to the part about her daughter, Savannah—funny, loves comic books, hates the rain—I start thinking she sounds like the kind of person I could be friends with.

"How old are you?" Marlene asks.

I say, "Almost eighteen."

She purses her lips, giving me a knowing look. "So you're seventeen."

"Yeah," I say, deflated, and Marlene chuckles. "My birthday is in a few weeks, though."

"And then what?" she teases, which, I can't lie, makes me want to smile a little. I fight it. "Kids always want to grow up fast. But then what? I'll tell you: taxes, death, and childbirth if you want it. None of which are very fun or very easy. And you, you seem like a bright girl. So many emotions. You should enjoy it."

"But I can . . ." Marlene looks at me, waiting for me to finish my thought. I don't even know how to say what I feel. Besides, she's so worldly. She'll probably think it's stupid. My eyes fall back to my dish of half-eaten rice as I say, "But I can do whatever I want, like, actually. I'll be free. Right now, it feels like there are so many things I *have* to do just because people want me to. I kinda hate it."

"Oh, so would I," she scoffs with a roll of her eyes. "I hated it at seventeen and I hate it now at my age. But that never goes away. Freedom doesn't live outside you, you know." She reaches forward, hesitant at first, but then with that same familiarity, she points to my chest. "Freedom lives in here. Hasn't anyone ever told you that?"

I shake my head. "N-no. No one really . . . I mean, *I* don't really talk about my feelings, so no one's ever told me . . ."

"You're likely to explode that way."

She's probably right.

I finish off my rice and chicken and chug the water until I'm so full I could die. Marlene moves to take my plate, but I shift it away from her. "I'll wash up," I say, and stand, reaching for her bowl as well.

She smiles at me, proudly. "Well, thank you. I appreciate the company, and you listening to me rattle on for hours."

It really has been hours. As I scrub and rinse the plates and utensils, I think of the place I should be heading back to: Olu's apartment. I've pushed so much out of my mind to soothe the part of me that needed attention the most that I've almost forgotten that Olu might be looking for me. I'm supposed to be helping her with the venue and the concert. And Sid, too, I'm supposed to help him finish packing. Tanya. Even Jet. All these people I've been hiding and running from for the past year, just because I was afraid of my reality, the current situation, myself.

Still, when Marlene asks me if I have somewhere to go, I tell her, "No."

The lines of her face flatten out as she takes in my answer. She is calm, nodding, even though I know she doesn't believe me.

I'm surprised to hear her say, "We have a guest room." She gets up, smoothing down her shirt, and nods for me to follow her. I wipe my wet hands on the kitchen towel hanging by the stove and hurry behind her.

"It's actually my daughter's room, if that's okay with you," she says. I'm so distracted by my feet retracing these familiar steps that I barely hear her.

She nudges open the closest door to the staircase to reveal a bed facing the window, a dresser decorated with ornaments and framed pictures of a girl whose curly hair almost envelopes her face, and carpet that is new and springy under my feet. She shows me a closet that has boxes in it, but that I'm sure held clothes and boots and storage cases filled with old books at one point. She shows me a window facing the backyard. She shows me string lights and high bedposts and an old desk.

She shows me my room.

CHAPTER TWENTY

I AM ACUTELY AWARE OF the fact that it's Wednesday the moment the sun comes up. I normally don't pay much attention to the days of the week, because I have nothing in particular to do most of the time, but this heightened awareness surges through my body when my eyes snap open. It's Wednesday, I stayed here overnight instead of going home, and I smashed my phone so no one knows where I am. Or if I'm alive. "Whoa," I croak, and pull the covers over my head, both to block out the guilt and the sunlight coming through the window. I threw a skateboard at my mom's car? I *shoved* an auntie? I ran away? Everything plays out like some B movie in my head, fuzzy and nearly incomprehensible. What happened to me?

My head is throbbing when I force myself to sit up. It must be all that crying from yesterday. I think I cried myself to sleep, too, trying to pass out in my old room. I crawled into bed after I folded my socks and left them on the floor, then stared up at the same popcorn ceiling I had for so many years. I whispered, "I'm home," and shut my eyes, hoping to drift off to sleep, but it never came. Because it felt like a lie, me being here.

First of all, this bed isn't mine. It is harder and smells like a budget lavender or something, the kind that comes from an aerosol can at a flea market. And I used to have so many pillows that I could barely see around myself. There are exactly two pillows on this bed. Next, I kept my dresser against the right wall, not in front of the bed. Why would they decorate the room this way? Whenever Savannah woke up, did she like being able to immediately see herself in the mirror? Isn't that weird?

And then, now, feeling the sunlight hit me at a certain angle—not the same angle it used to—solidified it for me. This isn't my room. This isn't my house. I can feel betrayed, discarded, ruined by the truth of what happened with Mom and Dad, but I can't live here, in this room or this house, anymore.

Summer, take a deep breath and get out.

I need to go to the only home I have waiting for me: Olu's apartment. My heartstrings tug the moment I realize that it may not be my home for much longer because Olu is leaving, too. And that *sucks*. Fuuuuck. I swallow down a crass chuckle. The irony that this is happening twice. It's funny. In an alternate universe, if I was stronger and more honest, I would be laughing. But also, in an alternate universe, I would hope this wasn't happening all over again. I would hope I'd be worth choosing.

"So?" I whisper. "What are you going to *do* about it?"

I bring my knees in to rest my head atop them and sigh. Inhale; deep, shaky exhale.

What *is* there to do?

I think about my parents.

The thoughts are sentient, taking on a life of their own beside me here. The last time I saw my parents together was in this house, after all. And the last thing they did was disappear without a word. That's the legacy of this place. That's the program my brain won't stop playing—that I am always being left behind.

And now I've gotten used to running because of it. My god, I love the feeling of escape. I love the wind on my back when I skate, riding through unfamiliar territories, tracing my wheels against paths my feet could never cross. Cutting through the heat like an arrow. Running, running, always running, trying to go faster. Never going fast enough.

I'm tired of being this person who hides her insecurities beneath grip tape and worn-out Vans shoes. I'm tired of being that poor girl whose parents walked out and who abandoned herself in the process. I don't know who else to be, but with my forehead pressed to my knees in a room—in a *place* I used to call home—I realize it is not this. This is not who I am.

I need to go back to Olu's. I gotta stop . . . I gotta slow my feet down. I need to *try*.

I splash some water on my face in the bathroom, gather my things, and head downstairs. There's a white man standing in the foyer. I freeze midway on the staircase, but he smiles when he sees me, waving. "You must be Summer," he says.

"Y-yes . . ." I utter—and then I remember: Marlene told me about her husband, the one whose family is very into her being Black. This must be him. "Um, thank you so much for letting me stay here."

He waves away my gratitude, almost offended that I'd even be thankful. "It's no problem at all," he tells me. "You're doing my wife a huge favor. She still cooks like there are three of us in this house."

He smiles, so I smile, too, and I shock myself with how easy it comes to me. I'm so much more in control of my face and my body today.

He points to the skateboard left by the front door and gasps. "Is that thing yours?"

"Yeah." I take the last few steps down to the ground floor and reach for the skateboard to show him. He gawks, angling his head to the side so he can take it all in. Honestly, his enthusiasm is out of control. I don't have the energy to mirror it so I stand politely while he marvels at the design.

"This is amazing. I used to skate when I was young."

"A long, long time ago." Marlene comes down the hallway, chuckling. She reaches over to squeeze his arm, which earns a sympathetic look from him. "You're gonna be late. I'm sure Summer has places to go, right?"

"Right," I answer. So unconvincing.

The man smiles. "Well. It was nice to meet you, Summer." He turns to Marlene, saying, "I'll see you in the evening," before he leaves through the front door.

Marlene is smiling again when her eyes finally settle on me, and there's a freshness around her gaze as if she's really surprised I stayed. "Good morning to you."

"Good morning."

"Some food before you go?"

"Thanks, but I think I should get home," I tell her.

"No, but you should eat." Once again, she doesn't wait for my response. She guides me back down the hall into the kitchen. I don't protest.

Marlene is making breakfast sandwiches: bacon, eggs, and cheese on whole wheat bagels. "It's just easy to throw them together," she says as she begins what I'm sure will be a long ramble about breakfast foods. "And besides, when my husband is running late, or when Savannah didn't wake up on time, I thought it was nice to, you know, offer something you can grab. Like this." She hands me the bagel and gestures to the table. "But also, you know, if you run while you eat, you'll get a stomachache."

"Yeah, makes sense," I utter, because it feels like she wants me to respond.

Marlene is still talking when something, a small mark on the doorframe leading to the backyard, catches my eye. I nearly stop chewing when I see it. That's . . . oh god, I remember. Tears come to my eyes almost immediately. All the composure and resolve I had literally half an hour ago is melting away. Holy shit, it's so meaningless, a stupid mark on a doorframe, but now I can't stop crying.

Marlene notices—she quickly wipes her hands on the nearest kitchen towel and comes to join me at the table. "Oh no, what's wrong? Did I say something?"

"No," I murmur, shaking my head. Then I get to my feet, circling the table toward the doorframe. My finger runs over the mark that now comes up to my hip. My *hip*! "It's just . . . Your whole house has been repainted, so I didn't think I'd see anything I recognized."

Marlene's gaze lands on my finger. "And what's this?"

"I was eight," I tell her, and her features soften with the kind of knowing only a parent could show. I say again, "I was eight and I was growing. Dad was really proud. He marked it on the frame." I don't bother wiping my eyes, though the sting behind them gets worse and worse. Soon, I am sobbing, full-on wailing, and Marlene is pulling me into a hug.

I just don't get it. That unsettled feeling. I don't understand this.

Marlene sighs, "I bet your parents miss you a lot. They're probably worried sick about you," and I cry harder because she doesn't know—of course she doesn't. How could anyone have known? *I* didn't even know what kind of parents I had until yesterday.

I start whimpering, "They don't care about me, they don't care," over and over again. Marlene lets me. I like that she doesn't try to correct me or convince me that I'm wrong. She just listens to me sob. I lose control of myself, crying for what feels like forever, until the sound of my own voice becomes grating to my ears.

Marlene walks me back to the kitchen table and brings me a glass of water. I muster an apologetic smile through a wet face, and she reaches out to squeeze my hand. "It'll be okay," she coos, her voice soft and lithe. The kind of thing people say when they have more hope than you do. I want to tell her that I have no plans and no future. I can't even make a decision about school without feeling like I'm panicking. But Marlene is the type of person who will still say "It'll be okay" to that, too.

I nod slowly. "Thank you."

"Do you know where you're headed?"

"Lakeshore in the Port Credit area," I tell her. "My cousin lives there. I feel like . . . I mean, I'm such an idiot. I didn't call her to tell her where I was. And all she's ever done was try to be nice to me, include me, stick up for me . . ."

Marlene reaches out to touch my shoulder. "Let me call you a taxi or something. You can't take the bus like this." She gets up before I can protest or say thank you. She's been so nice to me, just like Olu has, even when she didn't need to be.

The taxi appears outside too quickly. I was feeling so resolved in going home, but as I walk to the door, retracing the familiar steps I took for years living here, I realize I'm not prepared at all. The warmth of my house—of Marlene's house—is so comforting.

But just like Marlene guided me in, she walks me out to the car whether I'm ready or not. She's had experience sending off kids, I bet, since her daughter is at school in a whole other country. I wait for her last words. She says, "You're welcome back here whenever you need."

I stammer. "O-oh, no, I c-can't—"

"I don't know you, Summer," she goes on, her voice calm and even. "But I know when someone needs help. You come back here whenever you need. I said what I said."

The taxi honks.

I shake my head again, but Marlene walks me to the door and pulls it open for me. "Safe travels, my dear."

"Thank you," I say.

I get in and she's gone. The street disappears behind me. I try my hardest not to look at it.

I spend the ride thinking about what I'm going to say to Olu when I get home. I wouldn't blame her for being mad. She doesn't seem like the type to hit people, but if she wants to slap me, I'll let her.

"I'm sorry, Olu," I whisper to myself in the back seat, practicing saying the words with as much sincerity as I can muster. The driver doesn't hear me, thankfully.

A sense of dread comes over me as the car pulls up in front of Olu's building. I hesitate getting out to the point that the driver casts a glance at me in his rearview mirror and asks, "Is this the wrong building or . . . ?"

"I'm going," I mumble and climb out of the back seat. My "thank you" falls on blocked ears as he speeds away the moment my feet touch the pavement.

I turn to face the apartment building.

No, this is terrifying. Facing the consequences of my actions. Maybe I am no different from my parents. *That's* real terror.

I thought I was ready, but readiness doesn't exist in my current state.

I set my skateboard down and ride my way down the sidewalk, farther and farther away from the front doors.

On my way to the beach.

The tree-lined path greets me, and I can't stop myself from thinking, *This is the last time. You'll never come here again.* That's not true. This version of myself won't exist soon, the version that's always running and always scared, but I can't imagine staying away from the beach. Even if I end up having to go somewhere far away, this will always be a place I can come back to.

But if I went to York, like, actually *attended, then . . .*

I scoff at myself just as my feet hit the sand. "How?" I grumble. Quickly, I take off my shoes and socks, clutching them in one hand with my skateboard in the other. I pad barefoot to the shoreline, relishing in the warmth of the sand between my toes.

Olu said she would pay.

"Olu is leaving."

Olu said she would help.

"She said a lot of things."

Why won't you let people be there for you?

The water is so pretty today. Looks like glass.

The sand is like nothing else and the feeling of it beneath my feet and between my toes coaxes me forward. The shore comes into view. I'm lulled by it, as if it's calling me or something. All I want to do is sit as close as possible, feel the air on my face if only a little, and be reminded that everything isn't going to get worse when I head back home.

"Summer!"

Someone's voice carries in the wind. I whip around and drop my shoes in the process. "Shit," I grunt, and kneel to pick them up.

"Summer?"

When I get to my feet, I feel arms around me, pulling me in closer. The force pushes everything out of my hands, just as I'm swept into the tightest hug. Jet shudders through a sigh, his breathing uneven. He keeps muttering, "Jesus, jeeez," over and over again, exhaustion digging into his words. The kind of exhaustion someone can only have if they've finally found something they were searching for.

I hug him back. My arms can barely move with how he's squeezing me.

"Jet, hey . . . ," I utter against his shoulder.

He loosens, taking a step back, his hands still grasped on my arms as if I'll disappear. His eyes search my face, then my forearms, then my knees, for anything that might indicate where I've been.

"Just 'hey'?" he shoots back. He winces at the sound of his voice; he probably doesn't expect it to come out as brash as it did. "Where the fuck have you been?"

I swallow, nervously, and glance at my feet. "I've just . . . I don't know."

"*What?* Nuh-uh." He shakes his head, frowning. "You gotta do better than that. We've been out looking for you since yesterday and all you can say is 'I don't know'? What do you think this is?"

My brows knit together while I try to process his words. "*We?*"

"Yes, *we.*"

"Who—"

"Sid found me and the crew at the park," he launches

into the story, counting off each person with a new finger as he goes. "He was like, 'yo, have you heard from Summer?' and we were like, 'nah, why?' and he said he spoke to your cousin, and *she* said you weren't answering your phone after you were supposed to meet her downtown or some shit. So me and the crew start looking, you know, in all the usual places. Nothing. Sid says he and your girl Tanya are circling your old neighborhood, your favorite hangout spots. No-thing. Your cousin is frea-king-out, fam!" That hits me in the gut. I blink it away, pushing the guilt of Olu's worrying out of my mind. "She's like, 'should we go to the police? Should we call someone?'"

"I'm sorry," I whisper, eyes downcast.

Jet either doesn't hear me or he doesn't care because he just keeps rambling on. "I had to tell her, like, the police *here*? Not the best. They wouldn't do anything; they'd say you ran away on your own or some shit like that—"

"Jet, I'm—"

"—and then what? That's not the point. They wouldn't get it. Even if you ran away, your cousin was concerned—I mean, *we*—"

"Jet—"

"—*we* were all concerned that something bad happened to you. That's all. I heard you, I hear what you're saying, but . . ." He sighs and steps back again. Rubs his eyes. Suddenly, the way his shoulders slump, the lilt in his words—I wonder if he was up looking for me. I wonder if they all were.

My bottom lip quivers but I bite down to get it to stop.

"Where have you been?" he asks, his tone so serious.

"I was . . . around," I tell him, and then, quickly: "I was lost."

He frowns. "Where's your phone?"

"Broken." Rolled over, more like.

"What? How?"

I step away, shifting until I can get a better view of the water. I walk a few paces toward it, and I feel Jet follow behind me. The sound of the waves overtakes my thoughts, and I stand at ease while I watch the shoreline. I force myself to smile, but it feels unnatural. I feel unhinged. What am I doing here?

Jet walks up beside me. He doesn't look my way when he says, "You gotta go home."

I nod. "Yeah, I know."

"Your cousin won't be mad."

"She'll be *furious*."

"She cares about you," he tells me, like it's the most obvious thing. "We all do. That's kinda what friends are for."

"Yeah."

"Family, too."

The water is so pretty. Looks like glass.

"Go home, Summer."

CHAPTER TWENTY-ONE

I BREATHE IN THE AIR—the *smog*—and the scent of open water. Voices in the distance tell me people will be descending on the beach soon. Jet can probably tell that defeated look in my eyes means I have no energy left to run. I turn to grab my board and my shoes, and I make the long walk back to the street. Jet is behind me, not hovering, but trailing. The moment my feet hit the wooden steps, I pause to wipe them of sand before wrestling my socks and shoes back on.

Jet walks me across the street and doesn't stop following until we get to Olu's building. "Will you be good by yourself?" he asks.

I shrug. "I guess so."

"You guess?"

"Thank you, by the way," I add sheepishly. "For looking. For everything."

He flashes a bashful smile, one more like the Jet I remember. "I'm just happy you're, uh, alive," he coughs out. "Bet your cousin will be, too."

Let's hope so.

I swipe into the building and look around the lobby.

The concierge doesn't bat an eyelash. Meanwhile, I tiptoe past him like there's a target on my back.

Every step toward the elevator makes my hands shake.

Every floor up, my head grows lighter.

The doors open on the penthouse and I march out, hearing my feet squish against the carpeted hallway. Step by step by step. Then, I'm in front of Olu's apartment. PH6.

I take a deep breath, *deeeeep* breath, and open the door.

There's a thin blanket sprawled on the sofa. It's the first thing I see because, as disorganized as Olu can be, she's never really come off as a messy person. If she left this here, is she . . . "Olu?" I call, stepping through the doorway. My own voice echoes back to me, filling the empty space. The empty apartment.

I circle through each room, feelings of anxiety spiking each time I come up with nothing. "She's not here," I mutter. I don't know if this is better or worse than the way I imagined this going down. The plus side is I can gather my thoughts, have some time to myself. The downside is that I'll have to sit with this guilt a bit longer.

So that's what I do: sit on the sofa, my eyes focused on the door, and pretend I'm still at the beach. Fear won't let me move.

Even in her absence, everything about this apartment reminds me of Olu. The way a recently lit candle sits on the breakfast table, the way there's always a cabinet that's not fully closed. How the blinds are never really shut, even in the nighttime. How you can kinda see the beach from here, just a little, if you really focus.

I realize I miss her.

And that I regret so much of the last twenty-four hours, but most of all, I regret believing so deeply that the family who abandoned me was the same as the one who took me in. Who tried to fix things for me. Who tried to understand me.

God, I'm so stupid.

I bury my head in my hands and—sit up straight when I hear the doorknob jangle.

I don't know what to do with my hands.

The door nudges open slowly.

My breath hitches in my throat as I watch Olu slip in, her face rife with disappointment, her brows knit together as if she's pushing away sadness. I watch it happen in real time. Her knowing. She shuts the door, then pauses when she feels the presence of someone else. She tilts her head as if to hear better; she blinks around the apartment, taking stock of everything as she'd left it.

Then, she sees me.

Sitting on the sofa.

Olu gasps, nearly stumbling back into the wall, and brings her hands to her mouth in shock, then relief, then frustration—her right eyebrow twitches; her jaw squares. It makes her look older than she is. Makes her really look like an adult. I've never felt more seventeen than I do right now.

She says nothing.

I rise on shaky feet and shuffle over. Olu's eyes graze over me as I approach. I can practically feel them on my arms and legs the same way Jet was examining me. Her thoughts are so loud: *No bruises, no marks, no injuries. Where did she go?*

Still, she says nothing.

We face each other in the center of the apartment. My bottom lip begins to quiver and I force myself to look away so I don't see the hurt reflected in her eyes.

Why won't she say something? Isn't she relieved to see me?

But then I hear it, the way her breathing thickens with each rise and fall of her chest. That's not relief; that's rage.

Shit.

She breathes out, her voice barely a whisper as she asks, "Where . . . did you go?"

I shiver at the coldness in her tone. "It's . . ." I clear my throat. "I'm s-sorry, Olu."

Tears sting the back of my eyes, but I'm too scared to start crying now. There's nothing in her pointed stare, in the way she inhales and exhales slowly from her nose, that says she'd show me any sympathy.

When I look away, from the corner of my eye I see her tilt her head to the side, following my gaze. Not letting me disappear for even one second. "Did you . . . ," she begins, still with that cold, measured tone, though now, I can hear how it trembles. "Did you know we've been looking for you since y-yesterday?"

I stay quiet.

"Me, your friends . . ." She counts off, each word coming out breathier, more stilted, than the last. "We were all . . . *so* worried."

My eyes still can't meet hers when I utter again, "I'm sorry."

"You didn't call, you didn't text," she goes on. "You just disappeared and went off on your own—"

"I said I was sorry—"

"Don't you know how many people care about you?" she snaps, finally, her voice rising to an uncomfortable level. I can see in her face that she's as shocked as I am. The hurt underneath the anger shines through. "Huh? Do you—do you think people who are adults don't have anyone who cares about them? That they just turn eighteen and everyone leaves? That they never rely on *anyone*? Is—" Her voice cracks. She brings a hand to her mouth the moment her tears start to fall. We're both inconsolable now, with no one but each other.

I wipe my face, softly at first, and then aggressively. She talks about family and being there for each other, but—but—"You were gonna leave, too, though!" I cry out. She stares back at me, blinking away tears. Neither of us has a place to hide anymore. "You can't sit here and pretend that—that you weren't, like, planning on going back to Japan, to your old life, by the end of the month. I overheard at the venue. 'It just can't be next month,' remember?" I bite back. She looks away, flustered. "This entire time, you were looking for a way out. Isn't that what you told me? You were just waiting to see what your manager said, a-and then you'd be gone. Just like everyone else. J-just like my parents."

She doesn't say anything. God, I wish I were wrong. I wish she'd tell me that I made a mistake or something, or that she—I don't know—she could *fix* this for me, that someone would fix this hollow feeling. Fill it. Take it away.

I think of the beach, of the rolling tide, and let another wave of tears hit me. It nearly knocks me over, and I curl into myself, hugging my arms. I say, "My parents never meant to stay. They *knew*—they *planned* it. My mom knows I'm alone—Dad knows I'm by myself—and they literally don't give a shit! So how is that fair?"

Olu steps forward and reaches for my hands. The urge to fight is real but my mind is too tired. I drop my arms, drop my head, and sniffle quietly as Olu squeezes my fingers, runs her thumbs along my palms. Tries to calm me down.

"It's not," she says. "It's not fair."

I look at her.

"And I'm sorry. I'm sorry you . . . were in such a shitty position," she tells me. Her voice is hoarse; her tears have dried. And when she gives my hands another squeeze, I know she understands something I don't. Maybe it's heartbreak, maybe it's disappointment, but I feel it so strongly when our hands touch that I'm so annoyed at myself for not seeing it before. Olu isn't my enemy. She is maybe the only one who sees me.

She says, "So many things happen that we can't control. But that doesn't mean we should just close our hands to things we're supposed to receive." She gives my hands another reassuring squeeze. "I can't . . . I don't know why your parents are behaving this way. I'm not going to say that I understand when I don't. And I can't make excuses for people like that. You're right. It's not fair. But, S-Summer . . ." Her voice breaks a little. She's losing composure. I can hear the tears pushing forward in her words, but she holds my gaze. Firm. Unwavering. "You are not *this* person . . . You're not the kind of person people don't care about. It's wrong that people made you believe this—people like *me*, like when I didn't tell you about the concert properly. I'm *so* sorry. It was selfish of me. I don't know what I was thinking."

I purse my lips for a second to get them to stop trembling. "It doesn't seem like anyone is."

"Anyone?"

"Is thinking. Adults. Everyone."

"Oh . . ." Her lips pull into a sad smile while she wipes both her eyes. "The only thing I am sure of now, at twenty, is that no one knows what they're doing."

"But that doesn't mean it's fair," I utter, my eyes downcast. "That we should all get caught in the crossfire because someone doesn't know how to act."

"You're right," she cuts in quickly. "It doesn't."

I feel Olu's arms around me before I realize what's happening. She is hugging me. I let myself fall into it.

Besides, her presence is so grounding. Kinda like the beach. When I think of her, I think of the waves. I'm not sure why.

CHAPTER
TWENTY-TWO

I DON'T KNOW WHEN I fall asleep, but I'm surprised to find myself waking up in my own bed. *My* bed, at Olu's apartment, where I live. It's a strange feeling, opening my eyes here and sighing in relief. Just a couple of weeks ago, I would've pulled the covers over my head and pretended I wasn't surrounded by a million large and small plush toys, but now? Now, I reach out and squeeze the nearest bunny. Having it so close by is a comfort.

I cried so much.

I feel like I spent forever just sobbing on Olu's shoulder, spilling everything about what had been going on the past few days—the deliveries, that letter, Marlene—until my tears dried up. It hurt to cry and it hurt to swallow, so we sat on the sofa, completely spent, unsure what to say. Or, maybe it just felt that way to me. The embarrassment of having blamed Olu for wanting to leave hit at once, and I could feel myself mentally trying to retreat.

So I told her, in a timid voice, "By the way, I didn't mean to say all that shit about you leaving me."

She looked at me with that warm familiarity, the same way she looked at me when I first moved in, and just shook her head. "Yes, you did. But that's okay." She took a breath so deep it seemed to shake her. "You've been through a lot, right? So, really, it's fine."

"That's no excuse," I murmured. She didn't say anything after that.

I stop squeezing the stuffed bunny and push the covers away from me. I don't know what time it is, but it must be pretty early if Olu isn't awake. I don't hear any movement through the walls.

Quietly, I crawl out of bed and step into the hallway. I peek into the living room to make sure Olu isn't passed out on the sofa, and then I head to the bathroom to shower and get ready.

When I reemerge from the bathroom, I make my way to the kitchen, ready to start on breakfast. I'm craving whole wheat breakfast sandwiches, like the kind I had at Marlene's place, but I don't know if we have all the stuff for them. We have bread, but no bagels, and we have eggs, but no bacon. A somber feeling comes over me when I remember how Mom used to . . . We were always out of bacon. It's so stupid to think of that now, and I hate that the thought comes into my mind and doesn't let go. I try to shrug it off, to shake it out of my shoulders, but it doesn't leave. I guess it won't be that easy to face these memories.

"Whatever, Summer," I sigh with a shrug, and get to work.

Olu comes into the hall in her robe once I'm done toasting slices of bread. She smiles warmly as she joins me by the kitchen counter. "What's all this?" she gasps, looking around. "When did you wake up? This is *so* much!"

I try to smile, too. I think it's working. "It didn't take too long. I wasn't sure what else to make, so . . . yeah."

"Nnn, this is fine," she says. Then, she grabs an avocado from the fruit bowl. "I'll slice some for you too. It can be like one of those sandwiches."

"What sandwiches?"

She pauses to think of the word. "Uh, you know, like the ones rich people eat," she snickers.

You're a rich person, I want to say. She's clearly trying to joke with me, so it would be weird if I just didn't say anything, but at the same time, maybe she wouldn't appreciate it as much as I'm thinking she would . . . I don't know I don't know I don't know.

"Summer?"

"Hmm?" I clear my throat. "Y-yeah. Sandwiches." The moment is gone. Next time, I won't be so damn weird.

I bring the food to the table while Olu makes us tea. "Green tea," she tells me, setting both cups down.

"Thanks," I say.

For a split second, we stare at each other before diving into our breakfast. The awkwardness lingers, whether I want it to or not.

"Before I slept, I called your friends so they know you're here," Olu explains as she takes another bite of her sandwich. "But you should call them, too. Tell them you're okay."

Oh shit.

She chews slowly, watching me as my eyes drop to the table. "Oh yeah, your phone got run over . . ."

I grimace. "I'm probably gonna need a new one."

"Ah . . . it's okay, I guess. We can go to the store and get one. Just tell me if there's anything else, okay?" She offers a polite smile, but I can see the hesitation and the fear underneath. Like if she doesn't offer me these things, I'll have reason to disappear.

I wish I could tell her I won't, and that I'll mean it. Yesterday and the day before were such a blur. The only thing I know for sure is that I don't feel the way I did before. My head is clearer, and even though at times I still feel weepy, I'm sitting in that uncomfortable place with the truth. I owe it to myself, anyway.

After I take a sip of my tea, I say, "My mom used to make the same thing for breakfast every weekend."

Olu's hands were midway to grabbing her sandwich, but they rest at the edge of the table while she pauses to listen. "Oh, really?"

"Yep." I nod. "And, um, let's say we didn't have something . . . well, she would just go out and buy it." Memories of that day she left, the way she told us she was going to get more ingredients, threaten to ruin my safe space. I sigh through them, feeling my chest rise and fall with unease. "She actually did that the day they disappeared."

Olu frowns. "So it was just like that? That was the last time you saw her?"

"Y-yep." My voice wavers. "Then, in the evening, Dad

just . . . *whoosh*. Fucked off." I run my fingers past my face to symbolize someone running. "I was alone after that."

Her frown deepens. She looks at me, looks at my hand, and I can tell she's not sure if she should reach out or give me my space. I'm not sure which I prefer, either.

"I'm sorry," she says. "That sucks."

She sounds so serious when she says it that I burst into a nervous chuckle. "Yeah, it really did."

"I know I said it yesterday, but your parents shouldn't have done that to you," she goes on, her voice still serious. A regretful look comes over her. "We don't always see that our parents are people, so it's hard for us to understand when they do things we don't like. Especially when they do things that are just wrong. It's a problem."

"Yeah."

"It's okay to hate them," she tells me. "It's okay to be angry."

I felt so entitled to my anger these past few days in a way I never had before. In the past, I would always say I was fine and brush things off, but it was like I wanted people to know I was mad. I think about turning eighteen and finally being free, but I won't forget how liberating actually feeling my feelings was. The way my body shook when I skated up to Auntie Dara's place. I couldn't contain it, and in the end, everything I wanted to say, everything I was trying so hard to hide, came out.

And only then was I free from it.

It's just like Marlene said. Freedom doesn't live outside you.

I hear Olu say, "We should get you a new phone. You should call your friends as soon as possible," but my mind is elsewhere. It's at Auntie Dara's house.

"Actually," I pipe up. "There's somewhere I need to go before we get the phone, if that's cool. You can come with?" I add, hopeful. Thinking about heading to Auntie Dara's place alone makes my heart beat faster. She practically threw me out, but I mean, I was pretty much feral. Maybe she'll listen to me if I'm down to talk. Maybe she'll be more open with Olu there, too.

Olu nods right away. "Of course. I'll go anywhere with you."

I wait a moment, and then—"That sounds kinda serious," I say with a hint of a smile.

It takes her a moment to clue in that I'm not being a raging asshole, and she chuckles. "Yeah, like . . . shin-zou-o-sa-sa-ge-yo." And she clenches her right fist to her chest, sitting up as tall as she can.

I blank. "I don't get it."

"What?" She gawks. "You didn't watch *Shingeki no Kyojin*?"

"My friends did."

She grimaces hardcore. "Oh my *god*. It is seriously the coolest anime of all time. We have to watch together."

That gnawing feeling that we won't have time to get through all of it before she leaves hits me, but I swallow it down. Instead, I focus on the fact that she asked me, that she wants to include me somehow. I smile and say, "Y-yeah, that'd be cool."

We finish eating in relative silence, with Olu humming a medley of every intro song *Shingeki no Kyojin* has ever had. It's a quirk that I never knew she had. I think about Jet, who's met Olu already, and how he might not know, either. I think of Sid and Tanya, who haven't spent enough time with her, but who would think she was pretty cool. Cooler than she seems at first, anyway.

Olu begins washing up before I have a chance to take over. She washes and I dry. We fall into rhythm easily. "Do you know what I thought of?" she asks as she hands me a plate. "How interesting people can be."

I raise an eyebrow. "By interesting, you mean horrible, right?"

It's supposed to be another joke. Jeeez, I suck today. Olu glances at me, a beat of uncertainty lingering in the air, and then she smirks. "Yes. Horrible, good, loyal, mean. People are so interesting." Then, her eyes light up. "Actually, there was a Japanese show my dad used to love. He made me watch it once. *Kurosagi.* One character would always say 'people are . . . interesting'—and he would have this expression on his face, like this." She does the look, narrowing her eyes and tilting her chin so she looks like she's a mafia boss or something. I snort, a throaty chuckle erupting from my mouth. I can tell it lightens her spirits, too. "It's an old show now, but I can show it to you if you want."

"With subtitles?"

"No," she teases. "*I* am the subtitles."

I remember now: Olu is funny.

We leave the apartment while she checks her phone every few minutes. At first I figure it's because of the ride-share she called, but then I start thinking it might have something to do with her show, the one I was supposed to help her plan before I ran away. She chews on her lower lip as she texts, her eyebrows knitting together while she tries to think of the right phrasing. I see her hit delete a million times.

When we settle into the back of the car, she gives a tired sigh and pushes her phone into her bag like she's trying to bury it in there.

Nodding to it, I ask, "Is that about the concert?"

She grimaces, casting a sideways glance at me. "Ah . . ."

Wrong question. "Sorry, never mind," I backtrack. "I overheard you guys at the venue, you know. About how you're on your own. Independent." I add extra emphasis on the last word.

She hums, "Mmm," and it sounds a bit like some sort of confirmation. For what, though, I don't know.

The car pulls down the road on our way to Auntie Dara's place. I am restless, jiggling my leg and touching my forehead, worried that maybe I offended her by asking. Who knows if she was planning to tell me in her own time? I probably ruined that now.

We get onto the highway. It's so different being in a car and seeing the scenery race by, because on my skateboard or in a bus, the path to get around looks different.

"They didn't like it."

"Huh?" I tear my eyes away from the window to look

at Olu, whose phone is back in her hand, whose eyes are blinking back confusion and frustration. "Who didn't like what?"

"My label, my manager," she goes on.

I slouch further in my seat.

"I don't understand—or, no, maybe I do." She tosses her phone back into her bag. "My manager has been with me since I was a kid, and he always looked out for me. He always believed in me. But with everything that's happened . . . I mean, I can't really blame him." She lets out a frustrated sigh. "I know what it can be like for female performers who get caught up in scandals. I'm not stupid. But I just thought that, you know, that he'd . . ."

"Be there for you?" I offer.

She nods right away. "*Yes*," she says. "That he would support me, maybe stand up for me with the label. But he's taking their side. He's in a difficult position, but still, he's *taking their side*." She scoffs at the thought, at the idea that someone she knows so well could do something so unpredictable. I can relate.

"You know, at the venue when you were supposed to come help me," she continues. "That was just after I had called my manager to cancel everything. My contracts with the label. My contracts with him. I was so angry. If you heard me, you would say, like, *Is that really you?*" A crass snicker escapes her lips and she clasps her hands together. "I know now that I can't work with someone who doesn't believe in me. A-and I'm still young, so my career can't end like this. That's why . . . Summer." She shifts so she's facing me as best she can. Her expression is somber, as if she's waiting for the opportune time to console me. "Summer, I *have* to go back to Tokyo to start fresh. There's another agency that says they might want to work with me. It's not guaranteed, but it's . . ."

"It's your life," I finish for her.

She pauses for a second, running the words through her head as if she was planning on saying something different. "Right," she concedes.

"I—I understand. We don't have to talk about that anymore." I wave away her prying eyes and focus on the moving road outside the window.

There's a beat of awkward silence before Olu pipes up, "Hey, but do you want to listen to it? The song I've been working on."

I turn back to her. "Is it done?"

"No." Olu pulls out her phone again and swipes it open, digging around for the music file. "But I was going to do it acoustic anyway. The production is kinda bad and some of the lyrics are weird. Well, I mean, you won't understand anyway, but the sound is . . ." She tilts her head a little. "Somehow."

I bite back a smile. Something being "somehow" is such a Nigerian thing to say—it reminds me of my parents and our household. My family.

She finds the song. "Ready?" she asks, her thumb hovering above the file.

I nod. "Ready."

She hits play.

Her voice filters softly through the phone on top of a beat that's both electric and gritty. I don't know the words, can't really understand what she's saying, but I bob my head to the rhythm. When we lock eyes, I smile and she gives a sigh of relief. It's just like I thought it would be: a dreamy sound and her voice turning into that soft landing place.

CHAPTER TWENTY-THREE

I DON'T HAVE TO RECOUNT the way to Auntie Dara's house using faded images from my memory to get me there. The car Olu called drops us off right in front of her place. The driver tries to catch our eyes in the rearview mirror as he pulls up to the curb. "This it?" he asks as if I will say no. The truth is that I barely recognize this house, the cracked driveway and the lopsided steps to the front door, without a car in the driveway. Without my mom's car.

"Yes, thank you," Olu says boldly like she's been here before. She reaches over to pop open my door and awkwardly shuffles me out before she climbs out herself. She could've just got out on her own side. When I flash her a disgruntled look, she turns to wave off the driver before saying to me, "Yours is the side with the curb," as if that suddenly explains so much.

"Is this a famous person thing?" I ask. "Because someone's always chaperoning you from a car to a building?"

She opens her mouth to disagree, but I can see that small flash of curiosity in her eyes that tells me she never thought of it that way.

"A-anyway." She nods toward the house. "So this is where Auntie Dara lives, huh?"

"Yep." I take the first step forward. My foot hits the pavement with purpose, but my second step is way shakier. I lose focus about three steps in, and I wait for Olu to catch up before I move any farther. What am I doing? I didn't call Auntie. There's no guarantee she's home. Or that she'll even want to see me.

And why do I want to see her? What do I actually hope to accomplish here?

Olu nudges me at the fourth step. "Hmm? What's wrong?"

I turn to face her. "What am I doing here?" I mumble just loud enough to be heard. "She told me never to come back last time."

"Yeah, but she *owes* you," Olu says sternly.

She does. Auntie Dara says my parents have been giving her money for her restaurant. They're obviously still helping her out. Who knows where my parents are even still getting that kind of money from. And if they're giving Auntie money, doesn't that mean she could be implicated, too? Is she okay with that?

Suddenly, Olu cuts in front of me and marches to the front door. I reach out a hand to stop her but she flies to the door with that same purpose I had a moment ago. And she knocks three times.

"Wait, wait!" I hiss, scurrying up behind her. "What are you doing?"

She flashes a bright, smug smile. "Being your guardian."

Oh my god.

Olu knocks again with more force.

A voice inside, Auntie Dara's, rings out. "I'm coming, I'm coming."

Oh my god oh my god.

Without another thought, I duck behind Olu, hoping her mane of curls and big "I just turned twenty" energy will protect me.

Auntie Dara's face goes from confusion to recognition in seconds. The way her eyes dart back and forth from Olu to me tells me she's piecing it together in her mind. Still, she stays, one hand on the doorknob as if she's waiting for permission to slam it shut. "What is it?" she shoots out, sharp and cruel.

Olu takes a deep breath and says, "You should apologize to Summer."

Something sparks behind Auntie's eyes. She narrows them, ready for a fight. "*Me?* Apologize, ke? For what?"

"For being selfish." Woooow, she didn't just say that! Auntie Dara looks as shocked as I am, but Olu doesn't care. "You weren't honest with her, either. She just wanted to know the truth about her parents. Besides, she's just a kid—"

"Ah-beg, are you not a child, too?"

"—and it was unfair." Quickly, Olu steps aside and nudges me forward. "Here she is. Apologize."

I don't have the courage to look Auntie Dara in the eyes. No matter what I thought I was feeling, I can't put into words the shame that envelops me just standing here. I was so stupid, believing her—but really, how could I have known how things would play out? This is someone who used to bring me food, someone who used to be a part of my family.

By the time I look at her, Auntie Dara is sneering. My bottom lip begins to tremble. I bite down so she doesn't see. She says, "Apology, ke? I don't owe anybody anything," with such vitriol that it's hard to believe she was nice to me just days ago. That she was someone I thought I could trust. "Your parents' wahala or whatever—it doesn't concern you. Stop trying to find my trouble, o. I'm not your mate, if you didn't know." She rolls her neck, scoffs, looks away.

I gulp, hard. "Auntie . . ."

Auntie.

"I don't . . . even care anymore," I say finally.

The air shifts around us. Auntie Dara bristles, visibly confused. I bet she was thinking she could dangle this in front of my face, me coming back every day to plead and beg with her, ask her this one favor. Whatever. What the fuck ever. Now, as my eyes scan her hunched stature, the apprehension she uses to cling to the door, all I can see is wickedness. Relying on her won't do me any good. I get it now.

"You said if my parents wanted to tell me where they went, they would have," I go on. "And maybe you're right. But then, if you could tell them something from me . . . Tell them that they shouldn't come looking for me, either."

Auntie's eyebrow twitches. She inhales and exhales through her nose. In her eyes, there is frustration. "You . . ." She takes another deep breath. "If you know what's good for you, you'll get away from my house. Nonsense."

Then, the door slams shut so fast that the sound seems

to echo around us. Olu glances at me but it takes me a few more minutes to really pry my eyes away from the door. "I'm never coming back here again," I mutter.

Olu notices the tremble in my voice before I can, and she puts her arms around me in a binding hug. "I'm sorry."

Then she says, "Let's egg her house."

And I laugh. Like, really, full-bodied and out loud. What's there to even laugh about? I'm literally about to be alone, like, truly alone. Olu, my friends, my parents. How can I be okay with this?

I wanted my parents to stay, and they didn't. I want my friends to stay here with me forever. Even Olu. But none of that is really in my control. So when I laugh, feeling my chest shake, letting my feelings shift, I know it's because this is the only control I still have. Everything with Auntie Dara proves it.

We don't egg Auntie's house. Instead, we sit on the curb while Olu calls us another rideshare to the mall. A new phone is the furthest thing from my mind, but Olu insists I check in with all my friends. And I agree. If what Olu says is true and they were out looking for me, then the person who actually needs to give an apology is me.

Olu squints into the sky, sighing. "She is not a good person," she tells me, and I know she's talking about Auntie Dara.

I shrug. "S'fine. I don't know what I was expecting, honestly. I just wanted her to s-see me." Olu pouts when I say it, but I quickly shake my head at her sympathy. "Not in a sad way or whatever. Just that, like, when I came here last time, I was . . . a *wreck*." I snort. "Like, tears everywhere, snot everywhere, couldn't breathe. It was so bad."

Olu's pout deepens.

"It's chill," I reassure her. "I wanted to come back and I needed her to just see my face. Feel guilty and shit. Understand that it's *me* she's doing this to . . . That's all."

"Well," she sighs, glancing away. "I think it worked."

I think so, too. Olu and I stare ahead, listening for the signs of a car turning down the street, but we know if we turn around, we might see Auntie Dara gazing at us from a window. I can feel her eyes on us. I keep thinking she'll come out and say something, but she never does. And when we leave, I realize I didn't really expect her to.

The last time I came to Sherway Gardens with Olu, I refused to let her buy me anything, but today, when she asks me "what about this?'" and "don't you think you'd like that?" I say yes to everything. This is as normal as it'll probably get for the two of us—me, with my parental issues, and her, with her career issues—so I don't wanna ruin it. If she wants to drop a million dollars buying me stuff because she feels a type of way, then I'll take it. Every ring, every watch, every sweater that I try on seems to fit me really well, anyway.

So much for just grabbing a phone and leaving.

We get to the electronics store, and I gravitate to the first Android I see. Sid has this one, now that I think about it. I pull it out of its display and flip it around in my hands just as the salesperson comes over. "Amazing camera, that one," he says, nodding to the device.

"O-oh." I poke around the display, getting used to the

weight of it. It's on a retractable line so I can't run away with it, but I shift it toward Olu as much as possible so she can get a better look. "What about this one?" I ask.

She's completely zoned out. Her eyes are practically glossed over. I can see the wheels turning faster and faster behind them.

"Olu?"

She snaps back to attention, blinking fervently until she realizes where we are. I hold up the phone again. The salesperson grins. "S-sorry," she chuckles sheepishly, and then takes a closer look at the phone. "It's nice! What's the camera like?"

"Amazing," the salesperson repeats.

"Looks good to me," she says, then peers in to get a better look at the screen. "So clear. We'll take it!"

The salesperson's smile stretches so wide it's like his eyes are being pushed off his face. "Perfect." He directs us to his computer at the end of the desk and begins typing right away. "Okay. So . . . would you like our two-year plan or did you want to pay for the full thing upfront? For this week only, both deals come with a key ring and a leather case." He shows us both.

I glance at Olu, which is a mistake because she's just staring at me. Her eyes are sending panic signals, but she's trying to keep it together. To be an adult.

She clears her throat. "Uh . . ."

"Upfront?" I offer, more so to her than him. "That way you won't have to, like—or, like, there won't be monthly payments and stuff. You know." *Since you won't be here*, I want to say. *I'm doing you a favor here, too.*

Olu deflates, a sad smile tugging at the corners of her lips. "Sure. Upfront is good."

"Okay." The salesperson continues typing rapidly on his laptop while we both wait for him to finish the purchase. Olu and I stay quiet. We're perfectly transfixed on the computer in front of us, so neither of us has to sink too deep into the reality that in about two weeks, she will be gone and I'll be gone, too, somehow.

As soon as the purchase is through, I spend the rest of the mall trip signing back into all my old apps and accounts. Olu dips into a store to buy this necklace she saw on display and I wait outside, trying to get this new phone up to speed. Fix the background image. Fix the ringtone. Alter the brightness. Contemplate texting my friends, but, I mean, is a text really good enough? I'll call them later.

"Ready to go?" Olu asks when she exits the store. She holds up a small gift bag with the necklace inside. "It was on sale! I'll show you properly when we get home."

"Sure."

"Did you call your friends yet?" she asks, nodding to my phone.

I hesitate, shifting back on my heel to create some distance between us. "I will, I will. I'm just kinda scared."

"They're your friends, Summer," she tells me calmly. "They only care that you're okay."

"Why is that so scary, though?" I blurt out. It feels strange to vocalize something so obviously insecure. When I hear my voice echoed back to me, I want to roll my eyes and ugh, just go lie down somewhere. "Never mind," I say hurriedly. "I'll talk to them."

On the way outside, Olu calls another rideshare.

"Actually," I pipe up, my voice timid. "Can you drop me somewhere else before we get home?"

CHAPTER TWENTY-FOUR

IT TAKES ME FOREVER TO get all my old contacts back through cloud storage, but by the time our car pulls up to the skate park entrance, I at least have Sid's number locked in. "Thanks," I say, both to the driver and to Olu.

Olu reaches out for my forearm before I push open the door. "What time will you be home?"

The subtlety in her voice. It's a silent ask. *Don't go too far, okay?*

"Maybe, like, a few hours. Three hours max," I tell her as reassuringly as possible. Even after giving her my new number, she doesn't seem any less tense. "You can even call Sid, if you want," I say, trying to lighten the mood a little.

That earns me a frown. "Stay close to him, then."

"I will."

"Don't disappear on me," she says.

"I—I won't," I promise.

I didn't bring my board, so I feel awkward shuffling into the park on foot. It feels like it's taking forever to cross the stairs and the bends, to circle the outer trees and park benches. I spend all day skating; this much walking is actual torture.

I bring out my phone and call Sid. He doesn't answer, probably because he doesn't recognize my new number. "Damn," I groan as the phone rings a second time. I scan the park, squinting into its far corners until I see someone I recognize. The park is littered with middle school kids, lots of first timers, and lots of Kirstens—friends who just come to chill instead of skate.

A lanky, tan-skinned boy skates up to me, then circles me expertly like he's in orbit. He chews on the end of a lollipop stick like it's gum. "Where's your board?" he asks.

I narrow my eyes at him as he skates around. "What?"

"You're Jet's friend," he goes on. "So I always seen you with a board. Wondering where it went."

"Is he here?" I ask, ignoring his commentary.

The boy points in the distance toward the group of trees Jet and his friends tend to hang out at. "He's running errands for his mom, but he said he'll be back."

"Can I wait with you guys?"

He smirks. "Sure."

I don't know any of Jet's friends by name, so it doesn't really matter that I'm in a group now. They have their inside jokes, chortling over things that happened yesterday or the day before. I toy with my new phone, trying to dial Sid's number and hoping he'll pick up. Who taught him to be this distrusting of unknown numbers? Quickly, I shoot a text over: *It's Summer, call back pls.*

I drift away from Jet's friends. My phone feels hot in my hands. Sid should see my text message and he should respond any second now. I try calling again—nothing. "Maybe I should've tried his house . . ."

The moment I step away from the trees and face the entrance to the park is the moment I see him. Sid—and Tanya, with her favorite large slushie, and Kirsten, with her customary I'm-too-cool-to-be-here shades—but mostly Sid, whose hand is suspended with his phone clutched to his ear. One second later and I realize my phone is ringing. It's him. My heart leaps and I answer, my feet speeding forward as I speak into the phone, "H-hey, hey—"

"Hey, wow," he sighs out. "You're—"

"I'm almost there, I'm hanging up," I say just as I reach them, just as Tanya launches herself into my arms.

She holds the slushie away from my back so it doesn't jostle and spill too much. "My girl, my Summer, aahhhh," she sings. Even without looking at her face, I can tell it's doing that scrunching thing, that grimace before the tears come. She sniffles, locks on to me tighter. "What the fuck, what the fuck is wrong with you?" she sighs into my shoulder, and it makes me sad to know I disappointed her this much.

Sid hugs me next. It feels deep and binding, and much more personal than anything else. I hug him back with more emotional energy than I ever have before. I hope he can tell. I hope he knows that I'm . . . I didn't mean for things to go this way. I was just so frustrated. So scared.

I gotta say it. I have to tell them.

Being vulnerable is hard. How can you know someone for so long and still not want to share anything with them? How is that okay?

When I pull away from Sid, I take a deep breath. He watches me curiously, staring into my eyes, trying to understand what I'm feeling or what I'm thinking. We have always communicated this way, but maybe it's time for me to try communicating differently.

"I'm sorry. I didn't mean to make you worry," I say evenly. Kirsten takes off her sunglasses in time for me to see how puffy her eyes are. How much she's probably been worrying, too. She doesn't make eye contact with me. I don't really blame her. As awkward as this is for me, it has to be worse for her. Now she's gotta admit she actually cares about me.

I glance away, saying, "I just . . . I was in my own head too much. I wasn't doing too good. But I think you knew that already. You guys could always tell that I needed h-help." I choke on the word. It sounds so pitiful in my mouth. Tastes like defeat somehow, even though I know that's not true.

The air is a vacuum around us. I don't know what else to say. Sid stares, his jaw tightening the more I apologize. If anything, hearing my voice is making his frustration grow.

He tilts his head to the side. "Where did you go? What happened? How come you didn't call?"

I grimace at the directness in his voice. "I . . . I went to a place I thought was home," I explain. "I kept saying I didn't care, you know, about what happened to my parents. About anything, really." My voice wavers the deeper I get into my feelings. It hurts to push through, but as I stare back at the faces of people I'd always called my friends, I realize I genuinely owe it to them to be honest. I owe it to myself, too. "B-but I *do*. I care so much, guys. And it fucking sucks." My heartstrings tug; my throat restricts. I press my hands over my face, groaning, "Oh my goddd." I'm unsure if I'm going to laugh or cry.

Suddenly, I feel another set of arms around me. I shift my hands just as—Kirsten. She's hugging me. It snaps me right out of my impending spiral, and I look at Sid and Tanya to make sure I'm not imagining things.

Kirsten pulls away, stepping back to create distance between us. She stares at the ground as she murmurs, "You can't just fucking disappear like that."

Wow. "I . . . y-yeah."

"If you're going through something, then go to therapy like a normal person. Fuck's sake, man."

I lock eyes with Tanya. She has the widest, most smug grin plastered on her face.

I chew on my lip, nodding. "Yeah, you're right, you're right," I concede.

Suddenly, Tanya's arms shoot up in the air as she cries, "Okay, we came here to skate, right?" Never seen someone who doesn't know how to skateboard be so enthusiastic about it before. It's like she hears my thoughts, rolling her neck in my direction, as she adds, "Relax, not me. Sid says he's gonna teach Kirsten."

I blurt out, "About time," and immediately regret it.

Kirsten purses her lips. "Actually? Yeah."

She's agreeing with me? My being gone must have really screwed her up. I put up both my hands in surrender and back off just as Sid drops his board and nudges it toward her.

Kirsten puts one foot on the board and breaks out into a whine. "I caaaaan't! It's—it's moving."

Sid bites back a smirk. "Because they're wheels."

"Sid!"

"You'll be fine."

"She will not be fine," Tanya stage-whispers to me, and we both chuckle. She skips over to loop my arm in hers, smiling at me like she has a secret.

We gravitate to the perimeter, then sit cross-legged under a tree where the grass begins and the pavement ends. It's rocky and not that comfortable, but it gives us a perfect view of Kirsten on shaky wheels and her death grip on Sid's forearms.

"You want your dominant foot to be here," Sid tells her, pointing to the back, "so you can push easier."

She wobbles a bit and grabs harder onto his arms to stop from falling. "This feels weird."

"Yeah, because you're pushing with your stronger foot and balancing with the other," he explains. "But you'll get used to it."

"Will I?"

"I'm gonna push you a bit—"

"Nooo, waitwaitwaitwait!"

Tanya snickers, but I smack her in the leg so she stops. Skateboarding can be stressful at first. I mean, not like I wanna stand up for Kirsten or anything, but when I first started, I could barely stay upright. Plus, Kirsten is trying. And trying is . . . something. It counts for something.

As she massages her leg, Tanya gives me a warm smile. She fake-punches me in the shoulder. "Girl, I've missed you," she coos. "The *real* you. Not that crusty version who was keeping secrets."

I snort. "You thought I was being crusty?"

She grimaces. "Uh, yes. But like . . . don't scare us like that again." She glances away, but I can still see in her eyes how uncomfortable this whole thing makes her. "We get that things with your parents were rough. Just . . . don't just leave, o-okay?"

Without another thought, I grab her hands and give them a squeeze, just like how Olu always does for me. "I won't. I'm staying. I'm . . ."

Jet comes into view just over Tanya's head. He grins, waving at me, before skating over at a ridiculous speed. "Summer!" he calls, making his presence known to everyone in a ten-foot radius. He kicks his board up and jogs to a stop before he crashes into Tanya. "Good to see you," he says with a chuckle.

His mood is kinda infectious. Jet is just that kind of person, I guess. I smile up at him, squinting through the sunlight. "Your friends said you were running errands for your mom."

"Yeah, yeah."

"How is she?"

He brightens up the second I ask. "She's good. She's looking into jobs these days. Grandma is trying to give her her space, but Mom knows she's gotta at least take a first step, you know? It's rough, though, still."

"Y-yeah," I say with a small smile, and gesture to the grass around us. He takes a seat next to Tanya.

"So, Summer." He shifts a bit while Kirsten comes skating shakily past him. He looks way less worried than he should be. That girl has no balance. "You're settled back at home? Everything's good?"

"Everything's . . ." I pause a moment—and shake my head. "Everything's kinda weird. My cousin is going back to Japan at the end of the month."

Tanya gasps, hitting me in the arm out of shock. "Whaaat! The end of *this* month?"

"Yeah, man."

"So what're you gonna do?" Jet asks, tilting his head toward me. He doesn't have to say it; his eyes are already asking if I'm planning on disappearing.

I shrug. "I don't know. Honestly. I have no idea."

"Stay at my place," Tanya offers. "I'll be at Mac, so you can have my room. Mom won't mind. You know her; she's probably mad she'll have less people to cook for."

"Or, or, hear me out." Jet waves his hand between us to get our attention. "My grandma knows someone who's looking for someone to rent their place. You'd have your own privacy. Your own laundry room, too."

"And then there's Sid's place," Tanya goes on. "His parents won't mind, obviously."

Jet nods. "Right, right—"

"Guys!" I interrupt, clapping my hands together loudly. Even Kirsten looks over from where she's wobbling. "I, um, I appreciate . . . all of this," I say, staring around at them. "But you guys have helped me enough. I'm—I'm gonna figure it out—"

"No, no." Tanya points a stern finger at me. "Do *not* say you got this and then you actually don't got this—"

"N-no, not that," I chortle, pushing her finger away. "I mean that I may . . . just go to York after all. Stay on campus and everything. I know the registration deadline is coming up close, so . . ."

The thought of going to university felt like such a waste before, but it's overridden now by the feeling of studying something I may kinda like and having my own place. Somewhere I won't have to move from every other week. Somewhere I belong.

Kirsten yelps—and Sid has to grab her before she skates away onto the grass. But they, and Jet, and Tanya, they're all looking at me like I just said I was planning on robbing a bank. As if me going to school is so unbelievable!

"But you weren't interested, like, at *all*," Tanya says, then looks at Jet. "She thought we couldn't notice, but we did."

"It'll be a place of my own," I explain as Sid wanders over. God, even saying that is making my chest warm with the possibility of finally settling down. "I know it costs a million dollars or whatever to get a place on campus, a-and I get that, you know, I'd obviously be there for school, but my grades are good and, I don't know, I guess I *need* a degree and stuff, so it's a win-win. Right?" Tanya and Sid nod their approval right away. Jet gives two thumbs-up. Kirsten mutters, "Sure."

"And anyway, it'll be a good new start for me, especially after everything that happened last year, last summer . . ." My eyes fall to my lap. My skin is crawling with embarrassment. I am too open, too available for comment. I kinda hate it, but parts of it aren't as bad as I thought it'd be. No one's yelling at me, for example. And the more I speak, the lighter I feel.

So I ramble on, "I met a lady—when I ran away, I stayed with this lady, and her daughter went off to Oxford. I know York isn't Oxford, but just hearing her talk about it, I guess, like, I was just thinking about how I could maybe make something of myself if I went to university . . . It's stupid."

"It's not." Kirsten crosses her arms as if she can't believe she's supporting me on this. "I think you're just hype because now you have some sort of direction. That's normal."

"Yeah, but not having a direction is also dope," Jet says with a childish grin. "It doesn't matter. As long as you're doing whatever makes you feel good! And, aren't hurting anyone in the process. That's most important. Can't support murderers."

Tanya throws her arms around me, squeezing me in an overbearing hug. "Girl, I'm so happy for you! It's like you've matured overnight. Where's this lady live? We gotta thank her and her smart-ass daughter."

I inhale—"Uh, she lives at my old house," I say—and exhale.

No one is surprised. Except maybe for Jet, who turns to Sid and frowns. "I thought we checked there."

"Yeah, but we didn't think you'd go *inside*," Sid grunts. "That's bold. That's a new level, even for you."

"I know, I know, I'm sorry," I say. "But! I think I'm . . . I think I'm good now." The words fall heavy in the air, settling around our feet with a thud. *I'm good. I'm good.*

Sid looks at me, peers into my eyes for a hint of our hidden language. "Do you mean that for real?" he asks. It's hard not to hear the hope in his voice. "No more pretending?"

An uneasy grin comes to my lips. I want to tell him there's no use looking for a hidden meaning because I can say what I feel this time. The urge to lie will always shoot up, but I know enough now to temper it. To realize it's not me. "No more pretending," I tell him. And I feel good. I'm good, at least for now.

The feeling remains even after I leave the park. "Olu's expecting me home soon," I tell them before hugging everyone and promising I'll call later.

Tanya calls me a rideshare because she lowkey doesn't trust me to take the bus back. "At least this way I can monitor the route," she tells me as I get into the car. I'm not even mad. She's only being overprotective because she cares about me. And isn't that good enough? Being cared about and all.

The car pulls up to Olu's apartment—my apartment. Well, it won't be either of ours for much longer, I guess. I text Olu to let her know I'm coming up soon, to which she responds with a thumbs-up emoji.

The moment I make it to the penthouse and push the door open, Olu greets me, tosses me a beach towel, and says, "Let's go!"

"What? Go where?" I look down at the shades she's squeezing into my open hands. "What's all this for?"

She circles the kitchen's breakfast bar, grabbing her key-card, a water bottle, her phone. "Let's go see the water. I'm just, I was thinking . . . S-since I'm leaving soon, maybe we should hang out more." She sounds nervous as she says it, and suddenly, I notice she's not looking me in the eyes, either.

"O-oh, okay?" I follow behind.

She doesn't say a word to me all the way to the lobby. Not as we exit into the hot, sticky air. Not while we head down the street, looking both ways to cross the road toward the boardwalk. Not while we see the first glimpse of water, feel the first touch of sand on our feet.

"Come on," she says, and beckons me farther down the beach until we're close to the shore. My favorite spot.

I lay out the blanket and we sit. From far away, I wonder if people would know we're related.

Olu's acting so weird. I want to give her space, but I mean, if I'm as serious about school as I say I am, then I don't have all the time in the world here. Finally deciding to go to York is one thing; asking Olu if she'll help me pay is another. She offered before, and the social worker is under the impression she'd be willing, but still. How do you just ask someone to pay your tuition?

Like this, I guess.

"Olu, I'm gonna enroll—"

"I'm keeping the apartment, so stay as long as you want."

Wait.

We both look at each other like it's the first time we've met. Her face is twisted with confusion, leaning toward me like she might have heard wrong. And I just . . . I mean, did *I* hear wrong? I ask, "Say that again?"

"No, what were you gonna say?" she prods. "You're enrolling?"

"I . . . okay, well." I clear my throat. "I think I will go to York after all. I wanna stay in the dorms and s-stay close to home and . . ." The more I speak, the wider Olu's eyes get, the more joyful her expression becomes. She gasps and grabs my arm like she can't wait for me to finish talking. I chuckle, "A-and yeah. That's it. That's it!"

"Oh my god, Summer," she croons. "That's amazing."

"I don't want you to worry about me," I go on quickly. "I figure it'll be smart for me t-to have somewhere to go. Something to do. If that's cool with you, of course. Tuition is kinda expensive . . ." I hide my face.

She nudges me in the side. "I can pay. Of course I will. I want you to be okay. Like, truly and really okay."

Her sincerity threatens to make me cry. I can barely stand it. "Y-yeah, well," I sigh out, a small smile coming to my lips. "Thank you."

"Yes! But I mean what I said. Even when I go back to Tokyo, I'm keeping the apartment. During Christmas, I can come visit you and we can hang out together, just like this." She waves a hand out to the water, grinning as a flurry of waves comes crashing onto the shore. "I want you to always have a place to call your own. To have a place we can both belong."

"Hmm . . ." I take a deep breath and press my hands into my eyes.

Olu giggles and does the same. "Hmm."

I feel soft. Maybe this is what happiness is like.

We sit on the beach, caressed by the thick air, held by the warmth of the sand underneath us. Olu dips her toes in. I do the same. The sun begins its descent. I should've brought lotion.

"You know," Olu begins, glancing at me. "It kinda feels like we're both starting new things in life. You with school, me with whatever I'm doing." She laughs at that. "Trying to find myself as an artist. Writing my own music. Ugh."

"You'd be good at it," I tell her, reassuringly. "You're . . . You're, like, funny."

She gawks. "What?"

"You have a good personality, I mean."

"I didn't know you thought I was cool." Okay, that's not what I said. She gives a fake hair flip, and I laugh because maybe she's more corny than funny.

After some time, when the sun looks like it will be swallowed up by the water soon, Olu gets to her feet. She grins and takes a deep breath as if the air is filled with goodness we can't see. She kicks her shoes away, starts stretching. It makes me laugh. "What are you doing?"

"Preparing," she says, then points to the water. "We're going in."

"Is that why we've been here all day?"

"Sunset is the best time to swim," she tells me, and grabs hold of my arm, leading me to the shore. The sand becomes cooler under our feet as we go. Soon, I can feel the spritz of the waves tickling my face.

"Are you ready?" she asks.

"I've done this before, you know."

She smirks. "I know you have."

Quickly, she runs and gets far enough into the water that she's able to belly-flop into the waves. When she reemerges, both arms in the air like she just won a race, I laugh. I have to. She's always doing such weird shit.

But honestly, I hope I grow up to be just like her.

ACKNOWLEDGMENTS

THIS STORY IS AN HOMAGE to one of my favorite bands.

I love music, and I've been really into this Japanese rock band called L'Arc~en~Ciel since I was about fourteen or fifteen. They're my heart. I remember being in high school when their album *SMILE* came out and feeling like I would explode from excitement all day, desperately wanting to listen to it but being stuck in civics class. Or something. It's been a long time, so I can't remember.

But I do remember how their music made me feel a little less lonely, a little more like a person. And for me, as an awkward teenager, I latched onto anything that reminded me I was alive. A lot like Summer, actually, with her skateboard and the beach.

L'Arc~en~Ciel has a song called "夏の憂鬱 (Natsu No Yu-utsu)" and a promotional single version called "Time to Say Good-bye." The title translates to "Summer Depression" or "Summer Melancholy," and both the song and title completely captured who and what I wanted Summer to be. Everything from the nostalgia in the sound to the longing in the words has stuck with me since I first listened to the song ages ago. I made that song my entire personality for a hot second (arguably, it remains a strong part of my personality now!), and those lyrics carried me through a whole lot.

I wrote most of this book trying to keep myself, my own

fears and insecurities, away from the page, but I fear they found their way there anyway. It's all good. I'm so thankful for the opportunity to have written Summer's story. I'm thankful that you are reading it as well. I'm thankful to my wonderful agent, Claire, and editors Foyinsi and Yash, who gave me the space and agency to tell such a quiet story; the marketing and art teams at both HarperCollins Canada and Feiwel & Friends, for their support; Steffi Walthall, for depicting Summer so whimsically; Nozomi 雷希望, for her expert guidance and keen eye during our sensitivity consultation; and, completely seriously, to *Tony Hawk's Pro Skater 1 + 2* for helping me practice skateboarding without having to bust up my legs in the process, because your girl has no balance.

And I'm thankful to my eternal faves, my favorite band, for being the soundtrack. *The* soundtrack. It's our thoughts that link us together. I won't forget you ever.

THANK YOU FOR READING THIS FEIWEL & FRIENDS BOOK.
THE FRIENDS WHO MADE

THE MELANCHOLY OF SUMMER

POSSIBLE ARE:

Jean Feiwel, *Publisher*

Liz Szabla, *VP, Associate Publisher*

Rich Deas, *Senior Creative Director*

Holly West, *Senior Editor*

Anna Roberto, *Senior Editor*

Kat Brzozowski, *Senior Editor*

Kim Waymer, *Senior Production Manager*

Dawn Ryan, *Executive Managing Editor*

Emily Settle, *Editor*

Rachel Diebel, *Editor*

Foyinsi Adegbonmire, *Associate Editor*

Brittany Groves, *Assistant Editor*

Lelia Mander, *Production Editor*

Trisha Previte, *Designer*

FOLLOW US ON FACEBOOK OR VISIT US ONLINE AT MACKIDS.COM.
OUR BOOKS ARE FRIENDS FOR LIFE.